# VIPER

Maurizio de Giovanni

# VIPER
## NO RESURRECTION
## FOR COMMISSARIO RICCIARDI

*Translated from the Italian
by Antony Shugaar*

Europa
*editions*

Europa Editions
214 West 29th Street
New York, N.Y. 10001
www.europaeditions.com
info@europaeditions.com

Copyright © 2012 by Giulio Einaudi Editore SpA, Torino
This edition published in arrangement with Thesis Contents srl
and book@ literary agency
First Publication 2015 by Europa Editions

Translation by Antony Shugaar
Original title: *Vipera*
Translation copyright © 2015 by Europa Editions

Library of Congress Cataloging in Publication Data is available
ISBN 978-1-60945-251-3

de Giovanni, Maurizio
Viper

Book design by Emanuele Ragnisco
www.mekkanografici.com

Cover photo © Dm_Cherry/Shutterstock

Prepress by Grafica Punto Print – Rome

Printed in the USA

Paola.
Every single heartbeat.

# VIPER

So tell me: do you know what love is?

You, who sell love for two lire a go, the privilege of panting on you for five minutes, not even the time to look you in the eyes, to whisper your name: do you think you know what love is? What do you know about endless waiting, anxious silences in hopes of a single word, of a smile?

With this smooth soft body that I can now feel moving frantically beneath me, with these long white legs clamped tight around my hips, do you think this is love?

I've seen love, you know. I've known it, I've experienced it. It's made of pain and sorrow, of anxiety and relapses. It doesn't burn itself out in a flash; it isn't born and it doesn't die in places like this, the sound of a piano downstairs, and everywhere the smell of disinfectant. Love is made of fresh air and flowers, tears and laughter.

You, dragging your nails down my back and thrusting your pelvis against me, you think you know love, but you don't.

You're always faking, you even fake the pleasure you don't feel. You pretend, with your black mascaraed eyes, with your mouth lipsticked into the shape of a heart, with the beauty mark inked on your cheek. All fake. Just like your expensive clothes, made of organdy, crêpe, and printed voile, fabrics that you alone, in this so-called house of love, can afford, like the French perfume that pollutes the air in this room.

I know what real love is: it wakes you up at night, your heart full of hope and despair, full of thoughts that become dreams and *dreams that become thoughts. It doesn't need music played by negroes, to make the blood pump faster through your veins, nor does it need perfume to muddle your senses.*

*What would you say to me if I asked you what love is, as you moan in my arms, as you press your breasts against me?*

*Perhaps you'd laugh, the way you laughed just a short while ago, with your white teeth and your dark eyes, one hand perched on your silken hip; and you'd tell me that this is love, a room in a whorehouse, lace bras, candles, satin, ostrich feather boas. You'd say that love is luxury, well-being, not having to think about how to get enough to eat. Or maybe you'd tell me that love doesn't last long, no longer than a hooker does: and that the rest of life must be spent living as comfortably as you can.*

*Don't be afraid, I won't ask you what love is. I won't wait to hear more lies from your painted lips. I'll settle for feeling what I feel right now: your warm body moving beneath my flesh, in time to your breathing. More and more slowly. More and more slowly.*

*I'll settle for not hearing any more of your muffled cries, under the pillow I'm pressing down over your face.*

# I

It was a few hundred yards from police headquarters to Il Paradiso—the final stretch of Via Toledo and a section of Via Chiaia. But it was a bad time of day: the sidewalks were crowded, the shops were open, and the sweet spring air beckoned people out for a stroll. Ricciardi and Maione shouldered their way laboriously through the crowd, doing their best not to lose sight of the old woman hobbling on her bent legs with surprising agility; behind them were officers Cesarano and Camarda, who kept exchanging conspiratorial glances. They'd started it when Maione told them the address, and they hadn't stopped smirking since.

Ricciardi didn't trust the spring. There was nothing worse than the mild breeze, than the scent of pine needles or salt water that blew down from Capodimonte or up from the harbor, than the apartment windows opening. After a winter of silence, of icy streets swept by winds out of the north, of chilblains and of cold rain, people's brooding passions have built up so much of that destructive energy that they can hardly wait to erupt, to sow chaos.

As he approached the corner where the street opened out into Piazza Trieste e Trento and the crush began to thin, the commissario let his gaze sweep over the dozens of heads crowded in the area in front of the Caffè Gambrinus: young men dressed in light colors, thumbs thrust into the pockets of their vests and hair brushed back, were talking in small groups, trying to catch the eyes of women that strolled past in pairs, well aware of the approbation they had so sorely lacked in the previous dreary months. Some of the men turned to the young women serving at the tables that had finally been set out along the sidewalks, drinking in the curves that could be glimpsed under their aprons. Strolling vendors hawked their magnificent wares, shouting and whistling. Children tugged on their mothers' skirts, demanding nuts or balloons. There were convertibles, carriages, and accordions.

Welcome to springtime, thought Ricciardi. Nothing is more dangerous than all this apparent innocence.

Right around the corner was the elderly man who had killed himself. The commissario almost walked straight into him; he dodged to one side and bumped into a nanny pushing a perambulator; she glared at him, straightened her bonnet, and then resumed her brisk pace toward the Villa Nazionale. The commissario remembered the report, from a couple of days earlier: a retired high school teacher whose wife had died that winter. One day he woke up, dressed himself nicely, said goodbye to his daughter with a kiss on the forehead, then set out for his usual morning constitutional. When he reached the piazza, he turned to face the café, pulled out the pistol that he still kept from his military service in the Great War, and shot himself in the temple. The case had quickly been filed away; there was even a suicide note on the kitchen cabinet at home. But the grief of his departure lingered on, suspended in midair, perfectly visible to Ricciardi, in the form of a short, slender man dressed in dignified but threadbare garb: a jacket that was too big for him, the sleeves hanging so low that only his fingertips, and a pistol, could be seen. The bullet went in through his right temple and emerged from his forehead, opening up his head like a watermelon. The terror of imminent death had prompted a stream of urine, leaving a wet stain on the front of his grey trousers. Beneath the blood and brains that were oozing down his face, his mouth repeated the same phrase over and over: *Our café, my love, our café, my love.* Ricciardi instinctively turned toward Caffè Gambrinus, across the crowded street: the tables buzzed with people and life. He would feel his grief and pain for days: the old man who couldn't bear to face the first season of fine weather without the companion who'd shared his life. The sudden stab of pain in his head made him reach his hand back to the scar, now healing, on the back of his head. If only the scar on my soul could heal as nicely, he thought to himself, the scar that attracts the whisperings of the dead, the awareness of their sorrow.

He made a mental note to avoid that corner and to cross over to the far side of the street in the next few days. At least until the echo of the old man's suffering had finally dissolved into the cool air of the dawning spring.

Brigadier Raffaele Maione pushed through the crowd with some difficulty: his bulk kept him from moving quickly through all those people, and the unexpected warmth of the day had caught him off guard in his heavy winter uniform, thanks to which he felt sticky and sweaty. The old woman, on the other hand, seemed a ballerina, the way she dodged oncoming feet and perambulators, vanishing now and again from his sight, only to reappear a few yards further on.

Not that Maione needed directions to find Il Paradiso. It was Naples' most famous brothel, strictly for the rich, and its blacked-out windows overlooked a street busy with strollers and lined with the city's most expensive shops; from the darkened windows came the sound of a piano playing and the laughter of the clients, and the passersby either looked scandalized or amused, but in either case, a little envious.

The old woman had been out of breath when she got to police headquarters. She was the bouncer at the high-end bordello, herself an institution, known in the neighborhood for the powerful arms which contrasted with her petite appearance, allowing her to function as a reliable one-woman security detail: she would easily give drunken and troublesome clients the bum's rush if they refused to leave when their time was up. Her name was Maria Fusco, and she was known as Marietta' a Guardaporte—Marietta the Doorkeeper—and she had refused to speak to the lowly police private manning the front desk, demanding an audience with the brigadier to report "the calamity that had befallen," as she said in thick dialect; Maione had met her once or twice and had won the woman's coarse respect. When she appeared before him, he had immediately understood that she was truly upset: her cheeks were red, she was short of breath, her face twisted with despair.

"Brigadie', come, hurry, right now. Something terrible has happened."

Maione had only managed to squeeze out of Marietta that there had been a murder, so he had sent for Ricciardi, motioned Camarda and Cesarano over, and headed off after the old woman.

As he strode along briskly, he pulled his watch out of his jacket pocket. Four in the afternoon. The bordello must be open for business by now. Who could say how many people would be there, in Il Paradiso's handsome drawing room, listening to music and watching the procession of scantily clad young ladies on the balcony, waiting to be chosen.

Suddenly the busy street was as empty as if a sinkhole had opened up, and the four policemen found themselves outside the entrance to the place. Marietta stood on the threshold, impatient. On the other side of the street, the inevitable crowd of rubberneckers, their heads inclined toward the windows, locked tight and covered by curtains; a subdued murmur of comments and speculation, some elbowing as the police appeared on the scene. Maione heard a woman laugh, but the laughter fell suddenly silent when he scowled in her direction. Death was death: it demanded respect, wherever and however it appeared.

## II

Ricciardi didn't like bordellos.

Now, to be clear, it wasn't a moral issue. It was his opinion that anything that went on between consenting adults was their business, and people were free to spend their time and money however they saw fit, and this was certainly a better way than many others. But he'd had plenty of opportunities in the past to see how the passion that swirled around sex could be a very difficult tool to handle, one that all too often caused only harm. He remembered the faces of men stabbed to death, despairing suicides, fathers who'd hanged themselves over the affections of one of those young signorinas who were in the business of selling pleasure; on the other hand, he knew all too well that love vied with hunger for the dubious distinction of first place in the contest of what could cause the most death and destruction.

But he knew equally well, he thought to himself as he climbed the stairs leading up to the front room of Il Paradiso, that love was a disease bound up in the very essence of the human race and that no one, no matter how hard they tried, could hope to remain immune. Not even him.

When she reached the landing at the top of the steps, the old doorkeeper stopped, turned to look down at the four men, and announced in a hollow voice:

"Enter. Someone murdered Viper."

When he first joined the force, he'd often found himself

rushing with his fellow officers to one house of ill repute or another, which were regularly the site of brawls, serious injuries, or cases of aggravated assault.

It was normal practice for every bordello to arrange for its own security force, usually consisting of one or two ex-cons who were willing, in return for a hot meal and a few bills, to shove their battered features and their tattoos into the faces of would-be troublemakers; that was usually enough to restore calm in a place made for pleasure not bloodshed.

Still, pleasure is a passion, and one passion tends to trigger others. Sometimes the hired guard wasn't enough and, in fact, when the custodians of law and order had to be summoned, this guard would frequently be among the injured parties, punished for his belief that he could talk reason into someone holding a knife.

Those bordellos, at least the ones that Ricciardi remembered, were tucked away behind the crumbling facades of old buildings; the way in was up a steep dark staircase, at the top of which was a room with a woman seated at a small table, with a padlocked strongbox where the money was kept. Along the walls were wooden benches, where factory workers, soldiers, and students sat waiting silently—staring into the middle distance, uninterested in conversation.

Another set of stairs led to the rooms, and in the rooms were the girls, who were often anything but. Ricciardi remembered one woman with a bloody gash on one cheek who was fifty if she was a day, and had no more than ten teeth: she'd inspired some eighteen-year-old customer to pull out his knife when she asked for more money than she was strictly due. In those poor, cheap whorehouses, the customers lined up on the steps in single file, letting those who were raring to go cut ahead because there was a time limit on every trick, and if you went past the few minutes allotted there was a surcharge.

The place that met Ricciardi's eyes, once the old woman

had made her dramatic announcement and stepped aside, was quite another matter. First they made their way down a hallway furnished with chairs, their seats upholstered in satin, their backrests gilded, a large, elaborately-framed mirror, and red silk wallpaper. A sign invited guests to leave their umbrellas and walking sticks on a rack. At the far end there was another door, and as she neared it Marietta came to an abrupt halt: clearly, this was the far boundary of the territory under her jurisdiction.

The drawing room was large, the size of a ballroom, and it was cloaked in shadows. Heavy curtains hung over the windows and the enormous crystal chandelier was dark, as were most of the dozen or so sconces lining the walls. A tapestry on which naked nymphs and satyrs chased one another gleefully through the woods dominated the room.

But the atmosphere was anything but cheerful. The sofas and armchairs sat empty, the grand piano had fallen silent; the wall hangings and the thick carpet muffled the murmers emanating from the small knot of people at the far end of the room; a woman broke away and came toward them.

This was no ordinary individual. Her imposing stature and physique were only enhanced by a black plume that rose above a sort of tiara in her hair; her dark dress fluttered delicately, a yard-long train rustling behind her over the carpet. Before the policemen, she stopped demurely: her heavy makeup could not conceal the grief-stricken expression and the bloodshot eyes.

She turned to Maione:

"Brigadie', you're here. How sorry I am to meet you again on this sad occasion."

Camarda and Cesarano exchanged a smirk that eluded neither Ricciardi's nor Maione's notice. The brigadier glared at them, and both policemen immediately bowed their heads.

"Signora Yvonne, the proprietor of this establishment; Signora, Commissario Ricciardi. We came as soon as Marietta summoned us, but you could have telephoned and we'd have saved a little time."

The woman waved one hand distractedly in the air, and a dozen or so rings sparkled.

"That didn't occur to me, my first thought was to send Marietta. What happened seemed so ridiculous to me, and it still does. This misfortune. This terrible thing."

Ricciardi had the impression that the woman was playing a part. Her exaggerated gestures, the artificial voice, the way she'd crossed the center of the room, as stately as an ocean liner sailing into port: everything about her seemed theatrical, designed to impress and intimidate.

"*Buongiorno*, Signora. Your real name, if you please?"

He took it for granted that the name she'd given Maione was a professional pseudonym, and he wanted to invite the woman to be more forthcoming. The self-proclaimed Yvonne took his point. She fluttered her eyelashes, heaved a sigh, and focused her attention on Ricciardi.

"Lidia Fiorino, at your service. But everyone knows me as Madame Yvonne; I doubt anyone will be able to give you any information about me if you use my maiden name."

Ricciardi hadn't stopped staring at the woman.

"I like to know the name of the people I met, that's all. The legal name. Now, tell us exactly what happened."

Madame Yvonne shot a quick glance over her shoulder, toward the group of people by the piano. In the half-light, it was just possible to glimpse women in dressing gowns and one could hear muffled sobs.

"One of my girls . . . my dearest girl, she was like a daughter to me . . . the prettiest one, the sweetest one . . ."

She loudly blew her nose into a handkerchief pulled from the sleeve of her dress. Ricciardi waited, Maione sighed and raised his eyes to the ceiling.

"One of my girls is . . . Virgin Mary, Mother of God, I can't bring myself to believe it, right here, in my own home . . . where love, peace, and pleasure reign supreme . . ."

Ricciardi shot Maione a meaningful glance, and the brigadier stepped in.

"Signo', please. We know perfectly well where we are and what goes on here. In other words, there's no need to explain. Please, just do us a favor and of tell us, in short, what happened."

Yvonne dried her tears and assumed a vaguely resentful tone.

"Brigadie', you must understand what this means for me, for all of us. It's a tragedy. Viper is dead."

It was the second time he'd heard that word uttered; Ricciardi decided it was time to clear things up.

"Her real name, please. And let's start from the beginning: who found her? When? And where is she now? Has anyone moved anything?"

The woman turned her head toward the group at the far end of the room and gestured; then she turned back to Ricciardi.

"Viper is the name by which, throughout Naples, the best, the most beautiful of all the working girls, as we like to say, was known. The name is Rosaria, Maria Rosaria Cennamo. But she was Viper to everyone. No one's moved her, she's in the bedroom, the bedroom where . . . well, where she worked."

The other question went unanswered, until finally Ricciardi made up his mind to ask it again.

"I asked: who found her?"

Madame hesitated, then she turned to the girls and called out:

"Lily, come over here. Don't pretend you don't understand me."

A young woman broke away from the group, reluctantly, and came toward them. Her halting gait was quite different from Yvonne's majestic stride, and the older woman introduced her:

"This is Lily. Bianca Palumbo, to be exact: our clients, you know, like names with an exotic flavor. She's the one who found Viper."

The girl was fair-haired. Her features were soft and rounded, her face marked by horror and fright. She was clutching the edges of a flowered nightgown to her chest, which was quite prominent, disproportionately so, given her height. Cesarano let a faint whistle escape him, which earned him a furious glare from Maione.

"Now then, Signorina: you're the one who found the corpse?"

Lily looked at Madame, almost as if she were asking permission to answer; the woman nodded her head slightly, and the girl turned to Ricciardi.

"Yes. I went past her door, I'd ... I had finished, and I was going to the balcony. And Viper's door was open, just a little, it was, what's the word ... ajar. And she was on the bed, and I noticed her leg, dangling over the side ..."

She reached a trembling hand up to her face, as if to chase the image away. Her voice, deep and mature, clashed with her evident youth and her delicate features.

Ricciardi asked:

"And you, what did you do?"

The young woman hesitated, glanced again in her madam's direction, then decided to answer.

"I stuck my head out the door and called Madame."

Maione broke in:

"And how did you know that Cennamo—I mean, Viper—was dead?"

Lily shrugged.

"There was a pillow on her face. And she wasn't moving."

What Ricciardi sensed in the girl's voice, and even more in

her reactions, wasn't grief, only fright. He decided to get confirmation of that impression.

"Were the two of you friends? Did you get along with Viper?"

This time it was Madame Yvonne who replied:

"Of course! We're like a big happy family here, Commissa'. The girls are all like sisters, they spend all their time together, and they love one another, both the girls who come here to work for a couple of weeks and then go away and the ones who're here permanently. And Lily, just like Viper, is here to stay, she's not one of the girls on rotation, and so they're . . . they were even closer. Isn't that true? Answer me!"

Suddenly called upon, Lily stared at her employer and slowly nodded. Ricciardi's first impression remained unshaken: the relationship between Lily and the late Viper would need closer examination.

"And then you, Madame, sent Marietta to get us. All right. And who was here, besides you and the girls I see over there?"

Yvonne spread her arms wide.

"Commissa', of course, there were the clients. Amedeo over there, our piano player, was entertaining them while they waited, and the waiter was serving drinks. The usual afternoon activity."

"So these customers, what happened to them?"

The woman shook her head.

"I'm sure you can imagine it for yourself: the minute they heard Lily crying and screaming, they vanished. I certainly don't have the authority to stop them and tell them to wait for you all, do I?"

Ricciardi nodded.

"Certainly not. But you must remember at least your regular customers, and you can tell us their names, I believe. Just so we can check them out."

Yvonne exchanged a look with Lily that didn't escape the commissario's notice.

"Of course. Though I might have overlooked a few, in all the chaos. This kind of terrible accident, it doesn't happen every day."

"No, luckily, this sort of thing doesn't happen every day. Signorina, earlier you said: I had finished, and I was going to the balcony. What did you mean?"

Lily answered:

"Do you see that passageway up there, with the railing? We call that the balcony. When we're done working with a customer, after we've washed up and straightened up the room, then we go up there, where they can see us, that way the customers here in the waiting room know that we're free and that they can pick us. The one they like best."

Camarda sighed, earning himself an elbow in the ribs from Cesarano. Ricciardi decided to overlook it.

"All right, I understand. I may need to ask you a few more things later. Now, if you don't mind, take us to Viper's room."

# III

What is this breeze on my face?

What are these scents, the flowers and the sea?

What does springtime want from me, why doesn't it go back where it came from?

I'm a dead man, don't you understand that, springtime? I'm a dead man.

I've been dead for years and years, even though I breathed, worked, ate, and slept. I talked to the people I met, and maybe to be polite I even laughed, pretended to be interested: but I was dead.

If your heart doesn't beat in your chest, then you're dead. And my heart wasn't beating. Not anymore.

It's better to be born blind. You can't remember colors if you've never seen them before. If you're born blind, then the sun is nothing more than warmth on your skin and the sea is just water on your feet; you can't imagine how the light shimmers against the blue, while clouds scud across the sky, creating and erasing shadows. It's better, if you're born blind.

But if you've seen the light and then they take it away from you, all you can do is remember. You just remember, you don't live anymore: you're dead.

Curse you, God, why did you force me to be reborn? Why did you give back the sight that you took away from me, and the hope that I'd long since forgotten? God, you coward, why did you make me breathe again, and laugh again, and make my heart beat again, wasn't the suffering you'd already inflicted on me enough? Did you know that you would kill me a second time? You know everything, so why? Damn you to hell: you sent me to the inferno, you pulled me back out, and in the end you locked me in there forever.

Leaving my soul trapped in a bedroom at Il Paradiso. Motionless, breathless, awaiting a word that will never come from her mouth.

From her dead mouth.

## IV

At the far end of the shadowy drawing room there was a podium, and on it stood a sort of lectern made of dark wood, behind which sat a very high-backed chair, giving the impression of a throne.

Madame Yvonne, sailing toward the podium, said with undisguised pride:

"That's where I sit. That's where I greet our customers."

Ricciardi glimpsed money on the counter, a pad of printed forms, and an open fan. Behind the desk, stuck to the wall, was a sign displaying the prices.

SINGLE 2.50 LIRE
DOUBLE 3.50 LIRE
½ HOUR 6 LIRE
1 HOUR 10 LIRE
EXTRA FOR SOAP AND TOWEL 1 LIRA
BAR OF SOAP 10 CENTS
COLOGNE 25 CENTS

Next to the cashier's desk was a flight of stairs with a red handrail, at the base of which stood two wooden statues of black slaves: one was holding a lantern that illuminated the desk, the other a tray in which the customers deposited their cigarette butts before going upstairs. Madame started up the stairs, but Ricciardi, before following her, turned and murmured something to Maione. The brigadier said:

"Cama', you stay there by the front door and make sure no one comes in and no one leaves. Cesara', you phone police headquarters and tell them to call over to the hospital, this is important, tell them to ask personally for Dr. Bruno Modo, and to send the photographer. Then station yourself here and don't let anyone come upstairs."

At the top of the stairs was a hallway, lit by wall lamps. The doors of the ten or so rooms were almost all shut, except for one which stood half-open at the end of the hall.

Ricciardi indicated it with a nod.

"Is that it, Viper's room?"

Yvonne nodded her head yes. She seemed to have lost the confidence she'd displayed downstairs; her hands were trembling. That hatless commissario, with his penetrating green eyes, had made her uneasy from the first and, now that they were close to the corpse, he inexplicably frightened her.

Maione broke in, asking:

"And which one is Lily's room?"

Madame pointed to one of the rooms closest to the stairs.

"That one."

Ricciardi gestured to the brigadier, who said:

"Stay here, Signo'. Don't move."

The two policemen separated. Maione opened the door to Lily's room, and Ricciardi headed for the door that stood half-open. When he came to the threshold, he looked inside. He saw a side table, a gleam of light on a mirror, the edge of the bed. A hand, fingertips pointing away from the bed, was the only sign of a human presence that could be glimpsed through the opening.

He took a step forward and crossed the threshold.

As usual, instead of looking, he let his senses become accustomed to the room. He had to establish contact with the atmosphere, with the emotions suspended in the air. He kept his eyelids shut.

The smell, first of all. While in the rest of the bordello the smell of smoke, with an undercurrent of disinfectants, detergents, and dust, dominated, here the scent was of French perfume, elegant and penetrating; flowers, once fresh, fading; a vague aroma of lavender; and the unpleasant tang of stale sweat. No blood.

Then he listened to his skin. The open door had brought the temperature to the same level as the hallway, but he sensed a slight breeze coming from his right, possibly a window cracked open, or else just a draft. The room lay immersed in silence, except for a slow dripping.

The time had come.

He opened his eyes and looked, starting intentionally from the wall farthest from the bed. In the corner he saw the sink with the faucet whose drip he had heard, and a pitcher and washbasin; a vanity and chair, on which a black silk dressing gown with a red pattern had been abandoned; a five-drawer marble-top dresser, upon which he could see a jewel box and a framed photograph of a woman, middle-aged and serious, sitting with a little boy in a sailor suit in her arms; a vase with a spray of fresh flowers; the window, covered by a red curtain imperfectly closed, through which the spring air was entering the room.

His gaze had come around to the bed.

The corpse lay awkwardly sprawled in the middle of the rumpled sheets. One of the legs, as Lily had said, dangled over the side, and the arms were thrown wide, like the wings of a bird that would never again take flight. The light-colored slip was pulled up over the belly, revealing the undergarments that the woman was wearing. The only piece of jewelry on the body was a silver bracelet in the shape of a snake with two green stones in place of eyes, on the left forearm.

The face, uncovered, bore the expression of someone gasping for air, and a section of blackened tongue protruded from the open mouth.

Suffocated. The girl had been suffocated.

Just inches from the head lay a pillow marked with traces of makeup and a patch of damp saliva where it had been violently pressed down onto the mouth and nose, which to judge from the silhouette must have been fractured in the process. Even in the final insult of death, the commissario could tell that Viper must have been very beautiful.

Ricciardi followed the victim's blank gaze, the direction of her eyes in the moment of extremity. He heaved a long sigh.

Before a mirror that didn't reflect it, the woman's image: standing, arms at her side, short dark hair framing her face; lips stretched in one last breath, black tongue lolling out.

Looking at its own corpse, the image kept saying: *Little whip, little whip. My little whip.*

Ricciardi ran a hand over his face. Maybe I'm just imagining it all, he thought for the thousandth time. Maybe it's just an illusion produced by my sick mind. Maybe it's some kind of absurd inheritance, a lurking, silent form of madness. Maybe it's my hundreds of fears, my inability to live life. Maybe it's just a way to escape reality, maybe there's really nothing in front of me.

Outside, in the street two floors below, an accordion struck up a tango. Life in the street was resuming its movement through the first day of spring.

Ricciardi lowered his hand.

Along with the pain and grief of departure, the now familiar sense of melancholy and regret, and the surprise at being dead that Ricciardi knew all too well, he could just make out the echo of Viper's last thought: *Little whip, little whip. My little whip.*

He turned around sharply and left the room, walking toward Maione.

They'll understand. They'll have to understand.

I did it for you, to protect you. So that you'd understand that it's me, I'm the right woman for you. So that you would know that I and I alone know what you are, and what you want.

I can see you now, that time you came into my room, gripping my arm so hard that it hurt, staring into my tear-filled eyes, whispering through clenched teeth: it wasn't me. It wasn't me.

But I don't care. Whether or not it's true, you're my man, just like I'm your woman. The two of us together, we'll get out of this. Because you'll finally understand that I'm the right one, the one who cares for you: because I've protected you, I've put your safety first.

Not like that damned whore, who stole your soul. Who blinded you.

Because you can work as a whore, or you can be a whore. And she was a whore right down to the bottom of her soul.

But now she's dead.

Which is better for everyone.

V

Augusto Ventrone looked the angel in the eyes.
He admired its light-blue coloring, its intense expression, which was at once pitying and determined; ready to provide comfort and to inflict punishment, annunciating and exterminating. That's what an angel should be like.

He put the statue back on its shelf, next to the shop's front door, and looked outside: afternoon sunlight filled the street, and a few flies were flitting around in the low light. Spring had come. Punctual as ever.

Augusto allowed himself a quick smile. Not that he was in the habit of smiling: he was the most unsmiling twenty-year-old in the neighborhood, and possibly in the whole city. And really, why would he smile?

First of all, the merchandise they offered in their shop had to be sold with earnest sobriety, in certain cases with something approaching grief: and he was a born salesman. Their customers came in expecting a murmured recommendation. "Award-Winning Purveyors of Sacred Art, Vincenzo Ventrone and Son," read the sign. Sacred art. Nothing playful, nothing funny. The religious expected a sophisticated adviser; private individuals interested in decorating a home chapel, a family tomb, or even just a nightstand in their bedroom, wanted the understanding of a professional: for smiles, they were welcome to try the undergarment shop, just fifty feet down the street, on the opposite sidewalk.

Nor had life given Augusto any particular reasons to be

cheerful. A mother who'd died too young, no brothers or sisters, and a father who'd lost his head over a whore.

At first, Augusto had actually been quite tolerant. After all, after five years as a lonely widower, one could understand why Vincenzo Ventrone, who wasn't so old that he couldn't hear the call of the flesh, should have gone in search of comfort. And all things considered, better a brothel—with a discreet side entrance where you'd pay no more than a few lire—than a money-grubbing young lady from a well-to-do family looking to get herself situated, or even worse, a fortune hunter with children of her own, who could replace him as the heir to the family business.

But then matters had taken a strange turn. His father's visits to Il Paradiso (how blasphemously ironic, that name: astonishing that the authorities should allow it!) had multiplied until he was going daily, sometimes even more frequently. It was inevitable that other customers, that even a number of high prelates from the bishopric, would see him emerge from the bordello with a stupid, ridiculous grin stamped on his face, his celluloid collar unbuttoned, his tie askew, traces of lipstick smeared on his cheeks. And the idiot, instead of hiding in the shadows, just doffed his hat and called out hello.

With a shudder, Augusto remembered how he had learned that his father's affair with a whore had by now become public knowledge. One day the Contessa Félaco di Castelbriano had come into the shop, an elderly crone who weighed at least 225 pounds and collected statues of St. Anthony; she'd stopped at the front counter and stood there for several minutes silently staring at him, wearing a pained, sympathetic expression. He'd waited, as was befitting a serious shopkeeper in the presence of a first-rate customer. Finally, in her cavernous voice, the contessa had told him: "Your poor mother is turning over in her grave over this indecency. For the shame that your father is heaping on her, even in the afterlife." Then she'd turned on her heel and left the shop.

At that point, Augusto had felt it was his duty to have a man-to-man talk with his father, in part because he'd recently noticed a slight drop in the number of customers, and he was a very keen observer of these kinds of things, having inerhited from his mother a certain, let's say, attention to the practical side of life. He'd said to him, not in so many words: Papà, if you want to have fun, that's your business; but discretion, in a business like ours, is a necessity. Given that, I have to beg you to stop letting people see you enter and leave that place, which after all is only a few hundred yards from our shop.

That fool had looked at him and said: my son, I don't know what you're talking about. I'm not doing anything wrong, I'll spend my money and I'll go wherever I want. And after all, I only play cards there. You know that I live for the memory of your sainted mother.

Augusto was left with no alternative but to pray that Vincenzo would come to his senses, while every day more and more people came to see him, feigning compassion, to tell him the details of his father's affair with the famous Viper, the most notorious prostitute in town.

That day, however, something new must have happened. His father had come home much earlier than he usually did, pale as a ghost and trembling, the very opposite of how he'd looked when he'd walked out, frisky and fragrant, into the fresh spring air. He'd muttered something about not feeling well and needing to go to bed (his own bed, for once). Augusto had told him not to worry, that he'd look after the store. As if that were somehow a novelty.

Dusting off angels and saints, the young man indulged in the second smile of the day: a real record. And he decided that there are times when prayers are even answered.

Especially if you lend a hand.

*

Maione had understood perfectly what the commissario wanted him to check up on, when he'd nodded his head in the direction of the door to Lily's room—she was the woman who'd claimed to have found Viper's body—and he'd understood exactly what doubts his superior officer was entertaining.

They went back down to the main hall, followed by an increasingly concerned Madame Yvonne. They went over to the group that had clustered in the corner furthest from the staircase, as if death was contagious, as if its miasma might condemn them too.

There were about a dozen girls, of varying ages: there were very young ones, no more than twenty, and women who were probably past thirty, the marks of hard living just beginning to appear on their faces, their expressions hard and suspicious.

All different in their features and origins, brunettes, blondes, and redheads, dyed hair and natural colors, shapely and lean. Clothing and makeup designed to titillate and attract, and in that new and terrible context it all seemed like a grotesque masquerade. A few of them were weeping softly, blowing their noses every so often.

There were also three men. One was introduced by Yvonne as Amedeo, the piano player: a fidgety little man with tapered fingers and a wispy mustache that was being shaken by terrified shivers. A dapper, elderly gentleman in a tailcoat was announced as Armando, the butler, who actually made a formal bow, as if he were at a ball. The third, a strapping, shifty young man who grunted hello, was Tullio, Madame Yvonne's son: the woman explained that he was a handyman, in charge of maintenance, and also took care of security. All three of them swore that they hadn't left the main hall all morning.

Once they'd taken names and gathered what little information was forthcoming, Ricciardi summoned Lily.

The girl hadn't changed expression or attitude; now that he'd seen all the girls, including the victim, the commissario had made up his mind that the blond was the most attractive, with the possible exception of Viper herself: but her physical beauty clashed with the girl's hard and determined features.

"Signorina, can you confirm the statements you made earlier? That you found the body, by looking through the half-open door in the victim's room, while you were walking to the balcony for a new customer?"

The woman held Ricciardi's gaze confidently; that didn't happen often.

"Yes, that's what happened. I found her. Around three."

"And did you call for help immediately, calling for Madame?"

"Certainly."

Ricciardi exchanged a glance with Maione, who was desperately trying to keep his eyes from resting on Lily's spectacular breasts.

"I don't believe you."

The young woman betrayed no surprise.

"Ah, no? And why don't you believe me, Commissa'?"

"First: because Viper's bedroom is at the end of the hallway, and you wouldn't have gone by it on the way from your room to the balcony. Second: because you said that you had finished and that you normally tidy up your room before bringing in another customer, and Maione saw for himself that your bed is rumpled and unmade. Third: because through the gap of the half-opened door you can't see the leg dangling from the bed, but only the fingertips of one hand."

Lily had listened to Ricciardi's tirade without blinking, her hands on her hips.

The commissario said:

"Who are you covering for, Signorina? And why?"

The question was met with silence. The girls looked at one

another, no longer weeping. Madame Yvonne was twisting her hands, in a state of anxiety. Ricciardi said loudly:

"If that's the way things are, then this establishment is going to remain shuttered and you won't get to leave until I've discovered who actually found the body and in what circumstances; this is necessary information, and without it you all can't get back to business. On the other hand, I want to be clear that finding a corpse does not amount to the commission of a crime, and therefore this stance may only be casting suspicion on an innocent person. We have all the time in the world. We can wait."

Madame Yvonne took a step forward, her eyes on Lily, and said in a broken voice:

"I can't allow this, if we have to stay closed, we'll be finished. Already, having a death in here is a terrible tragedy for our establishment's good name: our only hope is to get right back to work. Commissa', Viper's body was found by one of our clients: Cavalier Vincenzo Ventrone, proprietor of the sacred art shop."

## VI

D
r. Bruno Modo entered the large drawing room panting, his collar unbuttoned, his hat askew, and his bag in hand.

"Here I am, what's happened? Which girl was it?"

Ricciardi and Maione could hardly help but notice that the doctor's demeanor was quite different from his usual: normally, even in the presence of the most heinous murders, he remained detached and ironic, even as he brought to bear his vast and impassioned expertise, which is why the police continued to request his personal assistance.

This time the doctor's brow was furrowed by a deep crease under the shock of snow-white hair. He seemed pained and frightened, the way one would be when summoned to rush to a family member's aid.

Maione walked toward him.

"Dotto', *buonasera*. Unfortunately, there's no need to hurry. That girl's not going anywhere ever again. Her name is, or was, Cennamo. Maria Rosaria Cennamo."

Modo gave him a bewildered stare:

"Cennamo? Who's that?"

Madame Yvonne took a step forward as if she were stepping onto center stage, and intoned dramatically:

"Viper, Doctor. Viper, our own Viper, is dead."

The doctor took off his hat and scratched his head.

"Viper. Poor girl. Where is she?"

Ricciardi walked slowly over to him.

"Ciao, Bruno. So you knew her, this signorina?"

The doctor grimaced wearily.

"Oh, ciao, Ricciardi. At least it's you, on this case, and not one of your incompetent colleagues. Yes, of course I knew her. Everyone in the city knew her. In her way, she was a celebrity. And after all, I'm someone who knows all of these girls."

He waved to the group of women in nightgowns, who all responded affectionately in return.

Ricciardi sighed.

"I'm well aware that you're familiar with this place."

The doctor was preparing a retort when Maione broke in:

"Speaking of family members, Dotto', is that famous dog still with you?"

"Of course he is, Brigadie'. Why on earth would he leave me, with what I feed him? Sure, his ideal meal would be ground policeman, but he finds that all too rarely in his bowl."

Maione snorted.

"My flesh would be too tough to chew, Dotto'. You'd probably blunt the edge of your scalpel if you tried."

"In any case, the dog is downstairs. He's just like Ricciardi, he doesn't like to come into places like this. He waits for me, and if I'm in here too long, he even starts to howl. I've acquired a mother-in-law, not a dog."

Ricciardi pointed upstairs.

"Come on, let's go take a look at the young lady. After all, this lovely reception is being held in her honor."

While Modo was focusing on the corpse, Ricciardi examined the bedroom more carefully.

It seemed that nothing was missing nor, at first glance, was there any reason to suppose that theft had been the motive. The drawers were all shut, the jewelry box on the dresser was full, and in any case, none of the baubles inside seemed especially valuable, junk for the most part, gaudy but made of cheap metals. The chaos that reigned in the room was only the result of the girl's messiness.

He started searching more carefully.

He looked in the dresser drawers, turning up nothing other than a vast assortment of elegant unmentionables, culottes, brassieres, stockings, and negligees of every cut and color. No letters, no documents.

And no whips.

He looked on the floor, under the carpet, beneath the bed. He noticed that everything was very clean. But he found nothing.

He realized that in all likelihood there'd been a brief struggle: whatever had been atop the nightstand had been swept off, possibly by the woman herself as she thrashed frantically, seeing as her left leg had been very nearby; apart from a few hairpins and a nail file, there was nothing on the nightstand. It must not have made much noise, because some of the objects had fallen on the bed and the rest onto the thick carpet that covered the floor; nothing had broken.

The commissario focused on the objects that had been knocked off the nightstand, but here too nothing seemed out of the ordinary: a bottle of glycerine, a container of talcum that hadn't burst open as it fell; nail polish, a small mirror with a handle, a small bottle of perfume with the name "Fleurs Parisiennes"; a round tin of face powder without a lid, but practically empty; a brush made of inlaid wood, a comb, and a cigarette case. All of them scattered across the carpet, with the exception of the face powder, the perfume, and the brush, which were on the bed.

Ricciardi reflected on how grotesque it was to see all this makeup and cosmetics in the grim presence of death. Beauty, cared for, cultivated, and then wiped out with a single act of violence.

He noticed that on the pillow that had been used to suffocate the girl there were a number of blond hairs, as well as on the brush; he filed away that detail.

Modo called him: the doctor had completed his initial summary examination. In the meanwhile, the photographer too had arrived; the commissario warned him take particular care with his shots.

odo shook his head sadly.

"*Mamma mia*, what a shame. Believe me, Ricciardi, Viper was a very beautiful woman. So beautiful. I'm so sorry that you had to see her so beat up. She had dark deep eyes, glittering with life, plump lips, and a graceful way of moving that drove men mad."

Ricciardi was impressed: he'd never heard his friend so raptly absorbed in a description.

"What about you, Bruno, were you . . . I mean, did you see her?"

A melancholy expression appeared on Modo's face.

"No, no. I come here to have fun, to drink and to play cards. The young ladies who warm my skin are more cheerful and unassuming than Viper. Also, from what I heard, she had very few clients. For Madame Yvonne she was like a kind of publicity, a flesh-and-blood advertisement. Certainly, this is a major loss for her."

"Yes, so she told me. I might have some more questions for you about life in this place, that way you can raise yourself from necrophiliac butcher to police informant. But tell me something else: did you notice anything about the girl's body?"

Modo, in spite of himself, chuckled briefly.

"There, now I recognize you: the real Ricciardi, the one who, as soon as the conversation veers onto lighthearted topics, steers it straight back to his world of blood. Well, no, little more than what you've certainly already guessed: it must have been over quickly, the murderer or murderess shoved her onto the bed and put a pillow over her face, and that was that. Death by suffocation; nasal septum fractured, bleeding of the upper and lower lips due to pressure against the teeth. She didn't have a chance to cry out to anyone. She kicked a little: there's a small ecchymosis on her foot, it must have hit the nightstand."

Ricciardi decided that the picture he'd developed matched perfectly.

"What about her hands? Did she try to defend herself, did she manage to . . ."

"No, no scratches on the murderer, there aren't any traces of skin under the fingernails. Unfortunately, there aren't any fingerprints: she struggled to get the pillow off her face, that's the only thing she touched."

Modo had immediately caught Ricciardi's drift: the presence of scratches and cuts on the hands or forearms could certainly have helped to identify the murderer.

"Of course, I reserve the right to come back to you with more information after the autopsy, which I intend to perform with extreme care: anyone capable of murdering such a beautiful woman, a woman who definitely freshened the foul air of this city, deserves the worst punishment possible."

Ricciardi shrugged.

"That's the kind of attention that we give all murderers. One last thing, Bruno: I've heard that in places like this they sometimes, let's say, play games that can turn a little rough. That some people, in other words, like to use . . . things that could hurt. Sometimes, the games can get out of hand, and lead to uncontrolled violence, even to death."

Modo was staring at him, arms folded, and with an ironic glint in his eyes.

"Well, lookie here: the monastic Ricciardi, the high priest of self-mortification himself, the man who never has fun, not even by accident, is all caught up on sadomasochistic practices. Yes, of course, people like the oddest things: and in places like this one, people come to try out things that they'd never have the nerve to suggest at home. And I certainly can't rule out that poor Viper might have been particularly gifted in this sector, in fact, I think I even heard something to that effect, some time ago, in the waiting room. But I can rule that out as a contributing factor to the crime."

"And how can you be so sure?"

"Simple. As you saw for yourself, she was still wearing her undergarments. There was no sexual intercourse underway, nor was there afterward."

They walked downstairs to the large drawing room. Ricciardi addressed Madame.

"Signora, for now I'd ask you not to move anything, and of course, we can't allow you to reopen for business. An officer will remain here until the morgue attendants arrive. No one will be allowed to enter the bedroom."

The woman put a hand to her forehead and clutched at the side of the desk, as if she were about to faint.

"Commissa', you're going to ruin me! Already this is Holy Week and we get little enough business as it is, but if we shut down then we'll lose even those few customers and that's the end! How am I supposed to feed my girls and my employees?"

Ricciardi didn't blink an eye:

"I'm very sorry, but that's the way it is and that's the way it's going to have to be. A murder is a serious thing, you know. The most serious thing that can happen. I need more information: you are to draw up a list of the clients that were present here when it happened, aside from this Ventrone. Now, tell me: apart from the entrance where we came in, are there any other ways in or out?"

Yvonne shook her head no, to the sound of jangling earrings.

"Only the tradesmen's entrance, but that leads directly into the kitchen. They use the little side door, off the *vicolo*, but if a stranger or someone unusual had come in that way, the cook and his assistants would have to have seen him."

Ricciardi nodded.

"Fine. No one is to leave town without asking permission from police headquarters, and you, Signorina Lily, you are not even to leave the building or talk on the phone. Officer Cesarano will stay here to keep an eye out, and you, Maione, remember to send someone to relieve him, at least for the day tomorrow. That goes until you make up your mind to tell the truth."

The young woman smirked sarcastically.

"So it's more or less like being under house arrest. Hardly new to me."

Ricciardi looked at the girl's long blond hair, tied up in a bun.

"Tell me something, Signorina: could something that belonged to you have found its way into the murdered woman's bedroom?"

Lily shrugged her shoulders.

"Of course, we're always swapping things, makeup, brushes, soap. We all live here, we're all doing the same things."

Yvonne broke in emphatically:

"Just like I told you, Commissa', these girls are like daughters to me, so they're also like sisters. None of us could ever have hurt Viper."

Ricciardi headed for the door, then turned around and said:

"One last thing. I want to know the names of Viper's clients, the most frequent ones."

Lily snickered and said:

"That's an easy one."

Madame Yvonne shot her an angry look that the commissario didn't miss.

As soon as they were back out in the street, Ricciardi said to Maione:

"First thing tomorrow morning, go get this Ventrone, the merchant of sacred art who found the body. And do it discreetly: we don't want to stir things up for no good reason."

As they passed it, he shot a quick look up the *vicolo* that ran alongside the palazzo and got a glimpse of the small door that served as the tradesmen's entrance, right next to where a blind accordion player was trying to coax charity out of the passersby with the heartbreaking strains of his instrument.

The night of the first day of spring had by now fallen, but its smells still filled the air.

People were dawdling, as if they were disoriented by the warm weather, hungry for hours outdoors after struggling through a harsh and pitiless winter. The strolling vendors took advantage of situation, and went on hawking their goods much later than usual.

After two days of celebrations, the Festa di San Giuseppe—the Festival of St. Joseph—was still going, and the fry cooks continued selling their *zeppole* fried in black rancid oil; the acrid smell and the plumes of smoke filled every corner of the street, causing stabbing pangs of hunger in the bellies of those hurrying home for dinner.

You could see bird vendors, their stalls piled high with cages of all sizes in which birds thrashed in a frenzy, beating their wings against the bars, in search of their lost freedom; according to tradition, grace would be granted to anyone who purchased a bird for the festival of Jesus's father, and that belief was still popular. With the arrival of spring, the city's balconies filled up with goldfinches and canaries that had been blinded with a pin to encourage their beautiful, despairing song.

But the air was also filled with the irritating noise of the *zerri zerri*, the infernal wooden rattles that children whirled around on their handles, producing a clickety-clack that sounded more or less like castanets.

The last gasps of the Festa di San Giuseppe, however, were destined to die out: the heart of the populace had already turned to Easter, which was by now less than a week away. The countless catholic religious and pagan traditions would soon reclaim their rightful space, their enchantments commanding the attention of the entire city, throughout each of the various social strata that made up Naples.

Modo made a show of placing both hands over his ears to shut out the shrill whistle of a peanut vendor.

"I wonder what on earth these starving beggars have to celebrate, penniless in their tattered rags. And yet, for whatever reason, they're still in the middle of the street, laughing and dancing. Instead of understanding that they're living under the heel of a dictator, who actually forces them to count in order to figure out what year it is: can you believe it, Ricciardi? Year ten. As if Christ had been reborn. Incredible."

Now it was Ricciardi's turn to feign despair and cover up his ears:

"For the love of God, please! It's already been a hard day, don't you start in too."

Modo snickered, pointing behind him at a little white dog with brown spots trotting along with one ear down and the other up.

"You see? I have followers of my own. In fact, you know what I think? From here on out I'm going to force the dog to say that this isn't 1932, but the year fifty-six."

Maione poked him in the ribs with his elbow.

"Dotto', if you ask me that dog doesn't think about you at all, much less have any idea how old you are. He never even comes when you call him!"

The doctor heaved a sigh of annoyance.

"So what? We're friends, it's not like I own him. He can

stay with me as long as he likes, and when he chooses to he'll go his own way. We all should do the same thing, in love and in politics. Let people choose."

Maione snickered.

"Dotto', I can choose, no question. But say that I choose not to go home for dinner and instead, I don't know, go to a trattoria with some friend, my wife will choose to greet me with a shoe straight to the forehead, when I do go home. So what does that mean, that we're two free individuals?"

Modo gave up, disheartened:

"Nothing doing, I give up. You're a bunch of sheep, and you're destined to die like sheep, and I say this with a perverse pleasure now that Easter is almost here. But do you want to hear how low we've sunk? Well, the other day in the hospital a lawyer comes in for some stitches. His lip was split open, he'd taken a slap or a punch to the face. We're getting along, we get to talking, and finally he tells me that he'd been assaulted in front of the courthouse, in broad daylight, by a pair of these idiots in black shirts. And do you know why?"

Ricciardi shook his head no.

"No, we don't, but we're pretty confident that you're about to fill in this gap in our knowledge."

"In fact, I'll tell you straightaway: because he'd dared to defend . . . dared, you understand? . . . an accountant accused of 'offending the honor of the head of government.' And what do you think this offense consisted of?"

Maione spread both arms wide.

"Dotto', this is starting to sound like twenty questions. Tell us, just what had this accountant done?"

"He'd taken down from the wall of his office at the Provincial Bank the portrait of the Old Bull Head you call Il Duce, that's what he'd done. And it was only because he wanted to hang up his calendar, and he didn't have any other nails handy. So do you realize how low we've sunk? Already it's ridiculous to bring the defendant up on these charges, but then to attack his defense lawyer!"

"We hear these kind of stories all the time, Bruno. We hear them. And there's not much we can do about them, you know. If they decide to establish a new crime, however absurd it might be, complete with sentence and indictment, it's our job to enforce the law. Now, of course, there are some things you do with conviction and others you don't: in other words, we have priorities. At least, that applies to Maione and me."

The brigadier snickered.

"That doesn't mean, Commissa', that if the order came in to arrest a certain doctor for subversive activity, we wouldn't take a special pleasure in carrying it out. Maybe by then they'll have come up with some new kind of penalties, I don't know, say flogging or flaying."

Modo playfully waved his finger under Maione's nose.

"Ah, the worst thing they're going to do to me is this new internal exile, and they'll send me someplace with lots of sun and sand, far away, finally, from your ugly mugs. In fact, maybe one of these days I'll turn myself in after some especially serious crime, like blowing a raspberry or farting in honor of your Duce, and I'll get myself sent down intentionally. And do you know what I have to say to you, my dear brigadier? This dog, here, I'll leave him to you in my will. The day you no longer see me around, you'll have to take care of him."

Maione, poker-faced, lifted his hand to the visor of his cap.

"All right, Dotto', at your service. And next time you see him, do me a favor, and teach the dog how to do a proper autopsy. That way we really won't need your help anymore. Now, with your permission, and the commissario's, I'm heading home for dinner, because this smell of *zeppole* is driving me crazy. Tomorrow morning I'll bring you the merchant bright and early, Commissa'. Have a good evening."

Modo gave Maione a friendly slap on the back and turned to Ricciardi.

"Well, my funereal commissario, now that you've shut down the place where I was planning to spend my evening, I hope you'll at least buy me dinner?"

Ricciardi glanced at his watch.

"I wish I could, Bruno; but I have to get home early tonight. Maybe tomorrow, let's be in touch."

The doctor gave him a long look.

"You're not telling me the whole story, and you haven't been for a while. You're in too much of a hurry to get home. My old but exceedingly well trained nose catches a whiff of woman. Go on, go on: I give up here. That means that the dog and I will just have to eat alone tonight, in a trattoria some friends of mine own down by the sea. He's getting used to fish, turning into a real salty dog. Good evening to you, my friend."


What do you want from springtime?

What do you ask of this season, which brings you gifts of new flowers and new ideas, borrowed from the scent of the sea?

Maybe to get away from the cold and the damp of winter. Maybe only that. To take off the grey overcoats, the galoshes, to furl the umbrellas having waxed their canvases one last time. To cover your trousers with sheets of newspaper to keep them from creasing.

Or perhaps to eat fresh fruit and rediscover flavors longed for like relatives away on a trip, new and forgotten but still familiar.

What gift do you ask of springtime?

Not to have to lay eyes again for months on the heavy gloves, slightly worn at the fingers, and the woolen stockings with an impertinent hole that defies any attempts at darning.

And maybe to dig out a cheerful silk scarf or a straw boater that's survived the moths.

Perhaps spring can give you the gift of a deep breath of fresh air, scented by new budded leaves in the forest of Capodimonte, if the wind blows in the right direction; or the image of a coachman dozing in the seat of his carriage, a hazy smile on his toothless lips, lost in a dream of youth, indifferent to the flies attracted by the smell of his nag.

And even the *scugnizzi* dangling like bunches of raggedy grapes from the ends of trolley cars rattling up Via Medina will seem more cheerful in springtime, as they shout obscene compliments at the girls emerging from the boarding school in Piazza Dante, walking silently, their books bound together with a strap. And their fellow students, the boys who are head over heels in love with them, will shake their fists in the air and invite them to fight bloody duels, but by then the laughing *scugnizzi* will already be at the far end of Via Toledo, on their daily ride down to the sea.

What do you ask of springtime, while you melt into new hopes you never thought you'd have, as you start to think that perhaps a life of happiness may still await you?

Ask springtime, and perhaps she, in her giddy madness, will grant you your wish.

Ask her for death.

# VIII

Taking care to avoid the corner from which the suicide was calling to his lost love, as he returned home Ricciardi paid his own silent tribute to Dr. Modo's nose, which was certainly right: this was about a woman. But the matter was a far more complicated one.

Last Christmas Eve had certainly reshuffled the cards on the table as far as his relationship with Enrica Colombo, the girl who lived in the building across the street, was concerned. After all that time spent looking at her through the window—first of all because he was drawn by the allure of a normality he felt excluded from, then attracted by the faintly hidden delicacy of her features and by the memory of a voice that he'd once heard by chance in an interrogation—things had suddenly accelerated.

An hour before the city's bells pealed out in celebration of the birth of Our Lord, as he was hurrying back to his usual solitude, depressed and weary, he'd found her standing in front of the door of his apartment building as if in some dream, just as a fine snow began to fall; she'd walked right up to him and, as in a dream, she'd softly kissed him.

That kiss, nothing more than a faint wisp of breath on his lips, had given flesh and blood to his thoughts, unleashing an unceasing tempest in his soul. Ricciardi was a man just over thirty, sentenced to solitude because he was aware of the curse that he bore; but that didn't mean that his flesh and his hands didn't yearn to touch and move to the rhythm of his beating heart.

Ever since that strange Christmas Eve, rationality had begun to slowly succumb to emotion. Day after day, the commissario found himself imagining more and more frequently what it would be like to repeat that experience, or even just to see Enrica again up close; in order to understand what she felt, and to some extent, what he felt too.

As he climbed Via Santa Teresa, walking into the smells of the forest that mixed with those of the sea from behind him, Ricciardi thought about Rosa, his *tata*, who as always understood sooner and much more clearly than he just what he himself desired. Who knows how, Rosa had established a strange friendship with the girl, on the basis of which Enrica would regularly visit, sometimes staying until he came back; magically, she often managed to brush by him on the stairs or at the downstairs door, greeting him with a smile and a word.

By now Ricciardi—the man who was terrified of love because he saw its fatal effects every day, the same Ricciardi who had long since decided that it was impossible for him to have a woman at his side because she'd have to share in his curse, the man who never saw a future beyond the days necessary to complete an investigation—had begun to live for the moment when, returning home, he might possibly cross paths with Enrica. He didn't know what might happen, nor whether that emotion might have a tomorrow; he knew only that living without that glimmer of sweet tenderness at the end of the steep climb that was his daily lot was now something that seemed almost impossible.

He looked at his watch and quickened his step.

Rosa set down her cup, which she'd been holding with the hand that shook less; still, the porcelain rattled against the saucer, causing a few drops of tea to spill onto the tablecloth. Enrica bowed her head over her tea, pretending not to have noticed; the *tata* appreciated this show of tact. She liked this girl better every day.

She went on with what she'd been saying:

"Signori', you have to keep this in mind: the truly important thing about a Cilento Easter dinner is the first course, the pasta. Any housewife knows how to cook a nice piece of meat or a leg of lamb, even though we really ought to be talking about a leg of kid goat, which is no simple matter, either; but the *primo*, the first course is, as we say, fundamental. And every detail deserves careful attention."

Enrica listened, concentrating. She liked to cook, she did it every day for her own family and she was honestly convinced that it was be a good way to demonstrate love; but hearing Rosa describe the cooking of her hometown, the rigor with which she respected its traditions—she found it, somehow, deeply moving. She understood that it was something more than just a way of providing for one's loved ones, ensuring they were well fed while at the same time pleasing them. She knew that it was also a way of establishing a profound link with generations of women in love who had left behind not words, but aromas and flavors.

And she understood why the elderly *tata*, who knew that she was ill, felt the need to ensure that her way of loving the man she thought of as her child—the man who was now the object of her own dreams—could in some way be carried on.

". . . and so," the *tata* went on, "deciding which pasta to cook with the ragú becomes crucial. You can choose cavatelli or fusilli, it's the same dough. Of course, cavatelli are easier; but what my young master likes best are the fusilli, so I'd advise you to make those for him. First: you have to get yourself some rods from a broken umbrella; of course, you clean them thoroughly, in vinegar and boiling water. Then you put the flour on the *scannaturu*, which would be that plank of wood, what do you all call it? The cutting board. Form a sort of volcano, with a hole in the middle, and pour lukewarm water in a little at a time, until you've made a loaf of dough, smooth as can be, and soft to the touch. At that point," and here she acted it out with her hands, "flatten and roll out the sausages of dough around the umbrella ribs."

Enrica, satisfied, nodded her head.

"But none of this is the real secret. The proof of a good cook is making sure that the fusilli are all the same, because that ensures that they'll cook uniformly; if there are some that are thicker and others that are finer, it's practically impossible for them to cook right—some will be raw in the center while others will be overcooked. You need patience: the ones that don't turn out right have to be rolled out again. But once you have the touch, there are no problems and you can do it the first time. And I think you, my girl, have plenty of patience, am I right?"

Enrica sighed.

"Yes, Signora, I have plenty of patience. My father calls it being hardheaded, to tell the truth; but when he says it he smiles and strokes my cheek."

Rosa laughed, a fine infectious laugh.

"Well, that's certainly true, from a certain point of view you could call patience being hardheaded. And with my young master, one needs a great deal of patience. The point is that he doesn't know what he wants. Men never know what they want, and you know why not? Because they think that the world ends tomorrow, so they only worry about what's happening today. But we women can see as clear as the light of day what's going to happen next, and we have to be responsible for it. So a little at a time . . ."

Enrica continued:

". . . a little at a time we need to lead them to do what we want them to do, letting them think that it was all their idea."

Rosa clapped her hands, contentedly.

"That's exactly right, well done, my girl! But now you should leave, because he's about to get here and if you don't you won't manage to run into him on the stairs. By now he's used to that, you should see his face, like a corpse's, when he misses you by just a minute."

The young woman stood up and gave the elderly lady a kiss on the cheek, then she ran for the door. Rosa's words followed her down the stairs:

"And tomorrow we'll talk about the ragú!"

She had just stepped out the front door when he appeared before her, as if they'd made a date. *Buonasera*, she said to him. *Buonasera*, he replied.

She even liked his voice: deep and full of emotion. She found him irresistible; she could understand why a woman like that Signora from up north, that rich, elegant, and shameless woman who drove around in a car with a chauffeur, would have developed a crush on him, though she could have had all the men she wanted. But she was also convinced that the way to his heart that she had chosen was the right one.

She hesitated, then stopped and said:

"You know, Signora Rosa . . . that trembling in her hand is getting worse, I think. Sorry, I know it's none of my business, but . . ."

He interrupted her, in a sad voice:

"Don't say that. Your visits give her great pleasure; she's so happy, I leave her alone for far too much time. I know, she's not well. But it's not easy for me to think that she's growing older. You know, I . . . I have no one but her."

She wanted to hold him tight, crying out that it wasn't true—that he wasn't alone and would never again be alone, if only he could say that's what he wanted.

Instead, she just said: *buonasera*.

## IX

On the morning of March 22nd, the springtime decided on a sudden and precocious change of attitude. The sky turned gray and the wind sprang up, a hot wind that stirred the sweet smells together with the rank odors that rose from the *vicoli* down in the harbor and in the Spanish Quarter, disorienting dogs, horses, and people who had believed that the season had changed once and for all.

Ricciardi, as usual, got to police headquarters very early. He'd had a restless night; the thought of Rosa's worsening health gripped his heart in a clenched fist of anguish. Enrica's few words at the front door had made him think about how often the mind forces us to ignore what we fear; how unprepared we are when those we hold dear grow old and fall ill.

And as always, the murder he'd encountered contributed to his troubled dreams. In his dreams he'd found himself face to face with the corpse of what had once been a wonderful young woman, full of life and perhaps hopes for the future, and from her dead mouth the references to who knows what perversion continued. The commissario wondered, as he covered the last few yards of Via Toledo before turning down the narrow street that led to his office, what corrupt passion could have brought someone to suffocate that life and those hopes under a pillow.

There were two men waiting for him at the entrance. The sentinel saluted and said:

"Commissa', *buongiorno*. These two men here have been waiting for you for some time now, they showed up in the middle of the night. Should I tell them to go on waiting or would you like to speak with them?"

Ricciardi walked closer. One was blond, with two deep circles under a pair of light blue eyes and a face creased with unmistakable suffering. The other one was little more than a boy, with similar features and the same light blue eyes, but with black hair.

The blond man stepped forward.

"Are you Commissario Ricciardi? The one who's . . . who's in charge of the murder at Il Paradiso?"

Ricciardi confirmed that he was, without taking his hands out of his overcoat pockets. The man's voice was deep and hoarse.

"Yes, that's me. And with whom do I have the pleasure of speaking?"

"I'm Giuseppe Coppola, and this is my brother Pietro. I believe that I was the last person to see . . ."

He ran a hand over his face. His lower lip was quivering, and he bit it to make it stop; he seemed to be gripped by powerful emotions. He went on:

"I was in Rosaria's room, before . . . before what happened to her happened. The last person to see her alive. Except for the murderer."

Ricciardi gestured toward the staircase and headed upstairs toward his office, followed by the two men. First, though, he told the officer on sentinel duty to have Maione wait for him with the merchant of sacred objects in a separate room. He had a feeling that for now it would be best to avoid any confrontations.

He pointed the Coppola brothers to the two chairs that stood facing the desk, then opened the windows on the piazza below, which lay immersed in the gray light of that morning, the branches of the holm oaks tossing their leaves uneasily in the wind. Strange weather, for this young spring; strange also not to have that moment of solitude that was the main reason he got to the office early, a time he used to reorganize his thoughts and plan out his activities for the day. But the two men he was about to talk to might well have very important information about Viper's murder.

He sized them up attentively. Giuseppe was a few years older, thirty or so at the very most, though hard work and general privation often made guesses at age spectacularly inaccurate; the man had a handsome face, even if his unmistakable grief and anxiety had deformed his features. He wasn't tall, and his taut, muscular physique spoke of days filled with hard labor, as did the gnarled hands, covered with cuts and abrasions, which he kept twisting.

The younger brother had declined the offer of a chair and remained standing, as if this were yet another way of expressing his subordinate role. He was a tall, powerful-looking young man, not especially intelligent in appearance, clearly ill at ease, like many people when they find themselves inside police headquarters.

Ricciardi sat down at his desk and said:

"Now then, from what you've told me, you were Viper's last customer. Is that correct?"

Coppola turned even paler than before.

"Commissa', I must beg you never to call her by that name. That's not her real name, her name was Maria Rosaria, and everyone who knew her called her Rosaria. If you call her Viper, you're doing her wrong."

It had come out in a whisper, uttered in a broken voice. Pietro, standing behind his brother, dropped his head in embarrassment. Giuseppe resumed:

"And another thing: I'm not one of her customers. I paid, that's true, otherwise they wouldn't let us be together; but I'm not a client."

Ricciardi refused to allow himself to be intimidated.

"Coppola, if we hope to attain any results from this conversation, then your hostility is useless. My objective is to identify the murderer of this poor girl as quickly as possible and to bring him to justice. If you have the same objective, that's all well and good. Otherwise, I'll have to question you in a very different manner, and in a different setting. It's up to you."

The tension drained visibly from Coppola's body, as his shoulders hunched and he once again ran his hands over his face. After a moment, he said:

"You're right, Commissa'. Forgive me. It's just that this *thing* . . . this news, you understand, it's got me upset. No, not upset, it's killing me. Because since last night, when they told me, I'm a dead man too."

"How and when did you learn about the girl's death?"

"From the cook. We supply fruit and vegetables to Il Paradiso, we bring them late every night so they have plenty of time in the morning to get everything ready. They have a large icebox and that's what they prefer. My brother, here, makes the last round: we're street vendors, we have a pretty big company, we have horsecarts and trucks. The cook told him and he came to me with the news. Right, Pietro?"

The younger man nodded his agreement; Giuseppe didn't even bother to turn around to look at him, and went on:

"It was late, very late. But still I hurried over. I had to see for myself . . . They wouldn't let me in. They said that at your orders the bordello was shut, and that in any case she . . . they'd already taken her away. And so I decided to come here, to see you, and to try to find out more. I've been here waiting for you all night."

Ricciardi nodded that he understood.

"Now tell me everything."

Coppola smiled bitterly, but on his careworn face it looked more like a grimace.

"It would take two lifetimes to tell you everything,

Commissa'. Two lifetimes, both ended together yesterday. Are you ready for that?"

Ricciardi spread both arms wide.

"I'm here in order to understand. Tell me."

Giuseppe seemed to be trying to gather his memories, lost in the void behind painful images.

Outside, a particularly powerful gust of wind rattled the windows. The weather really had decided to change its mood.

# X

The man began to speak, and his voice seemed to come from somewhere far away.

"I'm from Vomero, not far from Antignano. Now they have villas there, the well-to-do come in the summer to enjoy the fresh air; and ever since they built the funicular two years ago, some have even moved there to live full-time. But when I was a boy there was nothing but countryside, a few vegetable gardens, and the occasional farmhouse. There weren't many young people, everyone left early to find work in the factories, at the Bagnoli steel mill, or even overseas, to America. Hunger, Commissa'. Hunger is a nasty beast, it comes hunting for you at night and keeps you from sleeping, and by day it saps your strength and puts you to sleep on your feet, even though you're wide awake."

He paused.

"Among those few young people, there was us—me and my brother and sisters. My father died young: I'm the oldest, and I can just barely remember him; my brother Pietro is twenty and he practically never even saw him. My mother grew everything we ate, and we took turns standing guard at night to make sure no one stole the few crops we were able to grow in our little garden. Nearby lived our neighbors, the Cennamos. And there was Rosaria."

As Ricciardi listened, he noticed the reverence in the man's voice whenever he uttered the girl's name: as if she were a goddess.

"She has always been beautiful, Commissa'. Even when we were starving, in our privation, when her face was covered with dirt and her fingernails were ragged, her legs scratched by nettles: she was still beautiful. It's as if there's a light inside her, when she's there you can't look at anything else. She's always been so beautiful."

He jerked his head, as if a terrible thought had entered his mind, and he turned to his brother.

"Was. I have to remember to say 'she always was so beautiful.' Because she's dead now, no? She's dead, Pietro, and I'll never see it again, that light that was inside her."

There came a strange sobbing sound, a wail from his belly at once high-pitched and deep, that made a shiver go through Ricciardi. The young man standing behind Giuseppe put a hand on his brother's shoulder and whispered:

"Go on, Peppi'. Go on, the commissario is listening."

Coppola went on.

"As far as I can remember we were always together, me and Rosaria. We fell in love right away, and everyone knew that we would live our lives together. We dreamed of our children, the house we'd build, the things we were going to do. We spent our days immersed in thoughts of our future together. But little by little, as time went on, it became clear that there was a problem, Commissa'. There was a danger that threatened all our dreams. The danger was Rosaria's beauty."

A clap of thunder rumbled outside, from out over the water.

"Rosaria was beautiful, and she was becoming more beautiful with every day. No one who came through our farms, the merchants who came to buy broccoli, the butchers who brought us their hogs to fatten, could look at her without being tempted to touch. I was sixteen years old and she was fourteen, and I can't tell you how many times the others had to hold me back, to keep me from winding up in prison for stabbing someone. But now I understand that such a beautiful woman can't be born in a place like that. It's not right. Beauty, Commissa', it's something you have to be able to afford."

A few drops began to pepper the panes of glass.

"Villages like ours always have a master. A rich man, a nobleman, or a violent man who buys the world at gunpoint. That's the kind of man we had: he'd managed to become mayor through the power of fear. He was married, he had lots of children, and plenty more scattered throughout the countryside; he had a soft spot for beautiful women. A real weakness. One day, going by in his carriage, he saw Rosaria walking barefoot down the road, with a basket on her head; she was tattered, starving, filthy. But as always she was incredibly beautiful. That man was old enough to be her father, maybe even her grandfather: he had children much older than her. But he saw her, and he wanted her. And he took her."

Those last words told the tale of an old wound that had never healed. The man fell silent, and then sighed:

"There was nothing anyone could do. Of course, I could have killed him, and then I would have been dead: and afterward, who would take care of my family? My brother was still a child, and so were my sisters. My mother looked me in the face, begged me on her knees. That's how I lost her, the first time. I didn't see her again for years, that man had sent her far away from his wife. He'd lost his senses too: Rosaria's beauty is like the *vino novello*, the light sweet wine that, when the weather is hot, knocks you flat on your back before you know what's happened. Was. It was like the *vino novello*."

He seemed beaten by his inability to come to terms with Viper's death.

"I found out that she'd had a baby, a son. That's when I realized that I'd lost her for good. That child was the definitive destruction of our dreams, of our afternoons spent dreaming, sitting on the scattered straw under the sun. And that's when I started working hard: there was nothing else left to me."

Pietro, standing behind his brother, whispered:

"You cared about us, Peppi'. Your family."

"Yes, I cared about you. And it was for you that I really started working. I bought a horse and a cart, Commissa'. I brought vegetables into the city. I thought to myself: why sell them for pennies to wholesalers, when I could sell them directly? It wasn't easy, they don't let you just bite into their market: they split the districts up among themselves. More than once I found myself with a knife in my face, and I was forced to react. Maybe you know this, Commissa', but when someone doesn't care about his own life, it becomes difficult to reason with him. I didn't kill anyone, but I had no choice but to split a few skulls. But in the end, I won a place for myself."

Pietro, standing, had a clear surge of pride that Ricciardi didn't miss. The relationship between the two brothers, despite the younger brother's obvious subservience, must have been extremely strong.

"I spent all my days on that cart, I've always liked horses, and that's why I have the nickname I've had since I was a boy. As soon as Pietro here was old enough, we got another cart: and with the money we made we bought another garden, and my sisters started working that one. And then another cart and another garden, until we grew to become what we are today: the biggest fruit and vegetable company in all Vomero."

Ricciardi listened very closely.

"And Rosaria? When did you see her again?"

The momentary distraction of telling how he'd built his business was swept away like a cloud in the wind, and pain welled back up in the man's face.

"I hadn't heard from her in a couple of years. I'd learned that the bastard who stole her from me met the end he deserved: somebody took a stiletto and gutted him like a fish.

Rosaria had left, no one knew where; she'd given the boy to her mother, he still lives with her back in the village. I'd landed a number of important customers—when you deliver to them at home they're willing to pay extra; one of them was the bordello. One day when I was unloading crates, a woman came into the kitchen and said: 'Say, do you have any good apples like the ones we eat where I come from?' Commissa', you have to believe me: if she hadn't spoken, I'd never have recognized her. She'd always been beautiful, but the girl I was looking at wasn't just beautiful, she was a miracle. Still the voice, that voice, I knew it. And I said: 'Rosa', is that you?' "

Overwhelmed by the power of that memory, he was speechless. His brother, embarassed, once again put his hand on his brother's shoulder and he went on.

"She gave me a look, and who could forget that look. And she burst into tears, and ran upstairs. But like I told you before, Commissa', I'm a hardheaded customer; so I gathered my courage and one night I walked in through the front door, climbed the stairs, and sat down to wait. Every so often the Signora would ask me: young man, what, are you waiting for a train? And I would say: no, Signo', I'm waiting for a girl I like, the ones I see here are clearly rejects. Until I looked up at the little balcony where the young ladies parade, and there she was, my Rosaria. And she looks at me, and she doesn't say a word. I get to my feet, I wait until she gives me a sign, I pay what I'm required to pay for an hour, and I go up to her room. For a few minutes, Commissa', we don't say a word: we just look each other in the face. Then, we start sobbing like a couple of fools, and we embrace."

The rain, which by now was driving, left streaks down the panes like the tracks of tears. The piazza was filling up with people looking up at the sky in bewilderment, using both hands to grip the umbrellas that the wind was trying to tear away.

"Six months went by. I have plenty of money, I don't have bad habits, and the company's doing well. I'd go to see Rosaria every day: I paid for her time. I'd stretch out on the bed with her, and we'd talk; we had so many stories to tell each other. And of course we'd kiss. But not *that*, no, we didn't do that. I wanted to wait."

Ricciardi thought of the blond hairs on the pillow that had smothered Viper, identical to the hair of the man before him.

"What were you waiting for, Coppola?"

"I had found the love of my life again, Commissa'. The only woman I wanted by my side, the companion I'd chosen when I was still just a child. In your opinion, what else could I have wanted? I'd asked her to marry me. To leave that job, that despicable place, and to come live with me and be the queen of my home, to take the place that was waiting for her."

"When did you ask her to marry you? And what was her answer?"

Coppola ran a hand through his hair, the color of ripe wheat.

"I asked her many times, over the past few months. We talked it over, we talked it about it a lot. She was always vague, she said that by now everyone knew what work she'd been doing these past few years, that she would have brought me shame, thrown it in my face, that everyone would laugh at us. I told her that for her I'd be willing to move to a new city, that we could move somewhere no one knew us; I'd have taken her son with me, and I'd have raised him as my own. I'd talked her into it, I know that she'd made up her mind to marry me. Just yesterday, she'd asked me for a few more hours before making a definitive decision."

Ricciardi was listening carefully, attentive to every last detail.

"So you're saying that she had not yet given her answer. And what was your last conversation like? Did you argue?"

Giuseppe replied with great vehemence:

"No, absolutely not! She kissed me tenderly and told me: don't you worry. Come back tomorrow, and I'll tell you what I've decided. But she was smiling, and I knew her very well: she'd decided to say yes, I'm telling you. She was going to marry me. That's why they killed her, don't you see? Precisely because she had decided to marry me and to leave that vile place!"

He slumped back in his chair, overwrought, sobbing uncontrollably, both hands pressed to his face. His brother, wrapping his arms around his shoulders, turned to Ricciardi:

"My brother is innocent, Commissa'. He'd never have lifted a finger against Rosaria. When she died, he died too; he'll never have a wife now, never have a son or a future. It's up to us, up to his family, to stand by him now."

Ricciardi rose to his feet.

"All the same, I have to ask that you remain at our disposal and that you not leave the city without our authorization. For my part, I can only promise you that we will do our utmost, let me reiterate, our utmost, to make sure that the person murdered this young woman doesn't get away with it."

Giuseppe stood up, still sobbing. His brother accompanied him to the door, his arms wrapped around him. Ricciardi was touched by that immense and desperate affection.

"One last thing, Coppola: you said that you've had a nickname, ever since you were a boy. What nickname?"

Giuseppe seemed incapable of answering for himself, and so it was his brother who stopped at the door and, half-turning to speak to Ricciardi, said:

"We're a family that has always relied on horses, Commissa'. Everyone calls my brother Peppe' a Frusta—Joey the Whip."

# XI

The sudden rain caught Livia off guard. The night before she'd asked her housekeeper to put out a light flower-patterned dress, the skirt and jacket a color that contrasted nicely with her hair, bobbed short as was the fashion; but now that the weather smacked more of autumn than spring, it struck her as totally inappropriate.

Not that she really felt much like going out at all, to tell the truth. Perhaps it would be better just to stay home and read a good book, to seek distraction without going in search of company or noise in a smoky café.

She walked past the mirror and looked at herself: the silk dressing gown wrapped around her ample breasts and shapely hips. The food was just too good in that city: she wasn't worried, at least not yet, but she'd have to be careful; otherwise she'd become fat and ugly, and she'd no longer have any real chance.

Actually, she thought, running her hand through the hair whose cut she was still having a hard time getting used to, that was a fairly remote danger, at least to judge from the bouquets of flowers that arrived every day: men were as interested as they had always been in her. Married or single, soldiers or noblemen, government functionaries or Fascist *gerarchi*, men continued to proffer their chivalrous service to a woman who was certainly the most alluring of all the women who traveled in the best circles. But that mattered little to her. Very little.

Why are you here, Livia Lucani, widow of the tenor Vezzi?

she asked herself as she looked into the mirror. Shouldn't you really be in Rome, the center of the world, cultivating important friendships and possibly landing a man of enormous prestige, to whom you can hitch your fortunes? Shouldn't you, like every other woman in your condition, be thinking about your future in these difficult times?

For that matter, the increasingly infrequent phone conversations with her girlfriends in the capital gave her a picture of things that struck her, from a distance, as intolerable. The race to get close to the new potentates, vulgar self-important individuals who shamelessly ventured into the realm of the ridiculous, was one that took no prisoners. To join the competition with dozens of silly geese to win her way into the bed of some drooling Fascist was certainly not the most appealing of prospects.

In that case, what is it you want? How do you picture your life, Livia Lucani, the widow Vezzi, in a few years, when your charms are no longer quite so commanding, when men stop hanging on your every single word?

She picked up a silver hairbrush and lazily began brushing her hair.

The answer to her question materialized in the image of a pair of green eyes, clear as glass, watching her feverishly from the shadows.

Ricciardi.

He was the reason she'd come to this city; he was the objective she was aiming at, the goal she aimed to achieve, the summit she had to scale, the harbor at which she hoped to arrive.

She couldn't say why that man—not nearly as good-looking as so many others, less powerful, less wealthy than the men she could have had with a snap of her fingers—had captured her heart. But the thought of him caused her stomach to twist in a way it never had before, and would certainly never again. And she'd never be able to accept the idea that she couldn't have him.

The last few months hadn't been easy. Since Christmas he had been trying to avoid any situation in which he was likely to run into her, and when they did come face to face, he looked at the floor. Obviously, something had happened.

Still, she thought, looking at herself again in the mirror, it was hardly like her to lay down her arms. It wasn't like her to give up. Why, just a few days ago her girlfriend Edda, the Duce's daughter, had told her over the phone that, even though she did miss her, she had to confess that she could hear in her voice a new and captivating determination. And if Edda said so, then it must certainly be true.

She observed her own face more closely, in search of wrinkles she did not find. She opened her jewel box and went in search of something lovely to put on: nothing made of yellow gold, her friends in Rome had told her; the color white is all the rage now: platinum and diamonds. In Paris no one's wearing anything else.

Once again, she leveled her dark eyes at the mirror and smiled, accentuating the dimple in her chin. Look out, Ricciardi: Livia Lucani, the widow Vezzi, isn't giving up. No staying at home today, no reading books.

Today, lunch at Gambrinus.

# XII

Ricciardi headed for the little side room where by now the brigadier had arrived with Vincenzo Ventrone, the merchant of sacred art Lily had covered for.

The conversation with Coppola and the sorrowful tale the man told had left him baffled. Other times in the past he'd questioned brutal murderers who had so successfully buried their own guilt that they had convinced themselves that they hadn't committed the crime, even when confronted with unmistakable evidence. And the younger brother's declaration of innocence, when no one had accused Giuseppe of the murder, had sounded like an unasked-for justification dictated by a worried mind. And after all, this was a man who, by his own admission, had a certain familiarity with violence, and so the extent of his emotional involvement made it easy to imagine a disproportionate reaction if the woman had turned down his proposal of marriage.

Then again, the man's despair, his huge and overwhelming grief, could not have been concocted out of whole cloth. Giuseppe Coppola really had been madly in love with Maria Rosaria Cennamo, aka Viper.

Maione was standing by the door: in his sleepy expression and his relaxed features, Ricciardi recognized the brigadier's very particular way of disguising his anger.

"Commissa', *buongiorno*. The gentleman, here, is . . ."

The gentleman shot to his feet as if he were spring-loaded. His rain-drenched jacket, his dripping hair, his sopping hat, and his sagging mustache all gave a touch of the ridiculous to the man's angry expression, as he ground his teeth and bugged out his eyes.

"At last a sentient being, at least I hope so: Signore, you owe me not one but a great many explanations. A brute of a uniformed policeman knocks at dawn on the door of a more than respectable family, a family with friends, let me make this perfectly clear, in very high places, and this oversized gorilla practically yanks me out of my bed where, incidentally, I lie quite unwell, and he conveys me by force, I insist: by force! and where? Where? No less than to police headquarters! Like some common two-bit street criminal, like some robber or pickpocket, like a burglar, like an . . ."

Ricciardi, who stood, arms folded across his chest, waiting for the tirade to run out of steam, chose this moment of indecisiveness to intervene.

". . . like an individual who is about to be indicted for gross insult of an officer of the law and taken to a cell."

The phrase, uttered in a soft, almost inaudible voice, had the effect of a further spray of cold water on Vincenzo Ventrone, proprietor of the award-winning company of the same name.

The man—short, smartly dressed, and in his early fifties—lost his swagger.

"I, I . . . but how . . . I certainly didn't mean any disrespect to anyone, but surely you understand that . . . in other words, a poor citizen is asleep in his bed on a rainy morning, getting over the flu . . . and all of a sudden he's in police headquarters, talking to . . . with whom do I have the honor of speaking, Signore?"

In the face of this hasty about-face, Ricciardi showed a smidgen of mercy.

"Commissario Ricciardi, of the mobile squad. The gentleman who, at my orders, came to ask you this morning if you'd be willing to come to this office for a conversation is Brigadier Maione, and you owe it to his delicacy of feeling and his professional courtesy that the matter was conducted with such discretion: if it had been up to me and in accordance with the dictates of ordinary procedure, we'd have come to your residence by car and with an escort of two additional police officers. That's standard practice, when the crime in question is homicide."

Maione adored it when Ricciardi talked that way.

Ventrone blinked and turned pale as a sheet. Then he said:

"I beg your pardon. I had no idea. May I sit down? I don't feel at all well."

Ricciardi gestured and sat down himself.

"As you well know, yesterday at the brothel known as Il Paradiso, in Via Chiaia, one of the working girls was murdered. The name of the murdered girl is Maria Rosaria Cennamo."

Ventrone murmured:

"As I well know, did you say? I don't know anything. And I certainly don't know this woman, what did you say her name was? Cennamo? In fact, I don't know anyone by that name."

Ricciardi didn't budge by so much as an inch.

"Ventrone, let's not play hide-and-seek. I would not advise you to follow this line, because it won't take you anywhere good, but rather directly to a criminal trial for withholding evidence, during the course of which a great deal of information would come out, information which, I'm sure, would be quite damaging both to your reputation and that of your family; that is, if we don't decide to bring other, far more serious charges. The stage name, shall we say, of this young lady was Viper. Does that mean anything to you?"

The man's head dropped as if the commissario had clubbed him. He muttered an incomprehensible word or two, coughed, ran a handkerchief over his face and then, finally, replied in a low voice:

"Viper. Yes, I know her. And I appeal to your discretion, to the fact that we're all men of the world here today, and beg you to promise me that what we say here in this room will remain confidential."

Ricciardi wasn't in the business of offering discounts.

"That's not a promise I'm able to make. If the things you tell us have any direct bearing on the investigation, they'll have to be made public. But I can certainly assure you of our utmost personal discretion."

Ventrone nodded. That was already something.

"I patronize the place, yes. A man, after a lifetime of work, has the right to a little enjoyment. And I, sadly, became a widower at far too young an age. And I met this woman, Viper, in fact, who showed . . . initiative, and plenty of it. And we had a lot of fun together. And as far as that goes, I paid, and generously. It doesn't seem to me that there's anything wrong with that, no?"

Maione broke in:

"No, there's nothing wrong with going to whores. But murdering people is quite another matter."

The man protested loudly:

"I haven't murdered anyone, why, how dare you?"

Ricciardi gave him a level look.

"According to our information, you were the woman's last client. Another prostitute, Bianca Palumbo aka Lily, did her best to cover for you by claiming to have found the corpse herself, but we forced her to admit she was lying. Why would she have covered for you?"

Ventrone seemed stunned by what Ricciardi had just told him. He hesitated, then made up his mind to speak.

"Really? I certainly couldn't say. Lily is . . . sometimes I go to her, when Viper is otherwise engaged. I imagine that she was just looking out for me. But I wasn't Viper's last client: whoever killed her was. I paid for my time, I walked into the room, and I found the door ajar: inside, Viper was sprawled on her back on the bed, with a pillow over her face. I assumed that she was playing some sort of prank, you understand, sometimes we play games. I moved the pillow and I saw . . . I saw that she wasn't playing, anyway."

Maione drove in:

"Then what did you do?"

"Then I ran out of the room without touching anything else, and I called for help."

"Who was the first to respond?"

"The first was Lily, who came out of her bedroom with a man who'd been with her and was just leaving. She came over to me and took me to see Madame Yvonne. Then they both urged me to leave in a hurry, to avoid gossip and scandal."

Ricciardi shook his head.

"That wasn't a good decision, as you can see for yourself. Tell me exactly what you saw in Viper's room."

Ventrone concentrated, and described a setting that substantially matched what Ricciardi had found in his inspection.

"Were you aware of the fact that Viper had received an offer to leave that line of work? That another man had asked her to marry him?"

Maione looked at the commissario in surprise. Ventrone heaved a loud sigh and shrugged.

"Yes, I'd heard. The other girls and Madame were talking of nothing else, and had been for the past few days. But she would never have accepted."

"And why are you so sure of that?"

"Simple: she liked the life she led there. The money, the luxury, and even the fun, the cheerful surroundings. And the men, of course, she liked them a lot. Believe me, I knew her well."

Disgusting though he might be, Ventrone seemed quite certain of what he was saying.

The commissario asked another question:

"One more thing. What do you mean when you say: 'sometimes we play games'?"

The merchant blushed to the roots of his hair.

"Commissario, everyone has his own personal tastes. I just enjoy . . . let me say this, I try to spice up my pastimes, that's all. There's nothing wrong with it, that's why men go to certain places, no? Sometimes, with Viper, we'd play innocently, she'd be the schoolmistress and punish me. As a joke, of course. And I'd react, also in play, and spank her. She had a . . . well, she was beautiful, as you know."

Maione and Ricciardi would have been very happy to throw that man in prison, but they realized they lacked the grounds.

The commissario stood up.

"You're free to go. You are not to leave town and you are to remain available for further questioning. And for the time being, you are forbidden to patronize Il Paradiso."

## XIII

How beautiful you are. I only feel good when I'm with you.

How I love to caress your neck, watch your eyes half close at the touch of my hand. I'd spend hours doing it.

She would have taken everything away from us. Little by little, her nature would have emerged. He was already her slave, and it would have just have gotten worse and worse.

Your warm breath, how wonderful it is to feel it on my face.

She knew how to make everything good disappear. Where she was, no one else existed, all that remained was her, with her desires, her moods.

He was no longer himself, you saw that. He no longer understood a thing. She had become the sole proprietor of his smile; the rest of the time he was distracted, confused, he didn't care about anything anymore. His life was just time spent waiting between helpings of her, an ugly parenthesis to be shortened, something without purpose.

You feel it, my hand, don't you? You feel its light touch upon you.

Because I love you, and I respect you. When a person loves, his touch is light.

You're relaxed, with me. Untroubled. Untroubled.

Because you don't realize that my hand can deal out death.

# XIV

Ricciardi brought Maione up to date on Giuseppe Coppola's story. The brigadier, watching the rain hurled by the wind against the windows of the commissario's office, murmured:

"No question, this Viper left a trail of broken hearts behind her. And these are just two of her customers, think if she had the same effect on them all."

Ricciardi wasn't convinced.

"No, I don't think she had many others. Coppola and Ventrone, from what I've been able to understand, tended to take all the time she had available. Certainly, we'll need to dig deeper. We'll have to go back to the bordello and have a nice chat with Madame Yvonne."

Maione said:

"And with Signorina Lily too, Commissa'. I certainly can't figure out why she should have tried to cover for Ventrone. There was nothing strange about saying that he was the one to find the girl. Why take the trouble to tell a lie, and risk ending up in a mess, as in fact she has?"

Ricciardi agreed.

"You're right, it was an apparently reckless move on the part of a woman who didn't strike me as reckless in the slightest. There must be some other motive. The problem is that both Coppola and Ventrone, if we limit ourselves just to the two people we've spoken to, for various reasons might actually have killed the girl."

Maione smirked:

"You must have guessed that I don't like Ventrone, not even a little bit. He's not right in the head, and this little schoolmistress game might have gotten out of hand. People who have these tendencies, sooner or later they're bound to do something wrong, because they're constantly pushing the boundaries: first once, then twice and a third time, and then the next thing you know, after they're done with the teacher game, they play the pillow game."

Ricciardi agreed.

"That's right. For that matter, as head over heels as Coppola was, how would he have taken a rejection? In his past, by his own admission, there've been episodes of violence, however understandable. He even told me that if it hadn't been for his obligations to his family, he'd have killed the man who raped Viper when she was just a girl. He might have been nursing his thirst for revenge all this time, who can say."

Maione sighed:

"There's no two ways about it, when women are involved it's always a cathouse of confusion, and in this case there's a real cathouse involved, namely Il Paradiso. By the way, Commissa', why don't we take advantage of the fact that the rain is letting up and drop by for a visit? Before coming upstairs I sent Piro over to relieve Cesarano, but we can't keep the place shut down for much longer. Plus, as you know, with Easter coming up we're short on officers."

"Right you are. Still, for the time being, until we get a clear idea of the dynamics in there, I'd prefer not to introduce outside factors. Let's walk over. And do me a favor, call Dr. Modo on the telephone and ask him to come along. It strikes me we're going to need our own Virgil, in that inferno they call Paradiso."

No one would have admitted it, but the rainstorm that Holy Tuesday really had been a stinging disappointment. Everyone had become happily accustomed to the scent of spring, the warmth of sunshine on their skin, the fresh new light: and instead here again was the wind, the rain, and the smell of damp soil.

What's more, those who had optimistically put away their winter clothing were caught unprepared, and they wrapped the collars of their light jackets close around their throats, trying to find some scarves and walking gingerly to keep from ruining their shoes. The umbrella repairmen, on the other hand, were reinvigorated, because among other things the rain came accompanied by gusting winds, scourge of umbrella handles and ribs; they hawked their services: "*'O conciambrelle, 'o conciambrelle*!" They'd taken the place of the vendors hawking balloons and wooden toys that the Festa di San Giuseppe had brought swarming out into the Villa Nazionale and the parks and playgrounds, to the disappointment of the city's children, who knew that Lent meant no more sweets.

Ricciardi and Maione weren't too drenched when they arrived at their destination, both because the distance they had to cover wasn't all that far and because as much as possible they walked beneath the overhanging cornices. The street door was shut, and a few well-dressed gentlemen stood holding umbrellas and chatting in undertones, right out front; the minute they spotted Maione's uniform, they hurried away. Ricciardi decided that Madame Yvonne had a point when she complained about the damage that an extended closure of her business would cause.

A few minutes later, Dr. Modo came down the street, hopping to avoid the puddles, and then hastening to seek shelter in the building's entryway; the dog came trotting after him, shaking the water off its back and settling down just a short distance away.

"Well, well, my friends, here we are again. Have you finally decided to have some fun? I understand now why you ordered

Il Paradiso shut down: you want the whole place to yourselves.
Thanks for inviting me to the party, in any case."

Maione laughed.

"Now, Dotto', whatever gave you that idea! We just
thought you'd want to get a hatful of rain along with us, it's no
fun getting drenched all by ourselves. *Grazie*, now that you're
good and sopping and you've ruined your two-tone shoes, you
can go. We don't need anything else from you."

The doctor waggled his forefinger under the brigadier's nose:

"It's just a matter of time, Brigadie'. Just a matter of time.
Sooner or later, everyone winds up under the blade of my
scalpel: and when that happens, I'll be sure to have some fun
with you, or what's left of you!"

While Maione went through a complicated series of gestures to ward off death and bad luck, Ricciardi got to the
point.

"Bruno, I need some information about the way this establishment works, and you're the only person I know who admits
to patronizing it. I'd like to know exactly what to ask to avoid
false answers I might not be able to pick out."

"Understood, I'm entirely at your service. By the way, since
I was working the night shift, I was able to complete my
autopsy of poor Viper and I can give you my findings in
advance, though of course I'll also forward them to you in writ-
ing via the usual delightful bureaucratic channels. Provided,
that is, you'll buy me lunch."

Ricciardi sighed:

"Why, of course, after all, I can officially claim you as a
dependent. Lunch at Gambrinus, as soon as we're done here.
But for now, what can you tell me about how this place runs,
especially when it comes to the people who work here?"

Modo shrugged his shoulders.

"First of all, it's a mistake to think that a bordello is just a
place where men go to buy sex; at least not a classy bordello

like this one. It's usually not allowed, but here you can dine—the place has a first-class kitchen—you can order drinks, you can play cards. There are even older men who come here who haven't been interested in women for years, because it's always a pleasure to be surrounded by beautiful girls."

Maione snickered.

"Ah, now I understand why you come here, Dotto'; this thing about the old guys who like to watch had escaped me."

Modo smacked his foot down hard into a puddle, splashing a jet of muddy water onto the leg of the brigadier's uniform.

"Uh, so sorry, Brigadie'. You understand how it is, I'm an old man, and my legs make these uncontrollable movments."

Ricciardi tried to bring the conversation back to the point at hand:

"What about the girls? Where do they find them?"

"Most of them change establishment every fifteen days. That serves two purposes: first, it keeps the clients from getting too attached to any one girl, which might lead to relationships that can result in jealousy and violence; second, it keeps them expecting novelties and surprises, you understand: let's go over to see what's new at Il Paradiso. Other girls, though, do stay for a long time, sometimes for years."

"Which is what happened with Viper and Lily, no? And why would that be?"

Modo thought it over.

"For Viper, I told you before, she was famous and Madame made use of her to attract the customers' curiosity. She was much more expensive, she had a rate sheet all her own, and there were lots of men who came in just to see her walk the balcony. I suppose I talked to her a couple of times, she was friendly and stunning. Lily too, in her way, is attractive. Her breasts, you saw for yourself: they can do everything but talk! Sure, she's no Viper, but she has her admirers."

"And as far as you know, how did the two girls get along?"

The doctor tried to recall:

"I don't remember seeing them much together, but as far as that goes, when there are clients around the girls tend not to interact much. Still, if you can stand to hear a secret without running screaming from the room, I can tell you that I know a guy whose friends, for his birthday, bought him a couple of hours alone with both girls, and according to what the guy had to say later, there was no apparent friction between the two of them. Quite the contrary. The birthday boy couldn't stop laughing like an idiot for two days."

Maione went on brushing his trousers:

"So right, then, just out of curiosity, how much could one of those little parties cost? Just to get an idea of how long a doctor's salary could last."

Ricciardi didn't want to encourage digressions.

"What about the hours? How do the schedules work?"

Modo laid out what he knew:

"Let's see . . . generally speaking the girls have the mornings free until lunchtime. Some of them see their boyfriends, you'd be surprised to know how many of them lead ordinary lives; they rarely go out to do any shopping, for the most part they ask those who work in the at the bordello to buy them cosmetics, undergarments, and so on. Around three in the afternoon, they start getting ready; half an hour later the bordello opens its doors, and they start parading on the balcony you've already seen."

"Which means," the commissario commented, "the girl's murder took place just as the establishment opened for business. This restricts the possible ring of suspects to those who were there in that short span of time."

Maione explained further:

"And therefore, the last two clients: Coppola, who says he left her alive, and Ventrone, who says he found her dead."

Ricciardi added:

"They're not the only ones . . . Any of the bordello's employees could have come in, or any of the other girls, or even one of the other girls' clients. The circle is still too large."

Modo broke in:

"You're right, Ricciardi. Also because pressing a pillow down on someone's face by surprise doesn't take all that much strength, and the lesions that I found could have been inflicted by a woman."

Good point, thought Ricciardi.

"All right, Bruno. I'm going up to have a chat with the ladies and the girls. You go ahead to Gambrinus and I'll be along in half an hour: I promised you lunch, didn't I? Come on, Maione. Let's go have some fun."

## XV

I n the large drawing room of Il Paradiso, the atmosphere was quite different from the last time. Horror, fear, and grief had given way to boredom and worry.

The boredom was all on the part of the young ladies, who lolled about smoking and talking, moving from one chaise longue to another. The pianist Amedeo was tickling the ivories halfheartedly, and a couple of the girls were pretending to dance to the waltz he was playing, sketching out off-kilter ellipses across the carpet.

Worry, on the other hand, was concentrated in the imposing person of Madame Yvonne, who hurried over the moment she saw them.

"Commissa', you absolutely must allow us to open for business, and immediately! You don't have any idea of the damage you're inflicting on us! Yesterday we had to throw away a huge amount of food, the tradesmen keep coming with their deliveries, we can hardly send them away. And I can't tell you how many phone calls we've received, our clients are bound to go elsewhere, you can't imagine how little it takes to lose a customer, it's enough for them to go to another establishment and have a good time once, and they'll never set foot here again! And what's more . . ."

Ricciardi raised one hand to halt the flood of words:

"Signora, please calm down. We need some information and then, if everything works out, you'll be able to open up again. After all, we only closed you down yesterday and there was a dead girl in a room here. That hardly strikes me as excessive, no?"

Madame had no intention of ceasing her litany of complaints.

"Are you dismissing the losses that we've suffered? The grief for Viper, who was like a daughter to me—dearer than a daughter!—besides, she was also the star of Il Paradiso. It was for her, just to see her, that many of our customers came! Not only is she gone and I have no idea who could ever replace her, but now you've also shut us down."

Ricciardi listened impassively, then said:

"I fully realize. That means it's all the more important for you to supply us with the information we need, and as quickly as possible."

Yvonne spread her arms wide in resignation.

"Ask away, Commissa'. We're at your service."

"Yesterday I asked you to give me the names of Viper's most devoted customers, and Signorina Lily commented that that was an easy one. What did she mean?"

The woman answered quickly:

"Nothing to hide there, even if we always try to avoid these kind of situations because of the dangers that they can entail. Viper had only two clients: two people who paid for all her available time."

"And was that expensive?"

"Certainly, it was very expensive. Viper's rates were quite different from the numbers you've seen posted on the wall, Commissa'. And her percentage was very different too, she kept nearly all the money for herself, we scarcely made back our money on the room, her food, and her cosmetics."

Ricciardi listened with keen interest.

"In that case, what was in it for you?"

"Like I told you, Viper was important. People came here just to see her—if you only knew how many tourists passing through the city. They'd ask at their hotels: who is the most beautiful whore in Naples? And they all got the same answer. Then, once they came in here, they'd choose one of the other girls, and we'd get their money. As for having her, it was those two and no one else."

"And that didn't bother you?"

Madame shrugged her ample shoulders.

"Why on earth should it? They paid, she was happy, and in a certain sense it was fascinating to see something beautiful and not to be able to have it. The other men let off steam by drinking, eating, and taking other girls to bed."

Ricciardi decided to try a sudden lunge.

"Were you aware that Viper had received a proposal of marriage from one of her two clients?"

Madame didn't blink.

"Certainly. She told us herself that the blond guy, Peppe' a Frusta, the one who sells fruit and vegetables, had asked her to marry him. We laughed and laughed about it!"

"You laughed? But why?"

"Because why on earth would Viper, the most famous whore in all Naples, want to give up her earnings, the veneration of so many men, and the lovely life she was leading just to be a housewife in a shanty in Vomero, to bring up children surrounded by steaming piles of horseshit? She would never have agreed to that."

Ricciardi wanted to understand fully:

"Still, my information suggests she didn't turn him down immediately. Apparently she asked Coppola for a few days to think it over."

"I'm sure she didn't want to hurt his feelings. After all they knew each other as children, Viper had told me that story. Still, he was just a tradesman, even if he spends—or rather spent— lots of money here. Maybe Viper, before telling him to go to hell, wanted to wring more cash out of him. Maybe she was afraid that when she told him no, he'd never come back. But no question, she was going to turn him down."

The commissario thought back to the sight of Coppola sobbing.

"What about her other client, Ventrone?"

"Ah, certainly, he's a real gentleman. A discreet and respected man, unfailingly polite. Also, he has plenty of money; his business selling saints and madonnas is very profitable and his company is well-known. He'd been our client for many years, then once he'd seen Viper he refused to go to bed with anyone else, except for every now and then."

"So that means you'd lost an important client."

Yvonne laughed:

"Commissa', you seem bound and determined to get me to say that I had it in for poor Viper, but that's not the way it was. First of all, Cavalier Ventrone brought lots of his friends here, and I made plenty of money off of them. Another thing, we work for our clientele's satisfaction, so if he was happy, I was happy too. Last of all, in order to spend time with Viper, Ventrone threw plenty of big parties here, which everyone enjoyed. In other words, I could only be delighted to see him becoming more and more attached to the establishment; after all, the girls aren't the only way we make money here, as I'm sure you know."

Ricciardi wasn't going to be shaken off this lead.

"So what can you tell me about the relationship between Ventrone and Lily? Why do you think she chose to cover up for him about his having been the first to find the dead body, and with your assistance?"

The woman saw she was cornered:

"I know, I was wrong there. But I didn't think it mattered much who had found her. Lily has been with us for years, she was here before Viper and she knows the Cavalier very well, they've been together so many times, and even now, if Viper wasn't feeling well, he'd go with her. I assume she did it out of friendship. To keep him out of trouble. You know, the Cavalier is a well respected man about town, and if word got out that he'd been here . . . after all, he has plenty of priests for customers. It's one thing to see him go in and out, it's quite another to know that he found the body of a murdered whore. Then there's his son . . ."

Ricciardi's ears perked up:

"Whose son?"

"The Cavalier's son. Just the other day he was telling me that he was worried because his son, a young man, just twenty, who runs the shop with him, let him know that people were talking about the fact that his father comes to Il Paradiso. I mean, he was starting to worry."

Interesting, thought Ricciardi.

"*Grazie*, Signora. If I need any more information, I'll be sure to call you. Now could you send in Signorina Lily, if you please?"

Lily came into the room, her slippers flapping on the floor, unafraid to display her hostility to Maione and Ricciardi. Once again, the commissario could not help but remark the dramatic difference between the youth he could gauge from her delicate features, which looked even younger thanks to her blond hair and blue eyes, and the age that emerged from her weary, apathetic expression.

"*Buongiorno*, Signorina. I'd have just a few more questions, if you don't mind."

"And why should I mind, Commissa'? Without men in here, we're all just bored. You're a distraction. And now that I'm getting a good look at you, you're not bad at all, you know, I might even see if I can get a smile out of you. What do you say, should we give it a try? Or are you one of those men that don't like women?"

Maione took a step forward:

"Hey, sweetheart, don't step out of line or I'll smack you into a jail cell so fast it'll make your head spin, and don't think I won't."

Ricciardi raised one hand.

"Don't worry about it, Maione. My tastes aren't up for discussion, Signorina: what is up for discussion is the fact that you lied about the discovery of the corpse, and unless you give us a satisfactory explanation that we find convincing, you'll be going to jail, all right, and for much more serious infractions."

The girl wasn't about to let herself be intimidated.

"You guys really don't have a sense of humor. I wouldn't take a policeman to bed, even for double my fee, I was just kidding. And as for who found the dead body, I saw it right after Enzo . . . after Cavalier Ventrone called for help. So whether it was me or him, the important thing is that we found it, no?"

"The difference has to do with the fact that Ventrone just might be the murderer."

Ricciardi's words had the effect of a slap on the girl's face. Her sweet features suddenly twisted into an expression of anger and indignation.

"Ventrone didn't kill anyone. He was very fond of Viper, and in any case he couldn't hurt a fly."

Ricciardi went after his wounded prey.

"And yet, from what I've heard, Ventrone's tastes were quite particular. Let's just say that, at least with Viper, he liked a little violence."

Lily flushed red.

"What we do with our customers in the privacy of our rooms is none of your business. And if Viper never complained, it must mean she didn't mind it either. And in any case, she made money doing it, and plenty of it."

Ricciardi fell silent. Then he said:

"Signorina, I'm going to ask you one more time, and I urge

you to consider carefully the answer that you give: what was your relationship with Viper like?"

"We're all in here together, Commissa'. Some for one reason, others for another. It's not an easy life, we pass the time together, we talk. It's like being in jail, when people are thrown together with no say in the matter. Viper and I were very different, but we respected each other. In a way we were even friends. I'm sorry about what happened to her: but it's the kind of thing that you have to take into consideration as a possibility when you're in this line of work."

She furrowed her brow and stared into the middle distance. Her deep voice seemed to drift in pursuit of memories.

"There were afternoons in here, with the rain coming down and no clients at all, when we'd get to talking, stretched out on the bed in her room or mine. All the dreams we'd thrown away, all the things that could have happened but never did. She had a son, did you know that? She never saw him, because she didn't want anyone to know that the boy's mother was a whore. She sent nearly all the money she made to her mother, for the boy. Poor Viper, if she'd known how things were going end up, maybe she would have gone to see her son. Secretly maybe. And there were times when they had the two of us work together, the blond with the big tits and the fiery-mouthed brunette; men are fools, Commissa'. They imagine things and then think they can see them. How we laughed, behind those fools' backs."

She shook herself.

"We weren't fond of each other, Commissa', that's true. In here people can't be fond of one another, they can only pretend. But Viper wasn't a bad girl, she was just like me: someone doing her best to live decently. She certainly didn't deserve what happened to her. Can I go now?"

Ricciardi nodded his head.

"Yes, Signorina, you can go. But remember to make sure

we can get in touch with you, if we should need more information."

Once the girl had left, he summoned Madame Yvonne.

"Signora, you can open for business tomorrow. Of course, the room where the murder took place must stay locked, and no one is to touch anything."

The woman sighed, in evident relief.

"*Grazie, grazie*, Commissa'. You've saved my life. May the Virgin Mary reward you!"

Maione snickered.

"Let's leave the Madonna out of this, Signo', I have a feeling she might not pass by these parts that often."

Before leaving, Ricciardi went upstairs and walked toward Viper's door. He turned the knob and walked in. Everything was exactly as it had been the day before, except for the corpse, which had been removed, along with the murder weapon, the pillow. Like a chilly breath of air, he heard the girl's hoarse voice, as she stood at the mirror. The voice made the hair stand up on the back of his neck: *Little whip, little whip. My little whip.* What is it you saw, Maria Rosaria Cennamo from Vomero, aka Viper? What did you think about as you died? As your fantastic body, the fantasy of hundreds of men, gave up its last breath?

Coppola had been known as Peppe 'a Frusta, Joey the Whip, ever since he was a boy: since the days when he used to run over the fields and through the gardens with his little girlfriend, laughing and dreaming of a happy future. But Ventrone, the slimy merchant who dealt in sacred art, had an unhealthy passion for violent games, and perhaps the whip was an instrument of demented pleasure for him. One of the two, Viper? Or both of them?

There were blond hairs on the pillow and on the brush. Coppola was blond and Lily was blond, and neither of them had denied spending plenty of time in Viper's room.

Who was the last person to be in this room? Ricciardi asked the ghost he could sense there. Why, now that you've decided to poison my existence like all the other hundreds of dead people I encounter in the street, won't you go ahead and tell me who decided to reduce you to this state?

But the woman turned her dead gaze to the mirror that refused to show her reflection, repeating over and over: *Little whip, little whip. My little whip.* The same thing she'd keep saying until the air had forgotten her emotions, and she'd vanished into the wind.

## XVI

D own in the street, they realized that the rain had been defeated by the wind. The clouds were scudding rapidly across the sky, creating a succession of shadows and light on the wet street.

At the corner of the *vicolo*, the blind accordionist was taking advantage of the increased pedestrian traffic to run his fingers over the keys, playing a mazurka that drew giggles from the nannies out doing a little shopping with an umbrella well within reach.

Ricciardi and Maione stood watching the little side door, the one that Madame Yvonne had said led into the kitchen.

"The murder, Commissa'," said the brigadier, "took place just after the place opened in the early afternoon. Honestly, I doubt there was enough activity at that time of the day to make it possible to get away with this thing in all the chaos. And I don't think that anyone could make it from the kitchen into one of the bedrooms without being noticed."

Ricciardi stroked his chin pensively.

"You have a point, it would have been hard to pull off. And anyway, we have plenty of suspects to check out already, without going in search of new ones. Madame, for instance, mentioned that Ventrone has a son who is upset with his father over his obsession with the brothel. The son's twenty; I think they would have seen him if he'd tried to get in, but he could have pretended to be a customer of one of the other girls. It should be checked out, don't you think? At that hour, the shop would have been closed, so the young man would have been free to move, even if he'd have run the risk of being seen by his father."

Maione listened attentively.

"And if you want me to tell you the truth, even that Lily strikes me as the kind who'll say one thing but think another."

The commissario trusted Maione's intuitions.

"So that's the impression you got, eh? I thought there was something odd about her too, and the same goes for Yvonne . . . You know what I think, Raffaele? I think the time has come to open a crack in this wall. You should take a walk to see that girlfriend of yours, the one who knows everything about everybody."

Maione waxed indignant:

"Commissa', what are you talking about, what girlfriend! First of all, she's not even a girl. And we're certainly not friends: she . . . he owes me a favor because I didn't throw him . . . her in jail when we first met, and . . ."

Ricciardi raised both hands.

"Oh, for goodness' sake, you're right, my mistake. All right, go visit this old enemy of yours, this almost-ex-con, and see if she knows anything about what went on at Il Paradiso when Viper was alive."

A metallic sound caught their attention: a man walking a little dog on a leash had dropped something into the blind musician's metal tray. The accordionist, still playing with one hand, used the other to lift his dark glasses partway, and when he realized that what lay in the plate was a nail, not a coin, he cursed under his breath at the pedestrian who was walking away and then resumed his masquerade, with musical accompaniment.

Maione called out in amusement.

"Would you just look at that son of a bitch!"

Ricciardi glanced at his watch.

"I have to meet Modo at Gambrinus, otherwise he'll tell anyone who'll listen that I refused to buy him lunch. You go ahead and take your walk, we'll meet back at the office."

Rain or no rain, Gambrinus was still a destination for those who wanted to eat well without leaving the center of town, so the inside tables were all full.

For that matter, however unpredictable the weather might be, it was by no means chilly, and so some tables had been put outside and piano music poured out the open windows; as a result Ricciardi found Modo sitting at the table most sheltered from the wind, raptly reading his newspaper and enjoying the view of pretty girls walking past. A few yards away, sitting up as usual, as if he might take off at a dead run at any moment, was the the dog with no name.

"Ah, there you are. I was just resigning myself to being stood up for the umpteenth time by you, my somber friend. But this time I would have forgiven you, because I like this new familiarity with the brothel. All right, for now it's just work: but perhaps, over time, you'll grow to like it and become a customer."

Ricciardi sat with his back to the street: the suicide went on murmuring, his face bloody: *Our café, my love, our café, my love*, and he knew that in time the litany would give him a splitting migraine.

"I wouldn't count on it, you know. Those places aren't for me."

"Because people have a good time there? So where *do* you spend your evenings, at the cemetery chatting with the residents?"

The commissario was willing to give as good as he got.

"You can kid around all you like. But you ought to know, with the work you do, just what happens to those who experience powerful passions. Knives, brass knuckles, billy clubs, and revolvers, in and of themselves, when left in a desk drawer, are innocent. It's the hands that are guilty: and the hands are driven by the belly, by the heart, and by the exact same emotions you go in search of in places like your Il Paradiso."

Modo stretched out his legs.

"That's the point. I know that's how you see things; and it's what makes you seem like a character who's just walked out of one of those gothic novels from a hundred years ago. But you also know that the main force driving mankind is emotion, and that in the end emotions are nothing but a fancy word for the blood that pumps through our veins and fans the flames of our desires. We're animals, my friend, and we should never forget it. In spite of the church, which does its best to persuade us that we're purely spirit, or our lovely current ruler, who sees us as lines of numbers on a sheet of paper."

Ricciardi considered the matter.

"So, in your opinion the bordello is a place of emancipation, is that right? And these girls who work there, don't you think about them? About their dreams, their hopes? The fact that they have to go along with who knows what perversions, however violent?"

Modo turned serious.

"The girls are there of their own free will. No one forces them into it, and I believe that freedom to choose what kind of life you'll live is also a mark of civilization. Believe me, they're safer in there, under constant medical supervision, with a minimal security detail and decent sanitary conditions, than they would be on the street. Plenty of times I've seen some drunk who'd stepped over the line being given the bum's rush; I've even helped toss them out myself. What do you think, that I'm the kind of guy who takes advantage of poor defenseless girls?"

Ricciardi shook his head vigorously.

"No, no, Bruno. I know who you are and the way you think,

of course. But the fact remains that this girl, Viper, was killed while she was working. And that one of her clients often dabbled in violent little games."

"Yes, I know that there are people like that. But believe me, there are more people who want to be hit than the ones who don't. And in any case experienced girls, and Viper certainly was one, know how to keep the situation under control. But will you let me eat now, or are you hoping that your ramblings will make me lose my appetite?"

They caught a waiter's eye and ordered.

Modo snorted in annoyance.

"The fact that we aren't free to eat meat this week oppresses me. I respect Catholics, why shouldn't they respect me? A nice sizzling steak is off the menu during all of damned Lent, including the bone that I would have given to my little four-legged friend over there."

Ricciardi, who as usual had ordered a couple of puff pastries and an espresso, shrugged.

"Oh, come on, you'll find something to eat. And your friend won't mind eating those scraps, just this once; maybe they'll remind him of his youth, when he had to paw through the trash for his dinner."

In the meantime the doctor was listing for the waiter the dishes he'd selected in the absence of his beloved steak: macaroni timbale, grilled snapper with anchovies and capers, and strawberries.

"And a bottle of white wine, which you'll open here at the table before our eyes, otherwise I know you'll water it down."

The waiter, an impeccably groomed little man, whose few remaining hairs were slathered in brilliantine, glared at him in an offended manner and strutted away.

Ricciardi said:

"Well then, Bruno, what do you have to say about the autopsy?"

"Nothing like a dead body to stimulate the appetite, eh? Well, there's nothing new with respect to what we'd already guessed. Her nose was broken without trauma, due to the pressure applied to the pillow, and not from a violent blow. The murderer gripped Viper's body between his or her legs, and at some point must also have placed his or her knee on her chest because a few of the ribs were cracked. The whole thing didn't last long; perhaps the murderer caught the girl by surprise and she never even had a chance to take a deep breath. There are no traces on her hands, I'll confirm that she could only have tried to push the pillow away from her face."

"Nothing more than that?"

"No. Viper was in excellent health, she was twenty-five years old and looked even younger. And for what it's worth, she was beautiful even when she was dead."

Ricciardi remembered the sinuous body sprawled out on the unmade bed.

"And her beauty was the cause of her downfall. Listen, Bruno, she didn't have . . . I mean, there weren't any traces of . . ."

Modo burst out laughing, scattering bits of macaroni all over the tablecloth.

"Do you realize that you can't even bring yourself to utter the words? How old are you anyway, eighty? And in any case, it's a silly question, sorry, if you remember what this girl did for a living. Still, even a silly question can have an unexpected answer: no, Viper hadn't had sexual intercourse recently, neither vaginal nor anal. At least not in the past several hours."

Ricciardi shot a quick glance around the room, to make sure nobody else had heard those words.

"Considering that they'd just opened, that might not be so strange after all. Viper had only had time for one customer, possibly two at the most. And with both of the regular clients

that she had, apparently, she didn't always have complete intercourse. So we're back where we started from."

Modo stopped chewing, and stared at something just over
Ricciardi's shoulder. His face took on a glow of boundless
admiration, and he said:

"Speaking of beauty, take a look at that spectacular sight!"

Ricciardi turned: stepping out of a car through a passenger
door held open by a uniformed chauffeur, was Livia.

# XVII

Toward the upper end of the Via San Nicola da Tolentino, as the buildings became more scattered, the wind could be felt more keenly. Maione walked, holding his hat to his head with one hand, to keep it from flying off to join the flocks of swallows sketching enigmatic paths across the sky.

The brigadier, dripping with sweat, wondered what mysterious factors had caused the person who knew most about everything that happened in this city—a veritable spider at the center of a vast web, as he'd always pictured Bambinella to himself—to live in such an isolated location. It struck him as a glaring contrast.

For that matter, it was actually better this way: the possibility that he'd be spotted, which would spell trouble in several ways—an embarrassment to Maione and the loss of his chief source of confidential information—diminished considerably in that far-flung section of the Spanish Quarter, behind Corso Vittorio Emanuele, hidden in the lush greenery of Vomero.

The spider at the center of her web opened the door and stood waiting for him at the top of the stairs, leaning fetchingly over the railing of the external loggia and walkway.

"Well, well, what a lovely surprise! My favorite admirer comes running to see me on the first day of spring: the most romantic thing in the world? Now, if we were in a movie on the silver screen, you can just imagine the background music that the pianist would be playing!"

Huffing and puffing as he came up the last flight of stairs, Maione retorted:

"If you ask me, you found an apartment on the top floor specifically to make sure I'd be so out of breath I wouldn't have the strength to kick you downstairs. Now I ask you, wasn't the practically sheer climb enough, without the stairs to top it off?"

Bambinella burst out with a loud laugh that sounded like a whinny:

"Oh right, I'd completely forgotten, Brigadie': next time you should warn me so I can make sure you find me stretched out nude on the ground floor, so that everyone will know how much we love each other."

The brigadier hauled off and delivered a straight-armed slap at the *femminiello*, who dodged it easily.

"Ah, how nice, I love it when you take it from conversation to physical contact. Come in, Brigadie', make yourself right at home, and I'll brew up a pot of ersatz coffee. How are you?"

Maione collapsed into a bamboo chair, evidence of Bambinella's passion for anything Chinese, whether authentic or imitation. The lightly built chair groaned miserably under his weight.

"Ah, look, Bambine', in theory we'd be fine; but no such luck, the minute the holidays roll around something always happens and we have to run all over the place. My family never seems to have a chance to enjoy a festival in blessed peace."

The *femminiello* turned from the waist, as she briskly took down demitasses and espresso spoons from the drying rack.

"Oh, you're talking about the murder of Viper, aren't you? *Mamma mia*, I'm horrified by what happened!"

Maione spread his arms wide.

"Of course you would know all about it already. For that matter, it happened on your territory, no?"

"Not exactly, Commissa', as you know. I work for myself,

all the times that I tried working in a place like that, things
didn't really go very well. Not that they don't want girls like
me, don't get me wrong: in fact, it's one more treat on offer for
their clientele and, if I do say so myself, I'm famous. You ought
to know that there's one thing I do, in a way that . . ."

Maione raised his voice:

"For the love of Christ, Bambine', don't you dare try telling
me about the things you do! I don't want to know, and I don't
even want to imagine them, because my imagination is all too
powerful already. Just cut it out, and promise me you'll never
talk about it again, because if you do I'll walk out of here right
now!"

Bambinella whinnied again.

"Brigadie', the last thing I wanted was to upset you. I
understand that I'll end up in your dreams and then normal
life will no longer be enough: what do you think, that I don't
know how men become helplessly obsessed with me?"

"There's no obsession here, if anything a healthy disgust, if
you want to be exact. But please, continue. What were you saying, about that place?"

"That it's not really the right place for me, you see. They
have a clientele that's just too normal, people who aren't interested in trying anything new. But quite a few of my girlfriends
work there, people I met . . . in other circumstances, so to
speak, and that's why I know all about the situation in there.
That's all there is."

Holding the cup in both hands, she started across the room
toward the brigadier, swiveling her hips as she walked. The
black silk kimono dotted with a red flowered pattern parted to
reveal a pair of long legs sheathed in flesh-colored stockings,
while a lace negligee was visible at the chest, beneath a pair of
broad shoulders. The long face, with its sharp features, was
embellished by a pair of large brown eyes, limpid, expressive,
and heavily mascaraed.

"You caught me unprepared, Brigadie', I was just in the middle of putting on my face. Business doesn't really get started, up here, until later during the holidays. You have no idea how badly people get the urge to do something fun during Holy Week. It must be a contrast with all the penitence that the parish priest tells everyone to do."

Maione retorted ironically:

"And in the end, they come up to your place to do their penitence."

"In fact. So, Brigadie', if it wasn't love that brought you all the way up here, what is it that you need?"

The policeman took a sip of the drink that was in the demitasse, and grimaced, disgusted.

"*Mamma mia*, this ersatz coffee is just foul . . . You know why I'm here, I need information. Both the commissario and I think that the madame of the brothel, Yvonne, and one of the girls, a certain Bianca Palumbo aka Lily, are telling us less than what they know. Maybe you know something that could help us understand the reason we're getting this impression, that's all."

Bambinella assumed a pensive expression.

"Ah, you're talking about a couple of interesting individuals, Yvonne and Lily. I don't know them well, because they've always been at Il Paradiso and like I told you, I've never had much to do with that place. Still, I have picked up a tidbit or two about them, though only secondhand."

"Like what?"

The *femminiello* put both her hands, with their long red nails, over her mouth and sat, concentrating.

"All right then, from what I've heard out and about, it's not smooth sailing at that bordello. Madame Yvonne is having difficulties paying her suppliers, that's something I heard from a client of mine who's a fishmonger and that's the reason—the fact that he wasn't paid what he was owed for his supplies—he asked me to serve him free of charge. Well, I told him, I said: hey, *guaglio'*, what do you take me for, an office of the Fascist charity organization, the *beneficenza fascista*? But he begged and pleaded until finally I . . ."

Maione leaned forward, as if to stand up.

"No, Bambine', if you're going to start rambling then I'd rather go. Today I just can't bring myself to listen to the story of your life."

"Why, what dreadful manners you have, Brigadie', if a girl can't talk to her friends about the hardships life throws her way! In any case, this boyfriend of mine told me that Madame Yvonne saw him personally, something she'd never done before, to ask him if he could wait a few days, that maybe she could fix the problem. And he heard that all the tradesmen are facing the same situation, except for the one from Vomero who sells her fruit, Peppe 'a Frusta, who doesn't want money on account of Viper. But that's a whole different matter."

"Wait a minute, first let's finish talking about Madame. So you're saying they don't have enough money. And that's odd because from what I understand they're running at full capacity."

Bambinella agreed:

"Yes, Brigadie', as far as that goes, no question. It's one of the most famous brothels in all Naples. But there's Madame's son, you met him, practically a mental defective who loves to play cards, and she takes care of his gambling debts because if word gets out that he doesn't pay what he loses at the tables, someone's bound to kill him. She already lost her husband that way, stabbed in the gut outside a tavern in Vasto years ago, and she doesn't want her son to meet the same ugly end. Which brings us back to that earlier question, the most important one: did you know that Peppe 'a Frusta, the fruit vendor with the fleet of carts from Vomero, asked Viper to marry him?"

Maione sighed in resignation.

"Yes, in fact, I do know. But my question is this: how on earth do you know?"

Bambinella smacked her lips.

"I know because a girlfriend of mine who works there every so often told me, though she works as a housekeeper, not a whore, but she still hopes to become a whore because she's very pretty as a picture, if a little bit rough when it comes to her manners, because she just moved to Naples from Frattamaggiore; I told her: don't give up hope, because the important thing is to be passionate about what you want to do, that and to have a nice big pair of tits and she . . . Oh, all right, all right, Brigadie', what's the good of you getting pissed off? In any case, the fact remains that Peppe, who was Viper's boyfriend when they were just kids, is head over heels in love with her and asked her to give up the working life and marry him. But she wasn't sure about it. She said within earshot of my girlfriend, when she was tidying up: If I marry him, I'll have a home of my own, and I can keep my son close. Because, you know, she has a son . . . Ah, you do know that already. But if I marry him, she said, I'll lose everything I have and that I earn, and I might even wind up with a guy who gets drunk or gets himself killed on some unfamiliar street. In other words, she wasn't at all sure what to do, and she said that she wanted to think it over. And just as she was thinking it over, someone killed her."

"Did you know Viper?"

"Only by sight, Brigadie'. She was beautiful but she did put on airs a little bit, she wasn't the most likeable girl in the business, in other words. Beautiful women are just like that, they believe that the thing they have, between their legs, will let them rule the world but let me tell you, you can do plenty without."

"I don't doubt it. But the proposal of marriage, how could it have led to murder?"

Bambinella explained with a cunning look:

"Ah, that leads to the other person you mentioned, the other whore, Lily. And that's where her position comes into play."

"What do you mean?"

"You ought to know, in fact, you probably already do know, that Viper had only two clients, even if there were plenty of people who went to see her at the bordello out of curiosity. One client was Peppe 'a Frusta, who was terribly jealous of her but who had to reconcile himself to her profession, at least until she married him and he took her away from there. The other, whom you've certainly already met, was Cavalier Ventrone, the merchant of saints and madonnas from Via Chiaia. You know who I mean, no?"

Maione smirked.

"Of course I do, I went to pick him up because he was the one who found the body in the first place."

"Exactly. Now, you need to know that before Viper came to work at Il Paradiso, Ventrone's favorite whore, and he spends every penny he has in the place, was none other than Lily. When a man has the bad habits that Ventrone has, then he has to have a perfect understanding with the whore if he wants to be happy: and Lily, who's a strong, no-nonsense woman, was perfect for doling out a beating. But then Viper came along, pretty as she was and clever too, and she took him away from her. But Lily told my girlfriend she hadn't given up hope, and she still planned to get him back under her power: the man was like a trust fund!"

Maione's face lit up.

"That hadn't occurred to me. That's why she claimed that she, not he, had found the body."

The *femminiello* clapped her hands.

"Bravo, Brigadier! And that's why, if you ask me, the real motive for Viper's murder was Peppe 'a Frusta's marriage proposal."

"And why is that, pray tell?"

Bambinella got comfortable and said:

"Easy. If she decided to marry him, she'd be putting Madame into a world of trouble, leaving the bordello without its main attraction just when she most needed the money; and Ventrone would also be left without his favorite whore, and perhaps in the rage at losing her, he might have got some ugly ideas. But if she made up her mind to tell him no, then Peppe 'a Frusta, jealous as he was, might have lost control and killed her; or else Lily, who was hoping to get rid of her once and for all, hadn't been able to resign herself to the fact that she was going to stick around and deprive her of her meal ticket."

Maione looked at Bambinella with a renewed sense of admiration.

"Where did you get all these deductive powers? What are you planning to do, take my job?"

Bambinella tittered coquettishly, one hand covering her mouth.

"Oh, Madonna, Brigadie', what are you saying, you're so dear to me. For me, you're like a grandfather. I'd never do such a terrible thing to you!"

"A grandfather, eh? Now you just watch how this old grandfather tosses you into a jail cell and throws away the key. And in any case, if you hear anything else of interest about this crime, please send for me. And I'm warning you: stay on the straight and narrow, because I'll be keeping my eye on you."

The *femminiello* stood up to accompany Maione to the door.

"Brigadie', I'd be happy to stay on the straight and narrow, but I've never even been able to figure out where it is."

# XVIII

As if cued by a particularly theatrical director, the sun broke through the clouds just as Livia emerged from the car, appearing before passing strollers in all her glory.

Ricciardi tucked his head down between his shoulders, turning his back toward the woman and hoping he wouldn't be seen; Modo, for his part, didn't even make the effort to wrench his gaze away from the woman's magnificent figure.

"Say, Ricciardi, isn't that wonder of nature the widow of the tenor, the one who was murdered just a year ago?"

The commissario didn't have time to stitch together an answer of any kind, because Livia headed straight for their table. She'd only stepped out of her vehicle a few seconds ago and already at least three men were converging on her from different points on the piazza, all anxious to offer her their company: that too was an effect of the spring.

The woman wore an unmatched suit, with a lightweight wool skirt and jacket in two different shades of grey, clinging softly to her body, and a dark-blue silk blouse with raspberry-pink trim. Topping her short hair was a woolen beret, cunningly perched just off to the right side; a string of pearls and a pair of platinum and diamond earrings completed a stunningly elegant ensemble.

But it certainly wasn't on account of her beautiful clothing that everyone there, male and female, couldn't take their eyes off her: there was something feline about the way she moved, the way she looked around her, stirring both attraction and fear. It was immediately obvious that this was a woman capable of deciding what was going to happen to her, with only the slightest margin of error.

Livia took only an instant to recognize the back of Ricciardi's head, for the simple reason that she'd been looking for him. She looked for him everywhere she went, wherever she found herself in that city: she'd moved there specifically for that purpose.

She came over and spoke, addressing Modo:

"Do you mind if I disturb you, Doctor? I don't know if you remember me, we met a year ago in tragic circumstances. I see that you have company, and in fact I've been introduced to your luncheon companion as well."

Modo had leapt to his feet, knocking napkin and fork to the floor and making the table wobble.

"Signora, how could I ever forget you? What an immense pleasure to see you again. Please, do us the honor of sitting down with us."

She turned to look at Ricciardi.

"If it wouldn't bother your fellow diner, I'd be delighted to sit with you. In fact I'm here for lunch."

The commissario got to his feet, with a partial bow.

"I doubt I have much say in the matter, given the doctor's enthusiasm. Please, Livia, sit right down. I'm happy to see you."

The impeccably garbed waiter glided over with a chair and Livia sat down.

"Really?" she said. "You don't seem very happy at all, but I'll choose to give more credence to your words than to the expression on your face. For that matter, our man Ricciardi doesn't give his emotions much play, does he, Doctor?"

The three men who had hoped to squire her did nothing to conceal their chagrin, but quickly found new objects for their attentions. Modo, who would have agreed with Livia even if she had told him that the sun rose in the west, hastened to agree:

"I couldn't have put it any better myself, Signora: there's nobody like Ricciardi, when it comes to suffering. We were just saying, in fact, that . . ."

". . . that, in fact, this is—or was—a working lunch," Ricciardi interrupted. "And we were talking about a matter we're working on, at police headquarters, that the doctor examined just yesterday."

Livia batted her long lashes.

"Ah, I see. And I'm sure it's the not kind of thing a bored young woman should hear about, right?"

Ricciardi made a vague gesture with one hand.

"No, I rather doubt it. These are official matters, you see, and . . ."

Modo, on the other hand, couldn't believe his luck; he was delighted to be holding the woman's interest, no matter the subject:

"Actually, it's a very interesting case indeed, Signora. A murder, and of a beautiful woman."

Livia's jaw dropped, and she raised a gloved hand to her face.

"My God! And who is this murdered woman? I haven't read the paper this morning, and . . ."

Ricciardi shot Modo an angry glare.

"Because the investigation is still under way. The doctor was in fact just telling me about the autopsy, but it hardly seems appropriate to talk about it here."

Livia was looking at Ricciardi, but she spoke to the physician.

"You see, Doctor? Ricciardi not only denies me his company, he even refuses to engage in normal conversation with me. What do you think, why does he behave this way?"

"Signora, only a madman could think of denying any request you might have, trust me. I'll tell you: someone killed a prostitute, in a fairly well-known cathouse not far from here, on the Via Chiaia. She was a woman well-known in her field, renowned under the name of Viper, like the character in the song, do you know it?" and in a low voice he sang a few bars: '*Vipera . . . vipera, sul braccio di colei c'oggi distrugge tutti i sogni miei sembravi un simbolo, l'atroce simbolo della sua malvagità . . .*'"

The words ran something like this: "Viper . . . viper, on the arm of the woman who today has destroyed all of my dreams, you seemed like an omen, the hideous omen of all her evil."

Livia looked at him, captivated:

"What a lovely voice you have, Doctor! You know, I was an opera singer myself, and I'm a good judge of pitch: you're a very good singer!"

Modo blushed like a schoolboy.

"*Grazie*, really. In any case, this woman was suffocated with a pillow, and it's Ricciardi's job to figure out who did it. For my part, all I could do was determine the cause of death. That's all. We were done with our work and were enjoying a well deserved meal."

The woman turned to Ricciardi.

"This kind of work could easily kill your appetite, couldn't it? And do you have any idea, of who it could have been?"

Ricciardi shook his head no.

"No, it's too soon to say, it only happened yesterday. We're following a number of leads. Certainly, around a woman like her there naturally swirled a great many passions, powerful emotions; it's hard to say which of these proved to be the most lethal."

Modo was chewing again, having procured a clean fork. He pointed it at the commissario.

"There, you see? The blame must be put squarely on emotions. Our good Ricciardi would gladly go without emotions, he'd simply eliminate them. That's exactly what we were talking about when you arrived."

Livia was hardly surprised:

"I'm well acquainted with Ricciardi's views on emotions; I know how convinced he is about the importance of eliminating them from one's life. Perhaps he's right, after all. Emotions can bring pain, so much pain. I know it very well: when you tally up the love and the suffering in any life, the balance is always in the red. But then again, it seems to me that it's impossible to avoid love. Don't you think?"

The commissario said nothing, staring off into the distance. Modo understood much more than what Livia had said.

"You're quite right, Signora. From dawn to dusk, every day, I see people in the hospital fighting disease and death just for love's sake. And so many people come to me in tears, begging me to save the life of the person they love, because that person's survival is essential to their own. Love can destroy, that's true: but it can save too."

Ricciardi stared at his friend. Behind him, the elderly suicide was repeating, for his ears alone: *Our café, my love, our café, my love*, incessantly. The memory of love, he reflected, outlived him.

"What I do know is that maybe, if it hadn't been for love, Maria Rosaria Cennamo, known as Viper, might still be alive. And she'd feel the springtime on her skin, instead of the marble of your operating slab, Bruno. And in any case, it doesn't matter what I think about emotions: the important thing is to find out who felt they were so almighty that they had the right to take her life, a pillow pressed down on her face."

His tone of voice had been hard and brusque. Livia shot Ricciardi a glance of infinite sadness: and she thought that she would be willing to give everything, that she would give anything, just to bring a little love into that man's life.

After a moment, trying to steer the conversation onto another track, Modo said:

"It seems like the weather is bound and determined to prove the madness of March, don't you think? Now it's actually hot out, and this morning it was like winter again."

Livia was grateful to the doctor for trying to help out.

"And what nice plans do you have for Easter? I know that there's a festival at the Teatro San Carlo, I'd love to go but I have no one to accompany me."

Modo answered regretfully:

"Unfortunately, *cara* Signora, I have certain misgivings about attending social gatherings. Especially because these days those scarecrows in black shirts can even be found in the temples of high culture, even though they have no real culture of their own, and to see the wonderful floors of our royal opera house besmirched by their filthy jackboots would just break my heart."

With brutal irony, Ricciardi said:

"Watch out, Bruno. Perhaps Signora Livia, here, with the connections she has, could report your words and have you deported."

He immediately regretted what he'd said, the instant he sensed the chill that descended over the table. Livia was shocked by that unexpected and gratuitous insult, and tightened her lips. Modo glared at him in disgust.

"You know, Ricciardi, there are times I just don't understand you. I may talk too much and make no secret of my opinions, that's true. But of course everyone should be free to have the friends they choose."

Livia looked at him fondly.

"*Caro* Dottore, I am indeed friends with a few people in positions of political power, it's true. But I can ensure you that the last thing we'd dream of talking about is politics, and that my knowledge on the subject is far too limited for me to have any valid opinion; and in any case, I would never, under any circumstances, undertake such a despicable act as informing on anyone. I'm nothing but a stupid woman who loves beautiful things and the opera; and who, to her immense misfortune, still believes that love is not a catastrophe, even though I have excellent reasons to think that it is. I hope you'll forgive me, I'm no longer very hungry. *Buongiorno.*"

She stood up, unable to hold back tears of frustration, and strode to her car where her chauffeur stood smoking while he waited for her.

Ricciardi, mortified, tried to stand up and keep her from going, but then fell back into his chair.

Modo gazed at him with a pained expression: his friend had never stirred such feelings of sadness in him.

A waiter looked in their direction as he walked with a tray, tripped over a carpet, and dropped his tray to the floor as he fell.

## XIX

When Maione returned to police headquarters, he found an extremely grouchy Ricciardi.

He wasn't especially surprised: he knew how a crime, especially against a weak and defenseless person like a child, a woman, or an old person, left a deep wound in his superior's heart, a wound that went on bleeding for days afterward. But this time he detected a different kind of sadness that seemed to come from farther away, from a deeper, darker place.

He gave him a wide-ranging account of his meeting with Bambinella, including the *femminiello*'s theories of guilt and hypotheses on likely motives for the murder.

"So, you understand, Commissa'? She sat there and started telling me that, according to her, it could have been this person or that and why. Not that she ever expressed an opinion, though."

Ricciardi thought it over.

"Interesting evaluation of the situation. Practically speaking, this means that Viper's answer to Coppola's proposal was decisive. But the real question is this: did the girl give any answer at all? Aside from what her decision might have been, we need to find out what she said, and to whom."

Maione waved his hand in the air before him.

"In any case, if I may express neither an opinion nor an intuition, but a preference, I'd hope that it was the merchant of saints and madonnas. He disgusted me from the instant I first laid eyes upon him, and finding out that his secret thrill is violence just makes me suspect him even more. People who play around with violence will get serious about it too, Commissa'."

Ricciardi stood up and went over to look out the window; the late afternoon had finally shaken off the rain once and for all, but the sky was still veiled in gray. The traffic was light and irregular, and the few pedestrians carried furled umbrellas.

"Springtime. The weather changes every five minutes. When things are changing all the time, how can anyone plan or predict?"

Maione waited in silence, not knowing what the commissario was driving at.

Ricciardi turned to him.

"There are a few elements still lacking. I'd like a chance to look Ventrone's son in the eye, for example, because from what I understand he had it in for his father, and therefore also for the girl because of her relationship with the old man. It's not too late, the shop is probably still open. Let's go take a look."

Outside the office they ran into Deputy Chief of Police Angelo Garzo, Ricciardi's direct superior, as he climbed the stairs, whistling softly, heading to his office on the floor above.

"Oh, Ricciardi and Maione. How are the two of you? What are you up to?"

Maione decided that the man was even more unbearable when he was happy than when he was angry. An incompetent career bureaucrat with only a few talents: grooming his mustache and licking the feet of the powerful, he reflected; and putting obstacles in the way of people who were actually trying to do serious work.

Ricciardi replied:

"Very little, I'm afraid. We're investigating the Via Chiaia murder, a young woman who . . ."

Garzo interrupted him:

"Ah, yes, yes, I heard, a whore, right? A very beautiful whore . . . that's what they told me, of course. Famous, too, what did they call her? The Asp, perhaps . . . no, Viper, that's right, Viper! I even know the place, I've heard about it, Il Paradiso. Now that I think about it, yesterday someone at the home of the Baron Santangelo was complaining about the fact that the brothel had been closed, apparently in the aftermath of the murder, and I promised that I would look into it. What's the situation now?"

Maione observed Ricciardi; though he was never rude, whenever he talked to the deputy police chief, the commissario clearly betrayed the contempt he felt for Garzo in his every slightest action, from the expression on his face to his posture. Garzo never noticed it, thought the brigadier, only because he was too stupid and full of himself.

"We had to carry out the necessary examinations, Dottore. As you know very well, it was important to be sure we'd gathered all crucial information. The time to examine the scene, then the medical examiner and the photographer. We respected standard procedure."

Just as he did everytime he found himself speaking with Ricciardi, Garzo began to feel uncomfortable. He'd never liked that man, with his mocking air and those strange green eyes, nor did he like what he'd heard about him: a man without vices, without a social life. Plus, never once had he heard him say: Yessir. Certainly, he cracked cases, and therefore he deserved appropriate encouragement; but there were times when the man simply didn't know when it was time to obey.

"Come, come, Ricciardi, she was a whore, no? These are women who live in sin, and so also in violence. These are things that come with the territory. Certainly, we need to investigate, but it's not as if a respectable citizen had been killed. Anyway, has the bordello reopened for business?"

Ricciardi sighed with resignation.

"Not yet, Dottore. But it will be able to open again tomorrow; I issued the authorization."

Garzo seemed satisfied:

"Fine, that means I'll be able to tell that old satyr Santangelo that I was able to arrange for Il Paradiso to reopen. *Grazie*, Ricciardi, and remember: be discreet. At all times, be as discreet as possible."

"What does that have to do with anything?" Maione thought. Then, under his breath, as they walked downstairs:

"What an asshole deputy police chief we got stuck with."

Ricciardi gave no sign of having heard.

As they walked down Via Toledo and then along Via Chiaia on their way to Ventrone's shop, Ricciardi thought to himself that the week before Easter was the strangest time of the year. On the one hand, there was the sense of rapt engagement, the prayer and the sharing in the suffering of Christ on the part of the most observant Catholics, who looked to the dolorous end of the Son of God's time on earth as an occasion to repent and be even stricter with themselves; on the other hand there were the pleasure-loving agnostics, who bridled at the restrictions and obsessively sought ways, more or less clandestine, to have just as much fun as ever, in the proliferation of secret bordellos and gambling dens tucked away in the city's thousands of back alleys.

In the middle were the others, that is, most of the population, caught between the ritual of Christ's Passion and preparations for the holiday, with all the culinary traditions that entailed.

They passed by Il Paradiso, which was still closed; but they glimpsed Marietta at the little door, giving information to two men who were nodding happily.

The blind accordion player with the perfect eyesight was playing a vigorous polka, to the enormous satisfaction of a crowd of *scugnizzi* who were dancing to the tune.

A fat priest garbed in glittering vestments, followed by a pair of altar boys, was hurrying from one building to the next, engaging in the profitable ritual of blessing homes; one of the altar boys, forced to balance the pail of holy water and the aspergillum, was hurrying to keep up; the other boy, who was managing much better with only a cloth bag for offerings to carry, was mocking him.

Women were leaning out many of the windows, thrashing overcoats with carpet beaters before putting them away once and for all, or at least so they hoped, once the weather was done being so indecisive.

From certain balconies came the innocent cries of suckling lambs and kids, destined to be sacrificed just a few hours from now to the hot tears of the children who, over the past month, had become fond of those tender little beasts, unaware of their impending fate; on those same balconies the wings of the birds from the Festa di San Giuseppe fluttered frantically, as they sang their beautiful and despairing song.

Life goes on, Ricciardi thought. Life never stops. Except for you, Viper, and for you, elderly lovelorn suicide standing in front of Gambrinus. And for the many like you, whose last passions still hover, floating in air, singing their sad songs for me and me alone.

# XX

The award-winning company of Ventrone & Son operated in a beautiful shop with three display windows, right at the end of Via Chiaia.

The other specialized establishments were all concentrated in the streets adjacent to the bishop's palace, the Palazzo del Vescovo, in Largo Donnaregina, not far from the city's Duomo: instead Ventrone's grandfather had guessed that most private chapels could actually be found in aristocratic palazzi in the city's wealthiest quarter, and that's where he decided to set up shop. The idea had proved to be a winning one, and three consecutive generations of Ventrones had prospered off the guilty consciences of the heads of titled families, using a new statue or an expensive ex-voto to absolve themselves of a wealth that was too often indifferent to the suffering of others.

Ricciardi and the brigadier stood on the street admiring the objects arranged in the windows. In one, a crucified Christ about six feet tall enjoyed pride of place in the center, while grief-stricken angels, hanging from hooks on the wall, seemed to fly overhead. The Christ's expression was one of immense suffering and sacrifice. In the other windows, statues of saints alternated with various representations of the Virgin Mary, depicted with a light blue cape and a crown on her head, along with a great many silver ex-votos that recalled all the tragedies in human life that could call for divine intervention, including the pangs of love, for which a heart pierced by one or more swords was available.

The two policemen entered the store and found themselves in a huge room where hundreds of objects related to Catholicism were on display, including the unsettling presence of many life-sized statues whose dolorous eyes, both stern and pleading, looked down on them. Maione, somewhat irrationally, took off his cap and made the sign of the cross.

A tall and very slender young man, dressed in black, was assisting an elderly woman who wore a hat capped by a long black plume. With a demure air and a soothing voice, the young man was saying:

". . . absolutely, Duchess: your poor late husband, who was, as you'll surely recall, one of our faithful customers, will certainly like it very much. In an aristocratic chapel like yours, so spacious and elegant, an angel with a four-candle candelabrum is a lovely piece of decor. I assure you that, from the afterlife, he can hardly fail to send you a great many blessings."

The duchess lifted a shaking, begloved hand to the young man's cheek, as he made a slight bow, and said:

"You're such a good boy, Augusto. Your late lamented mother would be proud of you. You deserve the best: you'll see that everything will go back to normal, now that . . . You understand me, no?"

Ricciardi noticed a sudden blush spread over Augusto's face, although he gave the old woman a tight smile and kissed her hand. Then she left the shop.

Once they were alone, he approached the two policemen.

"*Buonasera*, Signori. What can I do for you?"

Maione replied:

"*Buonasera*, Signor Ventrone, the son, correct? I am Brigadier Maione and this is Commissario Ricciardi, of the mobile squad. We're here to ask you a few questions, if that's all right."

The young man stiffened.

"You want to ask me questions? Perhaps you're looking for my father: I'm afraid he's not here. He hasn't been feeling well these past few days. If you like, I can get in touch with him and arrange for him to be available at a time of your choosing."

Ricciardi took a step forward.

"No, we're not looking for your father. Not right now, in any case. No, we wanted to speak to you, if you can spare us a few minutes."

Ventrone thought it over in a hurry and realized that there was no good way out of this interview. He considered the fact that by now the street was practically empty and the shop deserted.

"All right. But if a customer happens to come in, you'll have to excuse me."

Ricciardi understood that he was talking to a thoughtful and intelligent young man.

"Why, of course. But why are you here alone? Your father . . ."

Augusto gave him a level stare.

"My father, as you know very well, has undergone a trauma. And it certainly didn't do him any good to be taken to police headquarters early in the morning, as if he were some two-bit criminal. It's been a few months since we were able to afford a shop clerk, we already have too many craftsmen in the work-shop, and in any case our customers must be given the kind of service to which they're accustomed. I'd prefer to take care of it myself."

Ricciardi gave a slight shrug.

"Your father, since you speak of him so freely, happened to find a dead body. He ought to have reported the fact to us immediately but he didn't: for us to go pick him up in such a discreet manner, believe me, was an act of courtesy. And even now, the fact that we're talking here in your shop and not in my office is thanks to your good name."

The young man took the point, blinking rapidly.

"Of course, of course. And I thank you for that. You certainly understand that our business is quite . . . singular, and a good reputation and sense of discretion are essential. Tell me, how can I be of assistance?"

Oh, at last, thought Maione: before people are ready to cooperate, you always have to give them a nice hard shake.

Ricciardi began:

"How's business? I imagine you do pretty well around Easter, don't you?"

Augusto grimaced.

"I wouldn't say so. People are feeling the economic crisis, and even saints have become something that most households feel they can do without. There are fewer and fewer wealthy families every day, the large apartments are being subdivided and rented out, and the first things to go are usually the private chapels. Offerings to the churches have dropped, and even the parish priests prefer to go on using vestments and stoles until they're threadbare, instead of buying new ones."

Ricciardi feigned astonishment.

"Will you look at that! And I was positive that your father had plenty of money."

The young man caught the subtle reference and blushed bright red. But his voice betrayed no emotion.

"I didn't say that we were broke, though. Three years ago we started a, shall we say, parallel line of products that are earning quite well: we make flags, pennants, banners, and pennons for regiments and brigades. Just now, demand is high, and so we make up for the decline in the religious market."

Maione underscored the point:

"So the army and war help prop up the church. We'd need the doctor here, who knows what he'd have to say."

"Excuse me?" asked Ventrone.

Ricciardi gave the brigadier a look.

"Nothing, just a little office politics. Now then, in the absence of your father, you're alone here at the shop."

"Unfortunately, that's right. Most of the time, anyway."

"So you don't have a lot of free time."

Ventrone sighed.

"Not much. Certainly, every so often, for instance, if I absolutely have to use the lavatory, I lock the door temporarily and I leave: we don't live far away from here, our place is midway up Via Filangieri, it only takes me a few minutes, at the very most half an hour."

Ricciardi asked:

"And are there times when you need your father?"

"It can happen. Unfortunately, he's the only one who can sign for merchandise from the various tradesmen."

"I see. So then you would need to go call him."

"That's right," the young man murmured. "I have to go call him. Good thing I've always known where he is. At least, until now."

His tone of voice, cold and cutting, made Ricciardi's ears perk up.

"Why do you say: until now?"

The young man answered brusquely:

"Commissario, let's be frank. My father was, quite simply, obsessed with that woman. He couldn't live without her. It would be pointless to deny it, and it would suggest I was trying to cover for him, and he doesn't need me to do that. Running away after finding her dead was a mistake, as I've told him. But he didn't kill her, he'd never have done such a thing. With time, perhaps, I might have convinced him of the absurdity of that relationship."

There was an awkward silence. Then Ricciardi said:

"And now?"

"And now, I truly hope that it's over. He'd always patronized that place, and I imagine that he'll go back; but in a less intense way, that's for sure. And that would be enough for me. It's not just a matter of our good name, you understand, it's also a matter of money. You can't imagine how much money he gave that woman."

Ricciardi was watching the young man.

"You hated her, didn't you?"

A look of sadness came over Augusto's face.

"No, I never hated her. But I can't deny a sense of relief, as far as the fate of our family goes, at the fact that she . . . that she's no longer around. You see, there's someone I care for. She's the granddaughter of the Duchess Ribaldini, the woman you saw leave a little while ago. We aren't engaged, even if I hope that someday . . . in other words, if things had kept on going the way they were going, I wouldn't have even been able to hope. So yes, I'm happy that it's over, though I certainly wish it had happened in a very different way."

Ricciardi was thinking about the power of love, and about money. He said:

"Where were you, when you learned of the murder? And exactly how were you informed?"

Ventrone furrowed his brow.

"I don't understand your question, Commissario. And I don't like it. I was here, in the shop, where I always am, as I was telling you. And I heard about it from the only person who could have told me: my father, who came back as gray as a corpse."

"I see. For now we have no need of any further information, Signor Ventrone. Forgive the intrusion, and enjoy the rest of your evening."

Once they were back in the street they noticed that nearly all the shops were closed.

Maione commented:

"Here's another person who, if poor Viper had said no to Coppola, would have had an excellent motive for wanting to get rid of her. His father was not only bankrupting the company, he was also blowing the guy's chance at a happy marriage."

Ricciardi walked along, hands plunged into the pockets of his overcoat, while the wind tousled the lock of hair hanging over his forehead.

"Yes indeed. And seeing that he went so frequently to get his father at Il Paradiso, it's entirely possible no one would even have noticed him going by. It seems incredible, but whoever we talk to, we seem to get new ideas about the motive for this murder."

"True enough, Commissa'. So what do we do now?"

Ricciardi walked briskly to the sidewalk on the other side of the street to avoid the suicide in front of Gambrinus, and Maione, lost in thought, followed.

"We'll need to go on a little outing to Vomero, tomorrow. Let's go visit the dead woman's family, and we'll take a closer look at Coppola's company too. I think that at this point, these are the pieces we're missing, no?"

Maione sighed:

"Yes, and let's hope it doesn't rain, there's no telling with this crazy weather. If I get my boots dirty one more time, my wife is going to shoot me with my own service revolver, at least that way the gun will get some use. *Buonanotte*, Commissa'."

# XXI

Ricciardi was walking into the wind; and as he walked he mulled over the way that the slight uphill slope of the street he took on his way home every night seemed to change from time to time, one day becoming an easy descent and just the next day a steep challenging climb, like a mountain he had to scale.

Viper's fate, such a young life cut short, now seemed practically predestined. The more the investigation proceeded, the more it seemed that Coppola's proposal of marriage, at first glance a favorable twist of fate, had actually worked as a death sentence.

As always, when he was confronted by a death caused by human hands, Ricciardi found himself thinking of hunger and love, the ancient enemies that regularly formed an alliance, each covering up the other's foul deeds, providing each other alibis, each concealing the other and helping to confuse those who were trying to figure out who was the guilty party.

Love, its manifold corruptions and the passions engendered by contagion which made it the worst of all diseases: Coppola confronted by rejection, Ventrone confronted by the possibility of a final farewell. But there was also Lily's affection for the merchant, and Augusto's hope for a brighter future. Hunger, greed, debts, and a blind and desperate need for cash: thus, Madame Yvonne, her son the gambler, and the possibility of losing the finest mare of her stable; and Lily, who might have wanted nothing more from Ventrone than the money he was giving to Viper. And who knows who else might be lurking in the shadows.

Sometimes, the commissario mused, it would be better not to see. Better to pretend to be blind, like the accordion-playing beggar sitting at the corner by Il Paradiso.

Il Paradiso, what supreme irony. A place inhabited by the passions of hell, but named after Eden. Perhaps, though, he reckoned, it was accurate. Maybe heaven and hell exist for that reason, so that they can switch places and pretend to be the perfect place for everyone.

*Little whip*, Viper had said, in the form of a ghostly image, whispering into the ear of Ricciardi's curse. *My little whip*. A pet name for her long-ago lover, a sign of the regret and pity she felt for having rejected him? Or one last desperate bid for a weapon of self-defense, an attempt to escape Ventrone's blind fury?

All that afternoon, Rosa had held a seminar for Enrica on Cilento-style ragú.

She'd begun by saying:

"Signori', do you know how to make Neapolitan ragú? You do? Well, forget everything you know. Clear your mind, this is a completely different matter, and if you want to do it right, you have to think of it as a way of saying 'I love you'; you are conjuring an expression of love into being. Your man should say: *Mmm!* And then he should turn to you, beaming. Men from Cilento aren't big talkers, you should be happy with that smile. Do you understand?"

Enrica felt a twinge of pity and more than a little fear when she watched Rosa holding the large wooden spoon the way a conductor holds his baton. The utensil trembled a little as her hand wavered, but it moved with the extraordinary confidence of everything the woman was doing.

Enrica had carefully listened to her description of the ragú:

eyes and words had arranged in the cookpot a piece of mutton, not lamb, with the bone in, and slices of pork laid out on the cutting board on top of which had to be arranged pieces of *caciocavallo*—a strong southern cheese—and prosciutto, parsley ("with the stalk!" Rosa had said, resolutely), raisins, salt, pepper, and garlic—then these slices of pork were to be rolled up tight, bound with twine, and sautéed briefly in a saucepan with a little garlic.

"Signori', and don't think for a minute that this is the entrée! After this comes the roasted kid goat."

At that point, she had stopped. She'd gazed at the young woman, at her tortoiseshell glasses, at the stray lock that had escaped the bobby pin behind her ear, at her cheeks reddened by the heat of the flame; and for the first time she got a sense of the young woman's charm, that silent, underwater grace that had captivated her young master from behind two panes of glass. Then she took everything she had made and put it away in a cabinet, and said:

"Now it's your turn. Let's see if you've figured out what you're supposed to do."

An expression of terror appeared on Enrica's face.

"Me, Signora? But I don't know how to do like you do. I cook in a different way and . . . I'm afraid to try."

Rosa softened.

"You think too much, Signori'. Instead of thinking, just love. Don't waste time. And I'm tired, my legs hurt: I'll sit down here, you see? I won't say a word. The ingredients are all in the icebox and the pantry, just cook without your head. Cook with your heart."

And she had sat down.

And Enrica had begun making Easter dinner for Ricciardi.

Just as he was about to start up the last stretch of road, Ricciardi realized that his mind was devoting itself to the thought of Viper in order to avoid another image, which unsettled him deeply: the image of Livia looking at him, wounded, desperately struggling not to burst into tears.

In a certain sense, the two figures—the prostitute murmuring about her little whip and the shocked woman firmly pressing her lips together at the little table in Gambrinus—both pierced his heart with the same pang of pity: something broken, something pointlessly hurt.

He really had been a son of a bitch, he thought to himself. He couldn't say how or why he'd come up with that inappropriate insult, and above all he had no idea why he'd said it, viciously slapping a person whose only fault was that she loved him.

He analyzed his feelings for Livia. He couldn't deny that he was attracted to her, in a way that had little to do with the thoughtful or the sentimental. She was flesh, an animal appeal to gut and to blood; her beauty, her graces pulled him out of the silent little room into which he'd retreated when he was just a boy, when it had become clear to him who he was and the nature of the verdict that had been visited upon him, making him different from everyone else. She dragged him into the eye of the maelstrom of human passions. The very thing that frightened him most.

What about Enrica? She too called him out of that room; and she was sweetness itself, the possibly illusory charm of a normal life, made up of small, sweet things, caresses, simple wonderful moments of mutual understanding.

Both women loved him, perhaps. Each in her own way. What about him? What did he feel, behind the veil of fear where he hid, incapable of looking love in the eyes?

Then he saw Livia's face again, beautiful and pained, as she bit her lip to keep from crying, the woolen beret fetchingly tilted to the right, atop her short hair. While all around her the world ground to a halt, and he listened to the beat of his own heart and the voice of the suicide who kept repeating: *Our café, my love, our café, my love.*

He slowed his pace and then came to a stop, just a few hundred feet short of home.

Enrica thought: love me.

As her hands, with calm determination, lay out the slices of pork on the cutting board, and her fingers sprinkle a pinch of salt over them.

Love me.

Rosa, sitting just a yard or so away, had told her: with your heart, not your head. And Enrica had floated out of the kitchen, out of her time and the world, and she'd sailed toward her true love to speak to him with the voice of the ever-growing emotion that filled her soul, with all the courage she lacked.

Love me.

As her hands carefully crumble the chunks of *caciocavallo*, the aged cheese so typical of the land that had seen her love grow from boy to man.

Give me the life I want, she told him; give me a home of our own, a place that doesn't seem too much like mine or too much like yours, a place that understands the spaces of our motion and our rest.

Give me the walls and the rooms, and I'll give you curtains and carpets. Together, let's fill our memories, let's bring the things that we had when we were waiting for each other without knowing it, and the new things we'll find together: let each and every one, be it a picture frame, a vase, or a chair, remind us for the rest of our lives of the moment when we chose it, as it gazes at us, silently.

Love me.

As her hands caress the prosciutto, seeking chunks with just the right mix of fat and lean, protein and flavor.

Love me.

Because I am the one who will give peace to your sorrow, whatever it may be, from whatever dark place and long-ago time it may come. I am the one who will watch over you as you toss uneasily in your sleep, who will silently stroke your forehead until I see the skin uncrease and grow smooth, until I hear your breathing calm itself.

As her hands carefully clean the *malevizzi*, the tender little thrushes caught in the branches of the olive trees where her true love played when he was a boy.

Love me.

And give me two children, so they won't be alone for the rest of their lives. Let them have your eyes, those wonderful eyes, the color of salt waves on the rocks on a sunny morning, but without the sorrow. Let them have your fine tapered hands, and my tranquility, my faith in the future. Let them have your sensitivity and my gentleness. Let them have your acuity, and my openness to the world around me.

Love me.

As these hands arrange laurel leaves and thin slices of lard around the *malevizzi*, and as they sprinkle them with the sauce of olive oil, lemon juice, and white vinegar, which these same hands prepared earlier.

Because I'm the one who protects your happiness. The one who will fight for your happiness.

Love me.

Rosa, pretending to be asleep, smiled.


Ricciardi waited in a doorway until he saw Enrica leave his building. Only after she stopped and surveyed the street, somewhat sadly, and went back into her apartment building, closing the door behind her, did he move.

# XXII

Just as they were getting ready to leave for Vomero, where Viper's family lived, Ricciardi and Maione received an unexpected visit from Vincenzo Ventrone.

In his features and his demeanor, this was a very different man from the swaggering, self-confident person they'd met the previous morning. He held his hat in his hands, nervously twisting the brim. His face, pale and feverish, bore the marks of two sleepless nights. His mustache drooped inertly around his bloodless lips.

"I heard that you were at the shop, last night. I'm sorry that I wasn't there, but I've really been feeling a little tired and I'd rather not let the customers see me, right now. For that matter, my son, whom you met, is well able to run the company. To tell the truth, there are times when I think that if I weren't around, things might go even better."

Maione, though he had instinctively disliked the man, felt a twinge of pity.

"A very accomplished young man, your son, no doubt. You can count on him."

"Yes. I'm lucky to have him. I've thought about it quite a bit, you know. I understand that from your point of view, I . . . in other words, it could have been me. But it wasn't me, you'll see that: I have faith in you. But that's not why I'm here now."

Ricciardi and Maione waited until the merchant felt strong enough to continue. He seemed truly overwrought.

"She . . . Viper, you know. I really don't know how to

describe her, what kind of woman she was. You go to places like that out of curiosity, and in search of fun. To keep from thinking. Then you find yourself buying time, it's the only place where you pay for time, where you buy a person's time so they'll listen to you. And so you start to talk. The first time, for a minute, the next time for five. And then it even happens that you find yourself just talking."

The strain was unmistakable; it must have been a challenge to express his feelings, there in police headquarters, and in the presence of two policemen.

"For me, and I won't be surprised if you don't believe me, this was a loss. I'm not saying she was dearly beloved—I have a son, as you know. But Viper . . . Maria Rosaria, was a friend. A dear friend."

Maione broke in, in a subdued, cautious tone of voice:

"Why on earth are you coming here to tell us these things?"

"Right. Right. Why am I coming to tell you?"

The question he had asked himself fell into a pool of silence. Then he said:

"Madame Yvonne explained to me, yesterday, that the doctor . . . in other words, that you're done with the corpse, in the sense that we can proceed with the interment of the deceased. That's right, isn't it?"

Ricciardi replied, hesitantly.

"Yes, I imagine so. The doctor is done with the autopsy, he told me so yesterday, so I believe that you can, yes, certainly."

Ventrone nodded.

"As you know, I work with religious men and women, so I have friends who can explain things to me. Catholic ritual denies religious interment to several categories of people: Freemasons and those who belong to heretical sects; suicides; anyone who dies in a duel; manifest public sinners. Unfortunately Viper was a member of that last category."

Ricciardi broke in:

"Ventrone, I don't see what we can . . ."

The merchant raised one hand:

"I beg you, don't interrupt, this is already very difficult for me. Last night I got practically no sleep; but at a certain point I dozed off, and I saw Viper, the way she was when . . . when I saw her the last time, in other words, still alive. And she spoke to me, she asked me to make sure she was given a Christian interment. That's right, those exact words, give me a Christian interment, she said. And I understood that I need to do something for her, to keep her from being tossed into a ditch who knows where."

He sighed, and then he went on:

"Tomorrow, as you know, is Holy Thursday, the start of the Sacred Paschal Triduum. A normal funeral procession is unthinkable, the so-called respectable citizens would raise an outcry. I've spoken to several of my friends, people I've worked with for decades and who, by the way, owe me money: there's a confraternity, a congregation that would be willing to accept the body for interment in a collective chapel, but under her own name. A Christian interment."

He repeated the phrase, as if it were a curse word.

"The procession will have to take place in the morning, at a very early hour, to ensure it passes unobserved. The girls who worked with her, who were her family, will be there, they want to be there. And so will Madame, naturally. I'll pay for everything, I've already made all the necessary arrangements, but I won't be able to attend: I have certain duties toward my son, toward my company, and to the memory of my wife. I can't possibly be there. But I owe her this, to ensure that she's buried as she would have wanted. It's a matter of mercy and simple humanity."

He seemed to be on the verge of tears. Maione and Ricciardi exchanged a glance, but they were at a loss for words. Once Ventrone had recovered somewhat, he went on:

"When they reach the cemetery, delivery of her body will be taken by the men of the congregation, and they'll see to all the rest. There will also be a priest, who'll remain inside the chapel to avoid being seen, and he'll give the blessing. I paid him too. All I had to do was pay, you know? All you ever have to do is pay."

There was an palpable bitterness in the man's voice.

"Nonetheless, they explained to me that this anomalous movement of the girls, all together, has to be authorized by police headquarters. They're prostitutes, and the fact that they're going out into the street together could technically be seen as a form of solicitation. But we know that that's not what's going on, don't we? They're simply friends who want to accompany a woman on her last journey. I beg you, Commissario: I beg you as I've never begged anyone else in my life. Ensure that she's not alone, in this journey. She was a woman who never did anyone any harm, in her all-too-brief existence. She doesn't deserve that."

After thinking it over, Ricciardi said:

"Don't worry, Ventrone. I'll be there. No one will interfere with Viper's funeral procession."

As they were walking to the terminus of the streetcar that would take them to Vomero, Maione said:

"Commissa', are we certain that this is a good idea? I mean, presiding over the funeral procession of a whore. Sure, I understand, many of them are good people; but they're still whores. And if anyone were to see you, and then went and told that idiot Garzo? The last thing we need is for you to be accused of patronizing bordellos."

Ricciardi walked with his hands in his pockets, his eyes fixed straight ahead of him.

"What Ventrone said made quite an impression on me, you know? We're investigating everyone else, all the people who might have killed the girl, but we're not investigating her at all, or very little. What did she want from life? What had she decided about Coppola's marriage proposal? And Coppola himself, for that matter, who was he and what did he really want from this woman? That's why we're going to the village where they both grew up: to understand who Maria Rosaria Cennamo was, before she became Viper."

Maione wasn't convinced.

"Forgive me, Commissa', but I still don't understand what the funeral procession at seven in the morning has to do with anything, and why you think you need to be there yourself."

Ricciardi smirked.

"You know as well as I do, Raffaele. There's nothing like a funeral, if you want to understand who a person really was. The faces of the people who attend, and the names of the people who don't, will give me some very interesting information. At least I hope they will."

They reached Piazza Dante, the point from which the city's streetcars departed for all the main destinations.

Although it was hardly late in the morning, the broad open space was already filling up with people heading here and there, in part encouraged by the weather, which, as opposed to the day before, was warm and sunny. There were university students and lovely young women getting ready to catch the Number 2 streetcar, which would take them to the quiet little streets down by the water near the Cape of Posillipo, where they could talk and kiss in secret; vendors of dairy products and pots and pans who were loading their merchandise onto the Number 6 streetcar, destination Torretta Market; and *scugnizzi* who were getting ready to catch hold of the back of the Number 11 streetcar, heading for Portici and the black sand beaches of that district.

Maione had done his homework:

"Commissa', we can choose between two possibilities: we

can either catch the Number 7 Red, which will take us to Antignano, climbing up by way of Infrascata, or the Number 9, which goes to Arenella by way of Via della Salute, but then we'd have to walk part of the way at the end. What do you say, which streetcar should we take?"

Ricciardi shrugged.

"Whichever one leaves first. Ask the conductors. I don't know the area, so I wouldn't be able to say. But why don't you just find out about the return schedules, I don't want to take all day on this."

"Commissa', when has anyone in this city ever known a schedule for the departures and arrivals of the streetcars? If you ask me, no one ever will. It must be some kind of state secret. In any case, if you had a word once and for all with that idiot Garzo and had him give you a car . . . are we or are we not the mobile squad? But mobile how, by riding streetcars?"

Ricciardi adored Maione, and he valued all his qualities, including those the brigadier himself didn't realize he possessed, but he was also well aware of the man's one grave defect: his inability to admit that he was incapable of driving a car, and that when he was behind the wheel he became a very serious risk to public health and safety.

He decided to leave him in the relative bliss of ignorance.

"Forget about it, Raffaele, you can understand that after the crash I was in on the Day of the Dead, I have a certain aversion to automobiles. Let's just take a nice ride on the streetcar."

And after all, it's such a beautiful day, he thought sadly; and for no specific reason, Livia's wounded expression appeared before him.

# XXIII

The first car to leave was the 7 Red, which went past the Archeological Museum and then made its way up Via Salvator Rosa, and uphill from there along Via dell'Infrascata, where a series of secondary country roads branched off toward trattorias and farms.

From the streetcar window, as they held tight against the jerks and jolts caused by the joints in the tracks, Maione and Ricciardi looked out on the changing landscape, as working class apartment blocks gave way to the sprawling and tangled mass of Mediterranean vegetation.

The Vomero neighborhood hadn't changed much since the Great War: in a way, in fact, it constituted a holdover from the turn of the century, in a city that was constantly in a state of chaotic transformation. The hillside surmounted by the Castel Sant'Elmo, the last sorrowful image in the eyes of the emigrants as they steamed away from the harbor of Naples, was still for the most part verdant and unspoiled. There were scattered mansions constructed in the fetching *stile floreale*, or floral style of Art Nouveau, or else in imitation of the Romanesque and Gothic styles, flanked by dirt roads running through orchards and vegetable gardens—and only a very few of those roads were open to through traffic. A nucleus of buildings similar to those in the center of the city—tall, austere, nondescript apartment buildings—had sprung up like an invasive species of vegetation around the funicular railway stations, but all around them, the countryside had remained unchanged.

During the ride up, Ricciardi caught fleeting glimpses of shepherds and peasants, the occasional bricklayer hard at work, and as so often happened, at the foot of a scaffolding he saw the image of two men, one with a vast concave depression on the side of his ribcage and the other with an unmistakable fracture to his spinal cord, both of them murmuring about the extreme terror that accompanied their falls. The foundations of these buildings are sunk in blood, he thought bitterly. One of the prices of prosperity, but not the only one.

The driver announced the Antignano stop, and the street-car stopped with a jerk. The brigadier and the commissario got out and found themselves in an open space, enclosed on one side by a wall of tangled vegetation and on the other by an agglomeration of shacks. A number of children, half naked, their skin dark as old leather, played with a rag ball held together with twine.

Maione got the attention of a couple of these urchins and, unlike their counterparts in the center of town, they didn't take to their heels at the sight of the policemen's uniforms. He asked them where he could find the Cennamo family.

Having been given directions, the two men headed toward the center of the village. On either side of the streets, little more than dirt tracks, larger buildings, relatively well kept and nearly all recently built, alternated with tumbledown shacks. The spring air brought scents of the nearby forest and the windows of even the poorest houses were adorned with vases of multicolored geraniums. There were children and plenty of animals, dogs and chickens and, in low enclosures, hogs, nanny goats, and sheep. The atmosphere was quite different from that of the rest of the city.

They found themselves standing before a building that, even though it was in the poorer part of the village, betrayed a different economic condition: pink plaster and wooden shutters painted green, balconies with bellied wrought-iron railings, and even a further vertical addition, still under construction. Ricciardi and Maione exchanged a glance and both mulled over the thought that, by a supreme twist of fate, money from Naples's most straitlaced and devout families had flowed, through Ventrone's perverse pleasures, into the pockets of a poor family that had given birth to a prostitute.

And both of them thought, sadly, that the woman had paid for that prosperity not only with her body, but with her life.

They knocked at the front door and were answered by a very young girl wearing a white apron. They even have a servant, thought Maione.

The housekeeper ushered them into a garishly furnished living room, which reminded Ricciardi of the bordello, with the exception of the statue of San Gennaro, which stood roughly a foot and a half tall, with an episcopal tiara and staff, under a glass bell on a mantel. Neither of the two policemen had any doubts about the gift's provenance.

The girl came to the door and said:

"The Signora will be right down," then dropped to her knees and went back to work, scrubbing the front carpet.

A few minutes later, a woman entered the room. She couldn't have been that old, and the life that she led certainly hadn't always been comfortable. Her face was wrinkled and most of her teeth were missing, but her back was strong and erect. She was dressed in black, with an ample skirt and a light shawl over her shoulders; her dyed hair was surmounted by a clasp made of horn.

She addressed them roughly, staring meaningly at Maione's uniform:

"What do you people want from us? We're honest folk, we haven't done anything."

Maione was accustomed to that kind of reaction.

"Signo', no one here is accusing you of anything. I'm

Brigadier Maione of the mobile squad, and this is Commissario Ricciardi. And you are?"

The woman didn't blink an eye.

"I'm Concetta Cennamo, the owner of this house. And you're the ones who came to call on me; what is it that you want?"

Ricciardi decided to speak up.

"Signora, are you the mother of Maria Rosaria Cennamo?"

The woman stiffened.

"I was her mother, yes."

"So you know that . . ."

She nodded again, just once. Then she said:

"Women like her, that's what becomes of them. I hadn't seen her in years, she was dead to me the day she became a streetwalker, instead of trying to raise her son like a respectable person."

Her voice was cutting and harsh, and she spat out the words with an icy indifference that sent chills down one's spine. That woman wasn't grieving in the slightest.

Maione said:

"Signo', can I ask you how you came to hear about what happened to your daughter?"

Concetta shifted her attention to the brigadier.

"I heard it from Peppe, Peppe 'a Frusta. His family lives nearby, right at the end of the road. I had to comfort him, he was sobbing like a little boy, he was inconsolable. He still loved her, as if she was the same girl she'd always been. As if she hadn't become what she turned into."

From the street came a woman's laughter and the bleating of lambs. Easter was coming out here, too.

After a brief pause, Ricciardi took a look around:

"You have a beautiful house, Signora. May I ask what line of work you're in, in your family?"

Maione struggled to suppress a laugh: he was curious to

hear how Viper's mother would answer that question. She sat up straight and proud in her chair.

"My husband, who was named Gennaro," and she pointed to the statue of the saint of that name, as if it were a portrait of her late spouse, "died young. I raised that shameless hussy and her younger brothers and sister all on my own. Children have a duty to help their mother, especially a mother like me, who sacrificed all her life for them."

Ricciardi didn't allow himself to be diverted from the point of his question.

"So Maria Rosaria's brothers and sister help you, monetarily?"

The woman burst into a mocking laugh.

"If only. If anything I help them, I practically have to feed them and clothe them myself, and there are three of them. My two sons are day laborers, and my daughter married a miserable wretch who's even more wretched than she is."

"So this house, the work you're doing on it, the money to feed and clothe your children, how do you pay for it all?"

Maione was enjoying this enormously. But Concetta didn't seem embarrassed in the slightest.

"The son of that whore lives here with me. The money is to make sure he's properly cared for. I'd like to see her try to keep all that money for herself, instead of paying for his expenses."

The brigadier broke in.

"So you say the child lives with you? And where is he?"

Without even turning around, the woman clapped her hands and, when the housekeeper came promptly, still with the scrub brush in her hands, she said:

"Bring the child."

After a brief interval of hostile silence, a little boy, about eight, came trotting into the room, his face and hands spattered with mud, his cheeks ruddy. Beneath a shock of midnight-black hair glittered a pair of gorgeous eyes. With a stab of pity, Ricciardi recognized the woman's features, delicate and fine-drawn as they had been, even in death; paradoxically, he also discerned the grandmother's features, though on her face they were shrouded by harsh anger.

"What's your name?"

The child looked at his grandmother, who nodded. Then he spoke:

"Gennarino Cennamo, at your service, sir."

Ricciardi signaled to the woman, who sent the boy away with a glance.

"He's a lovely little boy," he said.

Concetta retorted:

"He's a child of sin, born to a lady of the night who didn't know how to hold on to her man, the boy's father; she didn't know how to get him to marry her and she didn't even have the wit to get some other man to marry her; all she knew was how to be a whore, and there's not money enough in this world to wash away the shame that she's brought on her son and the rest of the family. I'd rather go on living in the mud and stealing food from the dogs and the pigs than bear the shame that one has made me suffer for the rest of my life."

She'd uttered that tirade without a shift in her tone of voice, without the slightest hint of anger. In the woman's heart there wasn't a speck of love or grief for her murdered daughter.

Ricciardi said:

"You wouldn't know who might have done this thing? You don't know about any enemies, or some jealous woman, for instance, or a man who might have hated her?"

During the silence that ensued, the woman displayed no emotion or uncertainy. Then she said:

"Someone always hates women like her. It was the same way when she was a little girl, just too pretty. Beauty, you know, is a sin. It's not like everyone can afford to be beautiful. If you're too beautiful, then you need to leave, otherwise this is how you wind up. Anyway, I have no idea who could have done it; she sent us money by mail, we hadn't seen her in years. Her son doesn't even know who she is. Who she was."

That final correction was the only hint of uncertainy.

Ricciardi said:

"One last thing, Signora. Did you know that Giuseppe Coppola, whom you know as Peppe 'a Frusta, had asked your daughter to marry him?"

"Yes, I know that. He came to me first, to ask my permission, can you believe it?"

The commissario was surprised to hear that the woman seemed to find the idea amusing.

"And what did you tell him?"

"I told him that as far as I was concerned he was crazy, that it was something that could never happen; that he'd just be throwing away his own good name and that his family would never forgive him. Peppe is a good boy, a *bravo guaglione*, he didn't deserve that curse."

Maione was disgusted. The two men stood up.

"Signo', thanks for your cooperation. I'd like to inform you that tomorrow morning, at seven, the funeral procession for your daughter will be leaving from Via Chiaia."

Concetta eyed him coldly.

"And since when do they give a funeral for women like her? They'll toss her in the gutter, where she belongs."

Ricciardi couldn't restrain himself:

"Signora, do you hear what you're saying? You're talking about your daughter, flesh of your flesh. A young woman, just twenty-five, who was no more than a child when she was raped. Don't you think that she has a right to a little pity?"

Concetta shot to her feet with astonishing agility. She stared at Ricciardi and said:

"All I know is that she was a whore. And now she's even left us saddled with debt. Do you want to tell me who's going to pay for the rest of this constructon?"

# XXIV

S he never expected to feel this bad. Still in bed, with the shutters fastened tight, in the darkness of her room, her pillow soaked with tears. She'd never have expected. Not now.

She had a past, a life that had been difficult more than once. The death of her son, just one year old, of diphtheria, had been the most painful moment of all, and she'd become accustomed to comparing everything terrible that had happened since to that event.

Her husband's domineering and violent personality—he might have been the most respected tenor in all Italy, a close personal friend of Il Duce, but his genius was matched only by the most staggering egotism she'd ever witnessed. She'd suffered—from his constant betrayals, from the loneliness into which he'd forced her, and from the silence in which he'd left her.

She'd held tight to the one thing she still had: herself, her beauty, a social circle of which she'd become the center through her loveliness, her charm, and her class; the same things that had brought her backstabbing, slander, insults, various other betrayals. Beauty is a crime that cannot be forgiven.

She'd stopped looking for love. It wasn't that she'd given up on it, no: she'd simply relegated that emotion to a lower rank in her soul. There had been men, men whose courtship she'd decided to accept, men who'd managed to charm her, or at least aroused her curiosity, in the hopes that they might be different from the rest. They all proved, however, to be no different from all the others.

And then there had been that meeting, that ridiculous acquaintance which had unhinged every resolution of solitude and serenity, every plan she'd had to renounce hope of a future. A meeting that took place in the most illogical circumstances imaginable: the investigation into the murder of her husband.

All it took was a glimpse of those eyes, those sea-green crystals into which she had sunk, and from which she could not seem to emerge. Livia had fallen in love with Ricciardi the instant she looked into his eyes, and now she knew it. Certain emotions leave their mark, they enter into uncharted territory in the soul, they cross an unknown threshold in the heart and take possession of it forever.

Livia was crying: because no one before him had ever triggered this feeling, a feeling that would never come again, and which she couldn't live without.

It was on account of him that she'd moved to that city, a city she'd learned to love, but a place where she'd always be an outsider; the capital—where she had been one of high society's most admired queens, where she had friendships at the very summit of political and economic life—had seemed to her as empty as the stage of a shuttered provincial theater.

She'd taken an apartment, and furnished it as if it was where she was to live as a newlywed. She'd once again welcomed hope into her life, she who had considered herself already dead.

She'd held him in her arms, in that apartment, on a night of fever and rain, when his eternal defenses had collapsed in the face of a stronger loneliness than usual, a disappointment of some kind, or something else, who knows, she didn't care: what she knew was that she had had him, on her flesh, in her body. That the kisses, the caresses, and imprint his body had left inside her hadn't been one of her many dreams, or one of the fantasies that accompanied her own solitary pleasure-taking, but a wonderful reality.

She'd hoped to chip away at his defenses gradually, to pull out whatever it was inside him that brought a perennial look of sorrow to his face, and to help him to erase that grief; she'd hoped for a future, something that fate had set aside for her in exchange for the many tears she'd shed; she'd believed once again that love existed, and that it existed for her too.

Against her own customs and her very nature she'd persisted, she'd courted him. She, who had always taken her pick of many suitors; she, who was gazed at with veneration by men and suspicion by women whenever she made her entrance—alone—into a theater; she, who every day received bouquets of flowers from admirers of all ages. And she hadn't allowed herself to be discouraged by the locked door guarding his heart, that he claimed belonged to another: Livia was certain it wasn't true. That he'd told her that just to keep her at bay, perhaps to protect her from some terrible unknown secret.

There couldn't be another woman. She'd have sensed it, she'd have seen it. He was always withdrawn, absorbed in his life which consisted of his work and his home, the elderly *tata* who still lived with him, and whom she had met after his accident, at the hospital, and another relative, a tall young woman who had left immediately.

All this was true until yesterday. Seeing him again had left her with her heart in her throat, as always; and she'd been happy to see the doctor, a likeable man, intelligent and one of his friends. She loved the idea of sharing every aspect of Ricciardi's life, and all the more so one of his very few friendships. And then that pointless, violent barb.

It hadn't been the words, that vulgar and inappropriate reference to her friendships. It hadn't even been his tone, flat and chilly as it all too often was. What had wounded her had been the obvious fact that he'd meant to hurt her. And the doctor's embarrassment had only confirmed that terrible sensation.

She'd started sobbing in the car, ignoring the driver's cautious words as he asked if there was anything she needed; she'd gone on sobbing when she got home, waving away the housekeeper who asked if she felt unwell; she'd sobbed all night long in her bed, without a bite to eat.

She was weeping over the death of her hopes, the mirage of lost love, the silence that would once again be her life's companion. Over her loneliness, which had come back, this time to stay.

She'd decided that she would leave. That she could no longer stand to stay in that city, where every day she risked encountering those eyes, the eyes that had once made her think life wasn't yet over, only to disappoint her in such a painful way.

She'd go back to Rome, where she'd rebuild, piece by piece, a modicum of self-confidence. Back to Rome where she was valued and perhaps, in some strange and unsatisfying way, even loved. Where some friendships remained to her. She'd once again be Livia Vezzi, queen of the night, the most beautiful one. At least she'd have that.

Meanwhile, as springtime was scheming changes all its own, outside the locked shutters, Livia decided that as soon as the holidays were over, she'd leave, and send for her things later.

Turning her back on love.

# XXV

R icciardi and Maione were used to it: in their line of
work, it was impossible to show up anywhere unexpected or by surprise.

In the best case, their arrival was preceded by word of
mouth—whispers and eyes peering out from behind shutters
and blinds, as the sound of their boots and shoes broke the
silence of secluded alleys. In the worst case, hordes of shouting
*scugnizzi* danced ahead of them like some irreverent fanfare.

Which is what happened this time, as a small flock of barefoot boys splashing through all the mud and puddles they
found along the way, laughing and singing choruses in dialect,
playfully darting to try to pull the brigadier's pistol from its
holster, as he tried to ward them off halfheartedly, like an ox
persecuted by a cloud of bothersome flies.

At the far end of the road, just a few hundred yards from
the Cennamo in-progress mansion, there was a fence with a
gate thrown wide open. On the ground it was possible to see
the tracks of countless cart wheels and, just as they were entering, a load of broccoli pulled by a mule came through the gate,
with a peasant on foot following the cart. The man eyed them
mistrustfully, neither speaking nor tipping his cap.

They found themselves in a large courtyard. The odor of the
nearby stables was piercing, as was the smell of vegetables that
were being stored in a building into which they saw the cartload
of broccoli enter. A broad-shouldered woman with a determined look on her face came toward them, wiping her hands on

her apron; from her blond hair and blue eyes, they immediately understood that she was kin to the Coppola brothers.

"Do you need something?"

The tone of voice wasn't hostile, but brisk: this was a workplace, and there wasn't time to waste. Maione said:

"Signo', is this where Giuseppe Coppola works? We're from the mobile squad, Brigadier Maione and Commissario Ricciardi. Can we speak to him?"

The woman seemed entirely unimpressed by the presence of policemen in her courtyard. She stared at them, mopping her brow with a handkerchief that she'd pulled out of a pocket in her skirt.

"My name is Caterina, I'm Giuseppe Coppola's sister. What do you want with him?"

She wasn't bad looking, the self-proclaimed sister of Giuseppe Coppola: her coloring was lovely, her eyes glittered in the sun like sheaves of ripe wheat; but her features were harshened by a strong-willed domineering personality, and she had a pair of deep creases at the corners of her mouth. Her powerful arms were accustomed to hard labor.

Maione set her straight on who was asking the questions:

"Signo', if we need to speak with him, then it's about something that doesn't concern you, otherwise we would have come straight to you, don't you think? Do me a favor: if he's here, would you please go get him for us?"

The woman gave the brigadier a long stare: she looked as if she was about to give him a shove. Maione put on the sleepy expression he used whenever he was interested in discouraging conversation.

"I don't know where my brother is. These past few days, no one seems to know where he's been going. Let's just hope that he snaps out of it soon, otherwise this whole place will go to hell in a handbasket. Why don't you go take a look in the stables? I have some broccoli to get unloaded."

She turned to the farmer that they'd seen enter the building and gave him an incomprehensible order in thick dialect. The man stopped short with a huge bundle of broccoli in his arms, as if frozen solid by her rough shout, and put the produce back on the cart, awaiting further orders, clearly frightened of the woman who was striding toward him.

The brigadier said:

"An energetic lady, eh? She's worse than any man."

Taking care to avoid the horse droppings that dotted the courtyard, where a dozen or so hens were busily pecking, they walked into the large farmhouse.

No matter what Caterina might say, the Coppola family company seemed to be humming along famously. On one side of the large shed were lined up a dozen or so carts, painted light blue, and there was still room for at least another dozen, which were no doubt out making deliveries just then. A number of men, each wearing a dark felt hat and a handkerchief knotted around his neck, were working busily around the carts, checking joints and axles and oiling hubs. At the opposite end of the room, the entrance to the stables could be seen, a high arch through which came the sound of neighing. Maione was reminded of Bambinella's laughter.

Seeing them come in, the workmen, clearly worried, made a show of concentrating even harder on their tasks: there was no one in that city who didn't have something to fear from the police. The two policemen headed for the horse stalls.

Inside they found a clean, tidy space, where three men and two women were hard at work, brushing and attending to the animals. Here too it was clear that only a small part of the fleet of horses were here, fewer than ten. Most of them were out working.

A man broke away from the group and walked toward them: it was Pietro, the younger Coppola brother, whom Ricciardi had already met at police headquarters.

"Commissa', *buongiorno*. Do you remember me?"

Ricciardi nodded, and introduced him to Maione.

"We've come to Antignano to meet Signora Cennamo, Maria Rosaria's mother. As long as we were here, we thought we'd drop by, just to see the place and maybe talk to your brother."

Maione decided that, his dark hair aside, the boy could easily have been Caterina's twin brother, except that he lacked his sister's massive musculature, despite his broad shoulders. But he must be better natured, because Pietro smiled and lifted both hands, displaying a grooming brush and a rag.

"Forgive me, Brigadie', I can't shake hands: I was just grooming the sorrel mare that you see over there. Pretty, isn't she?"

In fact the animal was magnificent: high and lithe, with mane and tail that seemed to be made of light brown silk, her eyes deep and expressive. Maione commented admiringly:

"She certainly is. She hardly seems to need the grooming. That's certainly not how I imagined a carthorse."

Pietro laughed again:

"Right you are. And in fact, it's not easy to persuade her to haul a cart like the other horses . . . Tell me, Commissa', what can I do for you?"

Ricciardi looked around: Peppe 'a Frusta was nowhere to be seen here, either.

"Where's your brother? The lady in the front, who said that she's your sister Caterina, told us to look in here, but he doesn't seem to be here."

The laughter vanished from the young man's face.

"No, in fact he isn't here. He's inside. He hasn't been out much for . . . for the past few days. Hold on, I'll send for him."

He gestured and a pretty brunette came over, young and not very tall.

"Allow me to introduce Ines, my fiancée. Ines, go in the house and call Peppe for me."

The girl sketched out a brief curtsey and then moved off. Pietro sighed.

"You know, we were planning to get married in a couple of months, we were hoping to do it in June. We've been together for a long time. But with my brother in the shape he's in . . . I just don't think it would be right, and so we've put it off indefinitely. Ines has an older sister, her name is Ada, she's been sweet on my brother for years, she's a schoolteacher, here in Antignano, and we all hoped it would work out. But then he ran into Maria Rosaria again, and since then he hasn't had eyes for anyone else."

Maione wiped his forehead with his handkerchief.

"So tell me, Coppola, what's the setup here?"

"Simple enough, Brigadie'. I take care of the horses and I'm in charge of supplies and deliveries. My sister Caterina supervises the produce, manages the farmers and orchardmen, and the loading and unloading of the carts. My other sister, the younger one, you haven't met her yet, Nicoletta, works in our gardens and orchards and supervises the cultivation of vegetables and fruit. And my brother's in charge of the money, he's the oldest one, you understand, he created this company and he's the boss. Which is why we're having some trouble now: we're doing the best we can, but if he doesn't get a grip on himself, things are going to go south."

He spoke in a worried tone. The company depended on Peppe; and both Caterina and Pietro hoped his morale would soon recover.

Ricciardi said:

"Tomorrow morning at seven there will be a funeral procession for Viper. We wanted to tell your brother."

The young man squirmed.

"For the love of God, Commissa', don't tell him! He's in

such bad shape, he'll do something reckless. He hasn't slept in two days, he's drinking, he won't eat: and no one knows what he might do, if he finds himself face to face with other people who went to Maria Rosaria! And if . . ."

He broke off suddenly when he saw his brother coming, accompanied by Ines. He was unshaven and he walked unsteadily, his hair was filthy and sweaty, his shirt was rumpled. It was immediately obvious to Ricciardi and Maione that he'd been drinking, and heavily, even though it wasn't even lunchtime yet.

"Commissario, greetings. Do you have any news? Any suspects?"

His slurred speech betrayed the grief that was filling his heart. And something else, too.

"Hello, Coppola. We're investigating. What about you, has anything occurred to you?"

Peppe looked around him, glaring threateningly. Ines moved away hastily, heading back toward the fountain to groom the horses. Pietro on the other hand remained nearby; he sat on the ground and started to whittle a piece of wood, staring worriedly at his drunken brother. Maione decided that the young man must feel a love for Peppe that bordered on hero worship; seeing him in that condition must have been true agony for him.

"Commissa', I've given it a lot of thought, and I have no doubts: the one who murdered Maria Rosaria must be that bastard, the one who sells saints and madonnas, Ventrone."

Ricciardi asked:

"Why would you think that? And how did you find out about Ventrone?"

"Rosaria told me about him, and I knew from what people said about the cathouse that her only customer, aside from me, was him. A bloodless man, with clean hands and a tie; but with more money than he knew what to do with. As long as he was around, she was making too much. I told her not to worry, that the money to finish her mother's house—you've seen it, right?—I'd give them to her. I work, you see that, Commissa'? The company is going great. She could have come here and been a queen, if she'd only said yes. A queen."

The brother stood up and started toward them, but Peppe froze him in place with a glare.

Ricciardi asked:

"Well then, what reason would Ventrone have had to kill the girl?"

An immense surge of rage disfigured Coppola's face into a terrible grimace.

"How can you ask me that, Commissa'? Because he would have lost her. She had made up her mind to marry me, I know it, I can feel it. She just needed a little time to tell the others. The same way I knew it, he must have known it too, and so he killed her. And you'll see, I'll kill him in turn, with these hands of mine."

Pietro ran toward him, in tears:

"No, no, Peppi', don't even say such a thing! Don't you care about me, about us? Don't you care about the family's shame, the end of the company you built yourself, doesn't that matter? What do you think, that if you get blood on your hands and you wind up in prison or, even worse, you get killed yourself, Maria Rosaria is going to come back to life?"

Maione placed a hand on Peppe's shoulder.

"Your brother is right, Coppola. You'll ruin your own life and you'll ruin the lives of those who care about you. Leave it to us, you'll see that the commissario, here, will find the culprit. It's just a question of time. Don't get yourself into trouble."

Peppe went on muttering disconnected phrases. A thread of drool dangled from his lips; tears streamed down his cheeks uncontrollably. The workmen had stopped brushing and grooming the horses and stood, horrified, watching the scene. Pietro, also in tears, had one arm around his brother's shoulders.

The first one to come to her senses was Ines, Pietro's fiancée; she clapped her hands in the workers' direction and, in a tone of voice that reminded Maione of Caterina's, ordered them back to work.

Ricciardi signaled to the brigadier and spoke to the young man:

"Coppola, we're leaving now. Listen, for your brother's own good, keep an eye on him: if something bad were to befall anyone, we'd have to consider him the prime suspect. Have I made myself clear?"

Shoving his brother toward the house, the younger brother replied:

"Don't worry about it, Commissa'. I won't leave my brother for a second. And tomorrow . . . a flower for her, from him."

Sitting on a bench by the streetcar stop, Ricciardi and Maione took advantage of the wait to take stock of the investigation.

The brigadier, fanning himself with his cap, said:

"Certainly this is odd, very odd indeed. We've talked to a lot of people, and everyone who knew her, for one reason or another, could have killed her, and the same is true of those who didn't know her. The most curious thing of all though is that everyone says they loved her: Coppola, Ventrone, Lily, and Madame. The only one who hated her was her mother, but she depended on her monetarily so I very much doubt she would have wrung the neck of the goose that laid the golden eggs. A lovely riddle, eh, Commissa'?"

Ricciardi looked into the middle distance, his hands in his lap.

"A complicated situation, yes. Nor does the scene of the crime help much, or the body itself, without any useful marks or wounds. And all four of them would have had the opportunity: one man had just left her, the other found her dead, and the two women were already inside the building. Still, the prime suspects remain Coppola and Ventrone."

Maione grimaced.

"Yes, but for one reason or another, I have to tell you the truth, the one I don't trust is Ventrone. Especially because of Coppola's reaction: you saw him, he's lost his mind. You don't do something like that and then end your life. The merchant, on the other hand, might be hiding his guilt by showing off how he's taking care of the funeral."

The commissario half-snickered.

"You really can't stand him, that Ventrone, eh? I, on the other hand, can't see things clearly even out here in Vomero. Viper's mother, for instance, strikes me as too determined: her hatred is excessive, if you take into account that she exploited her daughter's profession. And even Coppola has these overblown reactions, at times. Did you see how his little brother tries to keep him under control? As if he might explode at any moment. There's something that still doesn't add up."

Around the corner the streetcar swung, its steel wheels screeching, one of the new models with eight wheels and a green two-tone paint job. Maione laughed:

"Out here with all these plants, you'd never see the streetcar coming, it's so green. Lucky it makes so much noise!"

Ricciardi shook himself and stepped up onto the running board.

The spectacle of sunset was just beginning.

# XXVI

S pring night.
What do you want from a spring night?
You, an old woman, who can hear death breathing outside your door, waiting to come in; what do you ask of a spring
night?

That it bring you the time to do what you still must do, perhaps. That something might happen that doesn't entirely
depend on you, that someone might find the courage to speak,
that someone else might find the courage to say yes. That
someone who is in love might not condemn himself to a lifetime of loneliness, when you have gone for good. That spring
might make the blood quicken in the veins, that recklessness
might win out over fear.

This is what you'd ask of the spring night that scatters perfume through the streets.

And you, what is it you'd ask of a spring night?

You, who lie drowning in the silence of wine, and look at
your hands as you think of what they've done and in the fear
of what they could still do, what do you ask of a spring night?

That it might give you back that smile, perhaps. Even if just
once more, even just one miserable moment. To hear the word
that she would have said to you, and understand, and feel, so
that you can dream. To be able to breathe again.

This is what you'd ask of a night that brings wind.

And what would you ask of a spring night?

You who look back on the women of your past, so different

and so beautiful. So dead. With their bodies you tried to satisfy your own, from their hands you desired the pleasure that
you only ever had from one woman, one woman who is gone
now. What do you ask of the spring night?

That it might sweep her memory from your mind, perhaps.
So that you can bury behind the image of her corpse this side
of your mind, this shadowy side, this dark side. And that you
might see others respect you again, that you might see your son
respect you again.

This is what you'd ask of the night of new scents.

And you? What is it that you'd ask of a spring night?

You who continue to cry into your pillow, unable to find
peace in sleep. You, who are rich, and beautiful, and desired,
and loved, and who feel that you're the ugliest, poorest, and
most woebegone woman on earth. What do you ask of the
spring night?

That it might help you to forget about love, perhaps. That
it might chase away from your night those green eyes that stare
at you out of the darkness, making your belly churn and stabbing your heart. That it might help you to resign yourself to the
loss of hope.

This is what you'd ask of the night of sea foam.

What about you? What would you ask of a spring night?

You who sit up, wakeful, with your aching body, from the
thousands of bruises and aches and small wounds that you
know so well. Because you've lived through another first day of
this terrible profession, your body bearing the brunt of the
vices of so many men who lack the courage to seek from their
wives what they truly desire. What would you like from this
spring night?

Perhaps a man. Just one man. However many vices he may
have, however desperate he may be. No matter how much pain
he wishes to inflict, no matter how much pain he wishes to suffer. One man, who stays to sleep at your side, when he's fin-

ished searching for his own frenzied desire with blind fury. Just one man, who is still there when you wake up.

This is what you'd ask of the night of newly sprouted leaves. And you? What do you ask of the spring night?

You who have spent the whole day trying to fend off disease, pain, jealousy, anger. You who have administered medicines, you who have stitched up wounds and injuries. You, who when you finally got to bed, expected to drop into deepest sleep, and instead find yourself still there, staring at the ceiling that is a black screen for your memories. Tell me, what do you want from the spring night?

A new world, perhaps. A different world, where causing suffering isn't a virtue, a good to be pursued. Where one's true homeland is the whole universe, where borders don't need to be expanded with arms. Where pain comes only from natural causes, not from human hands. Maybe, not to feel that everyone else's suffering is also yours.

That's what you'd ask, of this night full of fresh magic.

And you, you: what is that you'd wish for on this spring night?

You who are so excited you can't get to sleep. You who are just discovering the smells, the spaces, the territories inhabited by the man you love, as you drink in his movements, as you imagine his expressions. You who caress his fabrics, his curtains, his armchairs, absorbing the glances of those eyes which preceded your touch. What do you desire from this spring night?

Perhaps that space might fill up for you, in your days and in your life. That he might understand, the way that you've understood, that the time has come, that by now the days of fingers brushing, the days of love are finally coming, just as the summer of light and dreams is on its way.

That's what you'd wish for, in this night of a thousand deceits.

And you? You, what is it you'd ask for from this spring night?

You who felt her presence in your belly, and now she's dead. You who saw her walk her first steps and heard her speak her first word, and who glowed with pride at how beautiful she was. Who dreamed of her as a bride, but never saw it. Who imagined her giving birth as you held her hand, but that too was denied you. Who tell everyone willing to listen how much you hate her, that you've never forgiven her for the shame she brought you, that you disown the whore that she became. So then why can't you sleep, on this pleasant spring night?

Perhaps it's because she's dead now that you find her sitting here on the edge of your soft feather bed, which she bought you in silence, without ever seeing what she paid for. Because her corpse looks at you and doesn't speak, it looks at you without reproof and without love, it looks at you and nothing more. And it waits for a word you can't utter, because corpses don't listen, because corpses have no ears. And in the sleepless night, you can't even think it, that word.

That's what you desire from this night of sad silence.

And you? You who never ask anything, what would you like from this spring night?

You who are no stranger to nights spent staring into the darkness in pursuit of a dreamless sleep that is always slow to come. You who feel echoing in your chest the voices of the living and the dead, and chase after a logic you never find, what is it you seek and what is it you find in this spring night?

Perhaps you seek one face and find another. Perhaps you'd like to find the image that brings you peace, a sweet left-handed silhouette that moves placidly through its familiar spaces, dreaming of making those spaces yours. And instead you see the deep dark eyes that swim with tears thanks to your gratuitous insult. And you recognize this new fragility, a gap in the armor of a heart you long thought strong and independent, and you now reckon with a new tenderness.

And perhaps those eyes transform themselves into a dead face, expressionless, with a vague memory of beauty in its features, a face that demands justice without asking it, or revenge for the life stolen from it, for its unknown future.

You'd like just a little peace from the night of stirring blood.

And then there's you.

You who have killed. You who are one of these people, or who are something else entirely, you who waited until there was no more breath left under that pillow, for the body that was once warm to cool, for the blood to stop flowing through her veins.

You, what is it you would ask of this spring night?

Perhaps you'd ask it to rub out a shadow of remorse. You'd ask it to call you right, when you thought that there could be no life, with her still in the world. That there would be no hope, no peace, with her. That the spring night might convince you that it will be possible to go on living without her, that you weren't wrong, that everything will turn out all right.

That it wasn't revenge, that it wasn't anger. But necessity. Not despair, but hope.

That the spring night might convince you that there was only one way, and that you did what you had to do.

That in order to be reborn, one must necessarily die.

That's what you'd like to hear from the night that cannot give you peace.

Because it has none.

# XXVII

For Holy Thursday the springtime chose a gray outfit. The morning dawned misty, with a sickly, pale sun that hardly seemed up to that day's task. A milky light sketched the outlines of things, plunging them into a fog. The occasional early-morning pedestrians moved along the walls, intimidated by a damp and incomprehensible air: this spring continued to lead people on before brutally disappointing them, pretending to be herself before she really was.

Ricciardi left home half an hour earlier than usual, to be punctual as promised for Viper's funeral procession. The report from the hospital, which he'd found on his desk the night before upon his return from Vomero, informed him that the corpse had been released to the only person who had claimed it, Signora Lidia Fiorino, also known as Madame Yvonne; therefore everything had gone as expected, and the strange funeral would take place.

If he had requested authorization through proper bureaucratic channels, he'd been well aware, it would have taken days and in all likelihood the request would have ended up stranded on the desk of some sanctimonious functionary who, horrified, would have surely dismissed out of hand the idea of a group of prostitutes parading the streets in the middle of Holy Week. Quite likely, that functionary would have been Garzo himself, in spite of his friendship with the very men who patronized the bordello in question. It's one thing to keep the place open for business, quite another to allow a young woman who'd been violently murdered to be given decent interment.

There was nothing that disgusted Ricciardi as much as hypocrisy. Even violence, the outburst of rage that led to murder, was part of human nature: masking, concealing, pretending were structures erected in the name of convention, and they were undertaken in the name of personal advantage and convenience. Nothing natural about them.

How much better, therefore, to simply be present to settle any issues that might arise then and there. A commissario of police was a living, breathing authorization. Maione wasn't wrong, his participation in that unorthodox ceremony was a risk and a potentially serious infraction, in bureaucratic terms; but Ricciardi had glimpsed the ghostly image of the girl, beautiful and dead, standing before a mirror that did not bear her reflection, as she repeated ad infinitum her last, incomprehensible thought. In a certain absurd and inexplicable sense, he knew her: he couldn't allow her to be buried like some stray animal, nameless, in a mass grave.

As his footsteps echoed over the damp cobblestones of the deserted street, the commissario mulled over the meetings of the previous day. There was something he couldn't put his finger on, a distinct sensation of disorder; he hadn't been able to see clearly into that horrible story, his ears had somehow listened badly. Powerful emotions seemed to coalesce around Viper, and one of them had caused the murder: but which? Sometimes the best solution really was the simplest one, and that's why it wasn't seen. Murder was such a grave and majestic thing that it rendered the obvious inconceivable.

Perhaps Viper had told Coppola no, and in a burst of fury he'd killed her; and now he drank to try to forget that he had snuffed out with his own hands his one chief reason to live. Perhaps the mother had decided she could no longer bear the shame, or else she hadn't been given some extra sum of money she'd demanded, and she'd murdered her daughter. Or maybe Ventrone's son had thought this was the way to free his father. Or even Ventrone himself, when confronted with the possibility of losing his chief source of pleasure, had suffocated her in one final, terrible sex game.

And maybe not.

At the corner of Via Toledo, he crossed paths with a group of women dressed in black who were heading off to Mass with their heads covered; one of them was carrying a basin full of wheat for the Holy Sepulcher. One of the oldest and most distinctive traditions of the Easter season: kernels of wheat and chickpeas were made to grow in the dark, inside wooden chests, in broom fibers so that they'd grow strictly white, and thus be used to adorn the *sepolcri*, the sepulchers, altars put up in churches in celebration of the burial of Christ.

Ricciardi recalled that a professor at the university had traced this custom back to pagan fertility rites at the turn of spring. That connection made him think of how likely it was that restrictions, penitence, and taboos would lead to explosions of uncontrollable violence and therefore murder: on the one hand penitence, the commemoration of death on the cross, and on the other hand springtime, the rebirth of life. Perhaps Modo wasn't entirely wrong when he called, in his interminable political tirades, for liberation from all forms of social coercion.

In the street outside the building that housed Il Paradiso, a black van was waiting to receive its doleful cargo. The vehicle was nondescript, devoid of any insignia or embellishments: it could have been meant to transport any kind of merchandise. Ricciardi was impressed with the care Ventrone had taken to ensure that the matter be carried off without attracting more attention than necessary.

No one was there yet, he had arrived a good half hour early.

He slowed to a halt on the far side of the street, in the shelter of doorway. The city was starting to wake up, there wasn't much time if they hoped to pass more or less unobserved. He let his gaze wander over the facades of the surrounding apartment buildings, he saw a couple of women saying prayers on their balconies, rosary in hand and lips moving in a perennial murmur; a man sipping a demitasse of espresso, his expression sleepy; two maids airing out blankets and pillows, squinting and furrowing their brows as they scanned the skies to see if and when it might begin to rain.

A voice startled him:

"*Buongiorno*, Commissa'. This spring really seems reluctant to announce itself, eh?"

He had always been astonished by Maione's ability to move inconspicuously through the streets of the city. How a man of his size managed to move a frame that measured six feet, three inches in height and 265 pounds in weight, clad in a police uniform, so that it suddenly appeared without anyone having noticed its approach was, to Ricciardi, a complete mystery; but this talent was so useful in stakeouts and in tailing people that he had never bothered to investigate further.

"What are you doing here today? Didn't you say, and rightly so, that it was dangerous to attend this ceremony even without the famous written authorization?"

The brigadier replied:

"What can I tell you, Commissa': it just must mean you're not the only reckless fool at police headquarters. And after all, hearing the words of the mother, yesterday, I just felt sorrier than ever for this poor girl. It didn't strike me as fair that they should just haul her off like that: perhaps the father, if he were still alive, would be standing here today. Whore or no whore. And I'm not the only one who feels that way, apparently."

Ricciardi looked in the direction Maione was pointing and saw a white dog with brown spots, sitting obediently. A moment later Dr. Modo appeared, whistling a little tune, hands in his pockets and hat pushed back on his forehead.

"Oh, is it the police watching over the state of public safety from the shadows of an entryway? Yes indeed, I certainly feel much safer."

Ricciardi was surprised:

"You here too? Well, well, well, I thought I was here alone this morning, and instead without my knowledge someone seems to have scheduled an assembly of insomniacs. I understand that old people don't sleep much, but I hardly expected to see you here too, Bruno."

Modo grimaced.

"It's all a matter your point of view, my gloomy friend. I never actually went to bed last night, I worked until late while you were having your nightmares, and I indulged in a glass of wine in the very last tavern to lock up and then a cup of coffee in the very first café to roll up its blinds, practically simultaneously. And I thought to myself: I can't miss an old friend's last stroll. The dog agreed with me, and here we are. And we're hardly the only ones, I see: Brigadie', isn't that a close friend of yours, that young lady across the street?"

Maione peered carefully, then walked disconsolately over to the tall figure dressed in black, a shawl of the same color over her head, but with a pair of red shoes with dizzyingly high heels and fishnet stockings.

"Bambine', what on earth are you doing here, if you don't mind my asking?"

The *femminiello* uncovered only a pair of eyes with extremely long lashes and murmured softly:

"Brigadie', keep your voice down, I don't want anyone to overhear! And what, I can't come to a funeral too?"

"First of all, it's not actually a funeral, second it's something that we're trying to keep as discreet as possible, and I certainly can't say you're the type who's likely to go unnoticed."

Bambinella lifted a gloved hand to her face:

"But just look, I put on the only black dress I own! Only I had to wear a shawl, because I don't have any little hats with a veil. My girlfriend, the one who works here as a housekeeper and who wants to become a whore if she can, told me that the funeral procession would be held this morning and that Madame organized everything with Ventrone, the merchant, who isn't going to be coming because he's afraid of what people might say, and then . . ."

Maione raised one hand:

"For the love of Jesus, Bambine', I can't keep up with you first thing in the morning like this, have you ever noticed that I almost always come to see you in the evening? I don't care how you heard about it, I only want to know what you're doing here."

Bambinella burst out in a giggle, meant to be subdued, but actually more like the whinnying of a horse with a sore throat.

"No, it's just that whoever's in our line of work feels the obligation to show solidarity. It happened to her, it could have happened to any of us girls, in a bordello or at home or out in the street. So, I just figured I'd come too."

Maione commented, his spirit broken:

"Fine. That's all we needed this morning, the consolidated sisterhood of whores. Well, then, just keep quiet and out of sight. And above all, don't give anyone the idea that we know each other."

"Brigadie', whatever you want. The course of true love never did run smooth. I'll get well out of the way and I won't cause you any trouble."

For an instant the brigadier considered whether he ought to give the *femminiello* a kick in the ass, then he decided to put that off for the moment and went over to the doctor and the commissario.

Modo said:

"You two can't go on meeting like this, Brigadie'. Sooner or later you're going to have to bring this secret affair out into the light of day."

"Dotto', please, don't you start too. I was just flipping a coin as to whether I should stage a nice police raid, now that I'm here, and be done with that creature once and for all!"

Just then, the street door swung open and the pianist, the butler, Madame's son, and the van driver brought out the coffin containing Viper's body.

# XXVIII

Ricciardi saw exactly what he'd been dreading: from the balconies and windows of the surrounding buildings women and children were peering down, attracted by the unusual bustle.

Il Paradiso, as was appropriate given the activity that took place in that house, was tolerated because it was discreet: the windows were covered, the entryways were private, the tradesmen came in through the side entrances, the girls displayed themselves only to the customers, going out rarely if at all, alone and at special times of day. Even the music was played in an interior room, and couldn't be heard from outside. Everyone knew of the existence of the bordello, but no one spoke of it or mentioned it by name: this was a respectable neighborhood.

Naturally everyone had heard about the murder, even though the newspapers—which for years had been ordered to maintain complete silence on all reporting that implied violent crime—had made no mention of it; still, news had its own ways of traveling, and Il Paradiso was constantly kept under close surveillance by the neighborhood gossips in search of prurient tidbits.

And now, unbelievably, they were daring to hold a funeral. Of course there was no priest—I would certainly hope not!—nor was there a black carriage pulled by horses decked out in tall black plumes: still, there could be no question that this was a funeral procession, even if it was so early that no stores were open and there was no one in the street.

In haste and hurry, the neighborhood mothers shooed their children into windowless rooms in the apartments to keep them from seeing, and then ostentatiously slammed the shutters shut, only then to peek out from behind the closed curtains. A few men leaned over, shaking their heads, and from one balcony a burst of laughter could be heard.

The casket was set down carefully inside the van; then the men stood aside and out the front door of the apartment building, in double file like nuns emerging in procession from a convent, came Madame Yvonne and all the women who had worked with Viper.

No one could have had a word to say against the sobriety of the women's attire. Black dresses, hats with veils or shawls over the head to cover the hair. No hair dye, no low necklines, no legs appearing through a daring slit in a skirt; no high-heeled shoes, no heavy makeup. Aside from Bambinella, who was keeping well out of sight, half-hidden in the shadows cast by the building, and aside from the lack of male presence, you would have said it was the perfectly normal funeral of a respectable citizen who hadn't been able to afford an expensive service.

The silence was absolute, and the cutting gazes from the windows created a palpable tension. One of the girls approached the dark wood coffin and caressed it slowly with her gloved hand. After her, all the other girls, one at a time, said their own personal farewell to a woman who had been the city's most celebrated prostitute: perhaps, as Bambinella had put it to Maione, each of them was thinking that the young woman's fate could easily have been her own, or perhaps it was simply sadness at the thought of a young life cut short.

Ricciardi noted that Ventrone, as he had told them, was not present, and that Pietro Coppola had managed to keep his brother from attending, just as he'd promised. Not even the ghost of Viper's mother: the commissario had hoped the woman might have a change of heart.

The doctor went over to the accordion player, who, in order to hold onto what must have been a prime spot on the street, was already there at the crack of dawn, and murmured something into his ear; he slipped the man a banknote, and the accordionist thanked him with a tip of his hat. Then he began playing a very famous tango.

The melody, so out of keeping with both the hour of day and the somber occasion, caused a stir of surprise in the little procession and also in the few people who had remained at their windows to watch; a few slammed shutters even opened up again, revealing astonished faces. The melody was beautiful, and the setting—the gray light of that damp, grim morning; the white faces of the girls little used to the sun shaded under black hats—made it heartbreaking.

The doctor went over to Maione and Ricciardi and shrugged:

"It's the music that I'd like at my own funeral. You know it, don't you?"

Ricciardi nodded vaguely.

"I've heard it on the radio, certainly. But why this song in particular?"

"Because it's about a bordello, a place where people exchange love in secret, an apartment on the third floor of a building in Buenos Aires. It's called *A media luz*. In half light, in the shadows."

When the song came to its chorus, the doctor began singing along in a low voice.

"*Y todo a media luz, que es un brujo el amor, / a media luz los besos, a media luz los dos. / Y todo a media luz, crepúsculo interior. / ¡Qué suave terciopelo la media luz de amor!*"

Many of the girls turned to look at the doctor, who was singing in little more than a murmur. One of them blew him a kiss on the tips of her fingers. The doctor responded with a slight bow.

Maione asked:

"Dotto', what do those lyrics mean?"

Modo ran a hand over his face. He seemed deeply moved.

"They're words, Brigadie'. Nothing but words. They mean: 'And everything in the half light, because love is a sorcerer / In the half light the kisses, In the half light the two of us / And everything in half light in the interior twilight / What soft velvet is the half light of love!'"

From a balcony, impossible to figure out which, a red geranium was tossed. A pair of shutters slammed shut, a cracking sound like a slap. A girl was dead. A whore was dead.

The driver turned toward Ricciardi, who nodded his head. The man went over to Madame Yvonne, who looked like a mountain dressed in black, and whispered something in her ear. The woman turned toward the girls and clapped her hands to indicate that the service was over.

Just as the women were assembling to return to their building, a group of four men turned the corner from the *vicolo*; they were dressed in black, and they were laughing uproariously for some reason, mocking the biggest man in the group, who was clearly not enjoying it.

They were wearing black shirts.

As they lurched downhill they found themselves practically face to face with the little line of girls; they exchanged glances of confusion, clearly drunk and returning home from a night out carousing. One of the four, perhaps recognizing the staff of a place he frequented, said:

"Hey, wait . . . Are those the whores of Il Paradiso? All of them out in the street? What are they doing out here?"

Another member of the crew gave the accordionist a shove, sending him head over heels with a clattering honk. The instrument crashed to the pavement in spite of the man's attempt to cushion the blow, and he emitted a strangled shout.

A third man, the one who seemed to be having the most

trouble remaining upright, laughed and uttered a vulgar compliment as he grabbed the bottom of the girl nearest to him, who screamed. From one of the windows came a cry of: "Bravo!" and the man made an off-kilter bow in response.

The other men, unwilling to be outdone, reached out their hands, as rapacious as foxes in a henhouse. The women clutched at one another for safety and Lily dealt a slap to the Fascist who had first grabbed a girl; caught off guard, he slipped and fell. His friends began to mock him and he stood up, offended, and slapped the woman hard in the face.

It all happened in just a few seconds.

Dr. Modo was the quickest to react: he grabbed the closest one, who fell, dragging another of his comrades to the ground. The other two turned their attention away from the women and moved toward the doctor, menacingly.

That was when the dog took up a position between Modo and the Fascists, baring its teeth, raising its hackles, emiting a hollow snarl. One of the men pulled a knife: the situation was critical.

From the shadows of the entryway across the street emerged the considerable bulk of Brigadier Maione, who had waited until the last possible moment in hopes that the situation might right itself without his intervention. Before taking action he had whispered an aside to Ricciardi, who had already started to step forward:

"Commissa', wait, please. Let me take care of this."

He placed himself in front of the doctor, and brought his hand close to the holstered revolver on his belt. He spoke to the four men:

"Gentlemen, let's calm down . . . Are you sure it's in your best interests to pursue this?"

There was a terrible moment of silence: from the windows and balconies by this point at least a few dozen spectators were looking down, and the girls and Madame Yvonne had all withdrawn to the entryway and were watching the scene from there. The Fascists were annoyed at having to backtrack, but the enormous policeman seemed resolutely determined to stand up for the doctor.

After a long hesitation, the tallest one put his knife away with studied and ostentatious lack of care. The oldest, who seemed to be in charge, spoke to the physician:

"We know you. You're that doctor from the Pellegrini hospital. The one who likes to let his mouth run and always spouts nonsense. So you like politics, eh, Dotto'? You'd better be careful, though. If you practice the wrong kind of politics, you could wind up having a nasty accident."

Modo looked at him hard for a long time. Then he spat onto the pavement, just a few inches from the tip of the man's boots, and the man leapt backward in disgust, red-faced with anger and humiliation. The Fascist nodded his head, ostentatiously, never taking his eyes off Modo, as if he were memorizing that face.

He signaled to the others and then headed away up the street, followed by his three comrades.

After a pause, the driver hastily closed the van's door, got behind the wheel, and set off for the cemetery. The women went back inside, but not before expressing their appreciation and gratitude to the doctor.

Bambinella went over to Maione:

"What a man!" she exclaimed in an adoring voice. "You just slayed me, I'm covered in goose bumps!"

The brigadier made as if to punch her and the *femminiello*, with a lilting giggle, headed off into the back alleys.

# XXIX

O f all the holidays, the one Lucia Maione loved most passionately was Easter.

Certainly, Christmas had its charms, with its various pizzas—anchovies and onions or escarole—to be made, and the manger scene with a real flowing river thanks to an enema bulb hidden behind the papier-mâché, with the pastries and the beautiful table setting, and the letters from the children making resolutions for the new year; and then there was the Day of the Dead, with its nougat *torrone*; and the marvelous festival of Piedigrotta, so rich in music and songs. But Easter, Easter was springtime, the windows opening after winter, letting sunshine and the smell of the sea back in.

For Lucia, just like for all the mothers in the city, Easter began with Carnival, forty-one days before; and therefore with preparations for the feast of Fat Tuesday, or Mardi Gras, a feast for which she was renowned throughout the quarter, if she did say so herself: his majesty the lasagne, the dish of kings, with ragù and meatballs; sausages and rapini, the *fegatini nella rezza*, pork livers cooked in a mesh made of the pig's intestine and laurel leaves, and most important of all, the sanguinaccio, a sweet blood pudding made of cocoa, milk, and pig's blood garnished with candied citron, a treat that the children dreamed of all year long.

And it was at the end of every Carnival banquet that her Raffaele, slumping back in his chair after consuming two helpings of every dish, exclaimed the stock phrase: "Luci', your cooking is going to kill me: but what a wonderful way to go!"

The holiday that followed was Lent, a time of self-denial and penitence. Although she was certainly no *bizzoca*, no pious bigot, one of those women who passed every instant of their spare time in church saying rosaries, she did want her children to have a clear idea of the traditions inherited from their faith. That was how they had been raised, and that was how their children would be raised. And so for the next forty days meat gave way to legumes, which left little room for the imagination of a sophisticated cook; Lucia limited herself to the occasional preparation of the *quaresimali*, the dry Lenten almond biscuits made of candied fruit and topped with just a dash of cinnamon—treats that consoled the children during a period of relative abstinence that seemed even longer than it was.

Then came springtime, and the Holy Week that culminated in Easter. When springtime came before Easter it was hard to rein in your appetites, as nature stirred and the bright new sunshine tickled the skin, out of keeping with the last part of this period of penitence; but when springtime and Holy Week coincided perfectly, as they had that year, then it was twice the holiday.

As Lucia walked briskly through Largo della Carità toward the Pignasecca market, she thought to herself that everything was ready: she'd prepared the full array of her culinary armaments well in advance. The pots and pans glittered, the knives had been sharpened, the ingredients that could be stored had all been purchased, and the menus had been planned out thoroughly. There was nothing left to do but wait.

The last few days had been devoted to another domestic ritual of particular importance: spring cleaning. For the first time, Lucia had involved her eldest daughter, who had just turned ten, and Benedetta, who was the same age.

At the thought of the little girl, Lucia smiled. Raffaele had brought her home on Christmas Eve, after an absence during which she had feared he'd gone to commit a terrible crime, which thank goodness he hadn't. Instead, he came in the door carrying that serious-faced little lady, with her perfect manners and her quiet voice: Benedetta had lost both parents in a tragic fashion, and tenderhearted Raffaele couldn't enjoy the holidays knowing that the girl would be left alone in a religious boarding school. She'd lived with them since that night. The Maiones had obtained legal custody of Benedetta, and they were in the process of officially adopting her. Eight can eat as cheaply as seven, Lucia had told her husband, and after all the girl ate like a bird.

And so Lucia, Maria, and Benedetta had mobilized for the major operations involved in spring cleaning: carpets, curtains, and winter clothing to be beaten and brushed, with special care taken to turn out the pockets and clean out the white clumps of lint; the mending and darning of small tears, worn-out buttonholes and eyelets and pockets to be re-stitched, dangling buttons to be reattached, linings to be resewn; grease stains and smudges on cuffs and collars to be cleaned with hot bran. And then everything had to be stowed away for the summer in the *cascioni*, the ample trunks which would be tucked away in lofts and attics, with plenty of naphthalene mothballs, camphor blocks, and pepper, essential weapons in the fight against mites and clothes moths.

But soon the wait would be over, and the women of the Maione household would test themselves against the most challenging and serious obstacle course of Neapolitan cooking: the *casatiello* and the *pastiera*, respectively the savory stuffed bread and the ricotta cheesecake that were synonymous with Easter in Naples. Lucia would initiate the two girls into the family's most intimate and closely guarded secrets, the secrets that they'd be able to use to ensure that their own men looked to them with gratitude and bliss for every Easter of the rest of their later lives.

But first there was Holy Thursday, the day of the *struscio*, or the walk up and down the Via Toledo, and of the *sepolcri*, or the day in which the faithful remember the Lord's Last Supper. Culinary tradition demanded, in the name of that commemoration, the *zuppa marinara*, or seafood soup, the first fanfare of Easter cooking.

When she needed to purchase mussels, clams, and *fasolari*—giant clams—instead of going directly to the fishermen Lucia preferred to frequent a fishmonger at the Pignasecca market; he was a longtime acquaintance and she knew that, out of consideration for their well established business relationship, he'd never sell her seafood that was anything less than fresh. The soup also called for cuttlefish and octopus, and that shopping would demand patient and attentive evaluation.

The market was large and crowded: it was broken up into a multitude of stalls, counters, and carts that intruded into the maze of lanes surrounding the larger structure of the Pellegrini hospital. Lucia dove in, with the confidence and expertise of a sea captain navigating through an archipelago whose every reef and shallows he knows by heart. The blond hair that spilled out of the scarf knotted over her head, her brisk pace, and her lovely blue eyes attracted the attention and greetings of a variety of vendors and merchants; she replied with a nod of the head: never let yourself be led astray by things you don't need, she told herself. Straight to her objective; the fishmonger was at the end of the street, she'd have to walk past the hospital's side entrance.

Passing the entrance, she shot a glance into the courtyard. She dreaded that place as the policeman's wife that she was; every morning she instinctively recited a Hail Mary as she watched her husband leave for work: she remembered Commissario Ricciardi's time in that hospital, in the aftermath of that horrible car crash on the Day of the Dead, and how worried Raffaele had been. She herself had gone to visit the man, bringing him a *torrone*, the classic almond nougat, that she'd made with her own hands.

Just as she was about to hurry on, she glimpsed an odd movement: a small dog, tied to a pole by its leash, was furiously struggling to break free. On the far side of the courtyard, two men were conversing animatedly next to a black car, parked with the engine running. One of the men wore a lab coat and had white hair, and looked to be a doctor; Lucia wondered if this could be Dr. Modo, the physician of whom her husband always spoke with the greatest respect and fondness. The other man caught Lucia's attention because he was so well dressed, in a double-breasted suit and a hat of the same color; unlike the doctor, who was gesticulating angrily, this man stood still, impassive, arms at his sides.

Lucia stopped, her curiosity piqued. The distance made it impossible for her to overhear what they were talking about, but the doctor seemed to be in a rage. The dog was barking desperately. Oddly enough, there was no one walking through the courtyard, which was usually a busy place, and the hospital windows were all shut. At the entrance to the courtyard there were two stalls, but the vendors were making a great show of indifference, and continued sorting through their merchandise in its crates.

At a certain point, two other men climbed out of the car and flanked the doctor on both sides; they dragged him quickly into the car while the well-dressed gentleman, the one who'd been talking to the doctor up till now, walked around and got in the car on the driver's side. The car pulled away quickly, passing close to Lucia as it left the courtyard.

The doctor looked out, and for a second his gaze met the woman's. His face was red and upset, his eyes filled with anger and something else that struck Lucia as sadness.

Once the car had screeched around the corner, the woman recovered her wits and started calling loudly for help, but one of the two vendors who had feigned indifference walked over to her:

"Signo', take it from me: forget about this. If you don't want to put anyone else in danger, say nothing to no one about what you just saw. These are hard times."

In the courtyard the dog had finally managed to break free, and it shot off in pursuit of the car that had by now disappeared.

# XXX

From his vantage point, what had happened at the end of Viper's strange funeral rite had provided Ricciardi with plenty of food for thought. First of all, he considered what he'd observed of Modo. His attitude toward anyone who represented the regime, even if they were just a few young thugs who were taking advantage of their black shirts to spread a little mayhem, would sooner or later land him in seriously hot water. Even if it only meant—and that time he'd come dangerously close—he was going to catch a beating.

After the women had retreated into their building and the doctor, Maione, and the commissario were left standing alone in the street, the doctor had blithely ignored their remostrances to be more cautious and had in fact actually scolded Ricciardi for failing to intervene.

The brigadier had replied in his superior officer's place:

"I told the commissario, Dotto', to stay out of the way. We were here without authorization, and the last thing we needed was a brawl in the street, to give the deputy police chief, that good-for-nothing Garzo, an excuse to toss us both in a cell. I can always say that I was just passing by, but the commissario can't."

Maione had a point, but that wasn't what Ricciardi urgently needed Modo to understand.

"The point is, Bruno, if you keep it up like this, you'll get yourself into trouble we won't be able to get you out of. The problem isn't a crew of drunken hotheads looking for trouble;

the problem is their boss. I dealt with them, last summer, when the Duchess Musso was murdered, and I can assure you that they're capable of doing things you couldn't even begin to imagine. I beg you, if you won't listen for your own sake, listen for the sake of all those you can help. Control yourself."

Modo's tone of voice was venomous.

"Are you trying to tell me that we're just supposed to accept the kind of things we've seen here? That some little idiot, simply because he's wearing a black shirt and a pair of jackboots, feels that he has the right to put his hand on a woman's behind when she's in tears at her friend's funeral? Not me, I'll never accept it: and if they want to put me in front of a firing squad for it, they can go right ahead. I," and here he tapped himself on the chest with his forefinger several times, "I defended this country, on the Carso. I stitched up wounds with steel wire, I amputated arms with a bayonet. And I'm not going to let them turn this country to a stinking pile of shit!"

He'd turned on his heel to leave, then he'd stopped, as if in regret, and come back.

"I know that you're my friend, Ricciardi. And I love you too, even if you're a silent, taciturn bastard and there's never a way of knowing what the hell you're thinking. But I am who I am, you know. There's no switch you can flip. If they're going to come cart me off, let them do it: that just means it was meant to be."

And with that he left. The dog stared hard at Maione and Ricciardi for a second, then turned and trotted off after him, as usual trailing behind by a couple of yards.

Maione had commented:

"That dog kind of gives me the willies, Commissa'. He's like a citizen who can't talk."

Ricciardi had said:

"What can I tell you, Raffaele: let's just hope that our friend the doctor manages to stay out of trouble. Let's just hope."

From the street door of the building housing Il Paradiso, Tullio, Madame's son, had emerged. He'd stopped for a moment to light a cigarette and then had headed off, head down as he walked into the wind, toward Piazza Trieste e Trento.

After a minute, Ricciardi had said:

"There: that's one piece of the puzzle we've been overlooking, it seems to me. Why don't you see where he's going, Raffaele: and then you can come back and report on what you find. I'll be waiting for you in the office."

Maione had started off on the opposite side of the street, taking advantage, as was his custom, of the intermittent shade of the front entryways. Experience had taught him that this technique greatly reduced the risk of being spotted. Not that he was particularly worried the young man might see him: he'd craned his neck as he left the bordello, but he hadn't even glimpsed the brigadier and Ricciardi, who were talking in the atrium of the building across the street, making no effort whatsoever to escape notice.

He observed Tullio's shoulders, the head that appeared and disappeared as the young man made his way through the Holy Thursday crowd now filling the Via Toledo. He might have been twenty or maybe a little older, his face scarred by small-pox, his broad shoulders slightly bowed, his hair fair; he'd never heard his voice. Bambinella had been quite clear about him: a gambler, slave to the promise of easy winnings that never seemed to arrive. Maione had seen plenty of dreams just like his that wound up dying at knifepoint. Debts, and more debts contracted to wipe out the previous debts.

At a certain point the young man veered off confidently onto a side street. Maione wasn't caught off guard because he knew the locations of all the city's leading clandestine gambling dens, which did a brisk businesses even during the week of Easter. He'd already noticed a couple of touts, fairly shady customers who served both as lookouts in case of a police raid and as procurers, luring in potential gamblers who might happen by. From a distance he could see that the young man was trying to win admittance to a gambling den he knew quite well, a place run by Luigino della Speranzella, where the chief tout on the door was a certain Simoncelli, an ex-con whom Maione had run in a couple of times for purse snatching.

There was a discussion between the two men, short and intense. Maione could have repeated it word for word: Tullio wanted to get in to play some cards, and Simoncelli refused to admit him until he'd seen the color of his money. It was obvious that the young man had run through the line of credit that had been extended to him.

Their conversation was starting to break down, the young man was powerfully built and unaccustomed to hearing no, while the gatekeeper was well aware of his job. Then he saw something glitter in the dim light, and Maione decided that it was time to step forward; but the flash of the blade had been enough to persuade the young man to hurry off in evident fear.

The brigadier watched him try a few more doors, receiving an equally firm, if perhaps less violent, refusal each time, and in the end Tullio made his way dejectedly back to the bordello.

Maione went back to Speranzella's gambling den and, sneaking up behind Simoncelli's back, whispered from the shadows:

"Hey there, Simonce', how's it going?"

The man leapt into the air and emitted a high-pitched shriek, and swung around ready for trouble. He was a slight individual, with a sickly, treacherous appearance, hollow-cheeked, with small darting eyes. He wore a ridiculous tattered tailcoat and a pair of down-at-the-heel shoes. He'd slipped his hand into his inside breast pocket, the same pocket from which Maione had seen him pull the knife earlier.

"Ah, Brigadie', it's you, *buonasera*. You scared me. Listen to the way my heart is racing, try that again and you'll probably kill me."

Maione took a step forward, emerging from the shadows.

"And you, to keep your heart a little safer, you have a knife right next to it, eh? Who's inside, how's the game going today?"

The man put up both hands, as if to defend himself:

"What game, Brigadie'? You know perfectly well that the only reason I'm standing here is I'm sweet on a girl who lives across the way, not because . . ."

With a quick grab, Maione seized Simoncelli's wrist and began to squeeze it, without letting the broad smile splashed across his face shrink by so much as a millimeter.

"Sure, of course. She must be quite a pretty girl, because you never move from this spot, you're here all day long, seven days a week. Must be true love! I'm a romantic at heart, Simonce', and I want to believe you. Why don't I wait here with you for awhile, and we can even serenade her together, all right? Start singing, Simonce', and I'll come right in behind you."

The man had turned pale from the pain.

"No, stop, Brigadie', keep it up and you'll break my arm! All right, all right, there's practically no one upstairs, you know that there's not a lot of activity the week of Easter. Let me go, I'm begging you, Brigadie'. . ."

Maione let go of the arm and, with a disappointed expression, pulled the knife out of Simoncelli's inside pocket.

"What a pity, and here I was thinking that you really had fallen in love. You see how much your heart's well-being matters to me? I'd better hold on to this, otherwise you might manage to break your heart with it, where the young lady who lives across the way failed. Though you might get a little assistance from someone else, say the young man who was here earlier. Speaking of which, why don't you tell me his story? I get all emotional when I hear stories about young people; maybe I'll even get teary and decide not to throw you in jail today."

The ex-con was now sweating copiously:

"Who, the son of that lady from the bordello? No, Brigadie', what are you thinking, he's just a two-bit chump, he's no problem. I just wanted to scare him, otherwise he'd have started yammering and there'd be no end to it."

Maione grabbed the man's arm again, but this time without squeezing.

"Ah, so that's the way it is? Then why didn't you let him go upstairs, if business is so slow? Doesn't your boss want this sucker's money, too?"

Simoncelli looked at Maione's enormous hand on his forearm and decided to tell the truth. And to tell it as quickly as he could.

"No, Brigadie', that young man doesn't have any money. In fact, from what I hear, he owes money to everyone in the neighborhood. That's the way gambling is, you know that, don't you? When you start to lose, you just keep losing and there's nothing anyone can do to stop you. So we don't let him gamble, and neither does anyone else. Otherwise, as time goes by, he'll just keep digging himself into a deeper and deeper hole."

Maione acted deeply touched. He gripped the arm again.

"Oh, how lovely to see how conscientious you are, how you take the well-being of the young people to heart. I should nominate you for a medal, they'll give one to you right away."

The man sobbed in pain.

"No, no, Brigadie', I'm begging you . . . Oh, all right, the order is not to let him gamble again unless he brings cash with him and shows it here, at the entrance. And even if he does come with cash, part of it gets taken to cover the old debt. Otherwise, he can't come in. Even if I have to . . . to beat him silly."

"And this is what you were going to use to beat him silly, eh?" asked Maione, waving the knife in the man's face. "I'm tempted to beat you silly, I'm tempted. Now then, Simonce', listen to me and listen good: if anyone stumbles on this young man in one of these *vicoli* with any kind of wound, I'll come and drag you out of your bed and I'll throw you somewhere that the next time you want to serenade a young lady, you'll have to wait a good thirty years. Do you follow me, yes or no?"

The man nodded repeatedly, frantically massaging his arm all the while.

"Yes, yes, Brigadie', I understand. But I can only promise you that I won't hurt him—what about the others? That guy owes money to a thousand people around here! What can I do, it's not like I'm his guardian angel, cut me a break!"

Maione dusted off his arm, making a show of being gentle.

"I warned you, don't tell me I didn't. Happy Easter, Simonce'. Try not to ruin your holidays."

At police headquarters, after Maione reported back to Ricciardi on the outcome of his tail, the commissario asked him:

"What do you think, does the mother know everything about her son's situation? The risks he's running, the fact that he's still trying to gamble?"

The brigadier shrugged.

"I couldn't say, Commissa'. I think she knows that her son has debts, but she might not know just how big they are. Certainly, that young man isn't in good shape; if you ask me, he's bound to catch a serious beating at the very least, it's just a matter of time. The good news is, from the information I've gathered, seeing that he's playing in low-end gambling dens and he's young, it must not be huge sums: those people don't extend much credit to a young guy."

"Maybe, but there's still the fact of the bordello behind

him. Everyone knows that it's a high-end house, and so they assume that sooner or later the mother is going to cover her son's debts; but actually, according to what Bambinella told you, she's not even keeping up with what she owes to the tradesmen. And if Viper had decided to leave, it would have been a serious problem for Il Paradiso."

Maione retorted:

"Sure, but why kill her? Wouldn't that mean losing her all the same?"

"I'm not entirely convinced. So many people have demanded the speedy reopening of the brothel; maybe there are more people patronizing the place now, just to see where the murder took place. You know, the mind works in mysterious ways sometimes. We should think about all the different leads, I think we're missing something."

# XXXI

Bianca Palumbo.

Who is she, Bianca Palumbo? Or who was she, actually. If she ever really existed.

Lily thought back to the moment when that strange green-eyed police commissario had asked her her real name. She thought back to it as she draped the silk garment over her ample breasts, those enormous white breasts that had changed her identity.

Because it was when she was thirteen, when her breasts became so prominent, that she had stopped being Bianca Palumbo, the little girl from Porta Nolana who played with the pigeons and the rag doll in the garret apartment where she lived with her mother and eight siblings. Ever since that time that a fruit vendor passed by with his cart when she was out wandering through the *vicoli*, killing time, and asked her if she wanted a ride.

There weren't, after all, that many possible futures for a little girl from Porta Nolana; not if she was nice to look at, with blond hair, a cute nose, and huge breasts. She hadn't really done much worse than plenty of other girls just like her.

She left her bedroom, without looking down the hallway, and headed over to the little balcony that overlooked the drawing room. Amedeo, the pianist, was rapidly riffing over the keyboard, playing a fast-paced rhythmic jazz piece: the music he loved best, though Madame would have preferred more waltzes and tangos and less of "that negro music" that tended to rub Fascists the wrong way; but it wasn't as if the Fascists were flocking to Il Paradiso. They liked more unpretentious places, where nobody would glare at you if you just wanted to guffaw loudly, if you had too much to drink, or if you had a hard time keeping your hands to yourself.

Amedeo looked lovingly at the butler Armando, who returned the look as he went sailing past with a full tray balanced on one hand. Lily decided it was the height of irony that the only real love affair in that house of love without love should have been a love affair between two men. Amedeo and Armando had secretly been together for years, they spent all the time together that they could, they were terribly sweet when they were together and terribly shy around everyone else.

Just as it had been for most of the past two days, the drawing room was packed. Viper dead had brought in more customers than had Viper alive: who would have thought? The regulars had been joined by people who wanted to see and know, to breathe the air in a place where blood, along with all the other usual fluids, had been spilled.

To tell the truth, Lily thought as she swiveled her hips in front of all those open mouths, there hadn't been any blood. It was a pillow that had choked off Viper's breath. That's all. And that was ironic in its way, too, wasn't it? A whore killed with one of the tools of her trade: a pillow. You had to laugh.

Whatever the details, you couldn't keep the crowds away. Perhaps gawking at death was just one among many perversions. Or finding out more about it.

Out of the crowd she selected as her first customer a tall dark-haired young man with a narrow mustache. Perhaps that apparent shyness, that bewildered expression concealed a pleasurable surprise. In any case, *he* wasn't here, she'd seen that immediately.

For that matter, he never went through the drawing room. He knew the merchandise by heart, he had no need to look at the display. And he was willing to pay a premium, in order to pick first and exclusively.

That's what Lily had liked about him, at first. His decisiveness, his confidence, the way he knew what he wanted and how to get it. And then, in the bedroom, he turned into the opposite: weak, trembling, and then strong at the right moment.

As she stood waiting for the young man, whose hands were unsteady, to complete the transaction with Madame, she feigned an eagerness that she certainly didn't feel. She remembered what the madam had told her at the first brothel where she'd ever worked, when she was just sixteen: you have to practice your art, and you can't refuse any of the guests. Be cordial and accommodating; remember that your sole objective is to make sure they come back, and come back asking for you by name. Figure out what they want and give it to them, without putting up any resistance: act as if you're having the best sex of your life, moan, sigh, squirm and kick, ask for mercy, compliment them on their size and their vigor. Pretend to come, more than once, and make sure you come when they do; don't ever come for real, keep your wits about you, but do pretend. And since you're so young, tell them that you're here because of a terrible misfortune, because you were ruined by an old man, that you were pure as a lily. You'll see, the madam told her, that screwing is only one of the reasons we're here. Your pleasure is not one of them.

As Lily took the young man's hand, she went on remembering. Since then, since those words, there had been plenty of men. Lily'd never had to work very hard to keep from enjoying herself; nor to find her way easily and directly to her customers' hearts. She listened to the ones who wanted to talk, and there were plenty of them; they were the most remunerative because they'd buy hours of her time just to tell her the tangled, boring stories of their lives, stretched out on their backs on the bed, pants unbuttoned, staring at the ceiling;

she'd wait for the ones who couldn't seem to get an erection, letting them know that the secret of their impotence would never leave that room; she'd masturbate, pretending to rise to peaks of pleasure, with cucumbers or walking sticks, while old men with sagging guts and gold-framed spectacles watched her from the armchairs where they sat, jaws agape.

After just a year, there was no trace of Bianca Palumbo. Only Lily still existed, the whore with enormous breasts and no heart at all, who never lost her head and snorted impatiently at the love stories recounted by her tenderhearted colleagues. Anything but love, she thought to herself. The worst kind of back luck, the curse that never quits.

After closing the door behind her, she undid her silk gown and let it fall to the floor. The young man stared at her open-mouthed, unable to tear his eyes away from those magnificent mammaries, firm and erect in spite of their size. She led him to the sink and began unbuttoning his trousers.

When she met Enzo, she hadn't been at Il Paradiso long. She was one of fifteen or so girls, and she assumed she'd be sent away shortly. Instead he had found her, selected her, and made it clear to Madame, with cold hard cash, that he didn't want her shipped away from the cathouse with the other girls two weeks later.

They'd hit it off immediately. She'd had plenty of men like him before, men who were accustomed to giving orders, wealthy and powerful, but who turned back into children in the bedroom, eager to play: she didn't care if what they wanted was a couple of sharp smacks or a cigarette burn on the thigh. Actually, to tell the truth, it was the only part of the whole thing she truly enjoyed; those bastards deserved it. But he wasn't like that. He was looking for a different place—a mountain peak, the bottom of the ocean. For him, pain was something to say, a way of speaking. And Lily had discovered that she was built the same way. Exactly the same way.

She extracted the young man's flaccid penis and turned on the water, murmuring reassuring words. He'd never once taken his eyes off her breasts.

She'd heard about it from some of the older whores, but she'd never believed it: they said you could find someone *you'd* be willing to pay, instead of being paid. Not because he was so handsome, which she didn't care about a bit, nor out of tenderness, a sentiment she'd never experienced; it was actually about the sex. Lily enjoyed it, with Ventrone. It was as if he somehow knew how to push all her most deeply hidden buttons of pleasure, the buttons Lily didn't even know she had; and he quivered with pleasure every time that she, suddenly, surprised him with a bite or a pinch, smiling at her in gratitude.

She washed the young man's penis and then dried it. No sign of an erection.

With him, in an absurd and cerebral way, Lily was making love. She had become his slave, just as he had become hers. It struck her as almost inconceivable that Ventrone should pay to make her happy. She'd found a series of variants that drove him wild: objects, positions. He had awoken in her an unsuspected and marvelous creativity.

Until.

Until *she* arrived.

Viper.

The young man looked her in the face, for the first time.

"Are you the one who found her? Someone told me that it was you."

Lily'd never understood what it was that Ventrone had found in Viper's bedroom that she couldn't give him. All it took was one day of feeling under the weather, and she had lost him: he'd asked to try "that pretty one," the woman he'd heard so much about, and he'd never come back to her again, save intermittently, when Viper had refused to open her legs for him.

Lily hadn't asked him a thing. It would have been an admission of weakness, a flaw in that strong will that he so loved. Still, she couldn't imagine what it could be, and so one rainy morning, she'd asked Viper, as they were applying nail polish and smoking while waiting for Il Paradiso to open for business. That slut had replied: maybe one day I'll teach you.

Now he'd stopped coming to Il Paradiso.

He hadn't been there for two days now. Not since the thing had happened.

But Lily knew that he'd come back to her eventually. She wouldn't make the mistake of going to look for him, all she had to do was wait. He'd come back. Now that the spell had been broken, now that Viper would never ensnare him again, faking the things that to her came naturally.

And when he came back, she'd look him in the eyes, and everything would become clear. After all, she'd done it for him. And only for him. And an act of love like that could hardly go unnoticed.

Because it was in his eyes that she had seen his terror. His terror at what had happened. His terror at seeing her dead.

Dead.

God, what a bitch Viper could be. It really is true, a woman can work as a whore or she can be a whore: and the two things aren't the same.

But now she was dead. She was cold and motionless, in a casket, underground, with a black tongue sticking out of that lovely pink rosebud of a mouth.

"Yes," she told the young man. "I'm the one who found her."

In her hands the penis quivered, like a dying fish.

"If you want, I'll tell you all about it, my handsome friend. If you pay for at least half an hour, I'll tell you the whole story."

# XXXII

Ricciardi watched as night fell over the city, from his office window.

The sound of the *troccole*, the clacking wooden noise-makers, penetrating and repetitive, incessantly filled the air, which had once again turned brisk and effervescent. The children waited for the Easter holidays just to pull out those infernal contraptions, originally devised to replace the church bells that had been tied in place and silenced, and used to announce the services of Holy Thursday and Good Friday, only to become wood-and-iron toys, the perfect thing to torment someone who, like him, was just trying to concentrate.

He couldn't make heads or tails of Viper's murder.

The more he thought about it, the more every single passion the girl stirred in those around her seemed to him like a more than plausible motive for wanting her dead.

He had always thought that the genesis of every murder could be found in two primary compelling passions: hunger and love. The two passions found endless variants, mixing together infinitely, one becoming the thirst for power, influence, and envy; the other jealousy, loneliness, and despair. And they put weapons in people's hands, generating a tangled lust for blood and justice, slaked only in death.

Hunger and love also danced around Viper's corpse, and in every possible form: hunger was what gnawed at Madame Yvonne and her son; hunger engendered by gambling debts, by the fear of losing the greatest of their sources of income;

hunger was what tormented the girl's mother, accustomed to enjoying the money that came to her from a source she held in such bitter contempt, money that Viper herself might well have decided to cut off; hunger, in a certain sense, was what drove Augusto, Ventrone's son, who feared the destruction of his company because of his father's reckless squandering; and he'd detected something similar in Caterina, Coppola's muscular sister, while Giuseppe Coppola in turn was a slave to his love for the girl. And love was what Vincenzo Ventrone had experienced, in a perverse form that was incomprehensible to Ricciardi, and in fact Ventrone had even felt obliged to arrange and pay for the young woman's strange funeral; and love, perhaps, was what had led Lily, the blond prostitute, to claim she had discovered the dead body, instead of Ventrone. Or was it more about hunger? And who could say how many other emotions, passions, and sentiments had circled Viper like so many wolves, attracted by the scent of her beauty. Emotions, passions, and sentiments of which he had found no trace. At least, not yet.

In his mind he reviewed the room where the murder took place. The contents of the drawers, which revealed nothing; the objects scattered on the bed and floor, the silver of the flasks and the cigarette case. The horn comb, the brush made of inlaid wood with blond hairs that probably belonged to Lily, and the blond hairs on the pillow that probably belonged to Giuseppe Coppola.

The little whip mentioned by the corpse, the little whip which wasn't there now; if it ever had been.

The Deed, as Ricciardi mentally referred to the set of his perceptions, was all too likely to deceive: it provided only a reflection, a tangled echo of the last fragments of a life on the threshold of death's darkness, taking one last look back. More often than not the Deed had steered him away from the truth; only rarely had the perceptions that he sensed actually helped him toward it: very rarely indeed. That's why he always kept that evidence, the words that he heard, subordinate, because only afterward was it explained, only once the full picture had been sketched out, through a combination of hard investigative work and pure chance.

But this time the little whip that came out of Viper's dead mouth was still more equivocal. Was it a prostitute's working tool, a nickname addressed to her longtime boyfriend? And even if the latter were the case, was it a loving thought addressed to her executioner or a final appeal before being murdered by someone else's hand, some last cry for help?

*What would you have answered, Viper, to Coppola's proposal of marriage?* Ricciardi asked the window. *What were you waiting for, before giving your reply? Could it have been Easter, to celebrate your profane resurrection?*

The *troccole* in the street kept clattering, increasingly annoying, iron against wood. Ricciardi had been told that the sound of that ancient child's toy was originally intended to chase away evil spirits. He thought bitterly, for the umpteenth time, that not spirits, but the living, were the ones who were truly frightening.

That was something he knew all too well.

## XXXIII

Maione had carved out an afternoon off, as was traditional on Holy Thursday. It was a fundamental ritual that no one would ever have dreamed of missing: the *struscio* to see the *sepolcri*, the special altars representing the tomb of Christ.

After lunch—which revolved around Lucia's justly celebrated *zuppa marinara*—and the necessary nap that followed, all the Maiones dressed up in the spring garb that had been readied for the occasion, and went out: out in front, Mamma Lucia arm in arm with the brigadier, in his spotless, neatly pressed uniform and polished boots; behind them, hand in hand, their children, spiffy and well groomed: the boys in zouave trousers that covered their inevitably skinned knees, and the girls in starched pleated skirts. That year, the ritual included the debut of Benedetta, their brand-new adoptive little sister, the happiest one of all.

Actually, the excursion consisted of nothing more than a simple walk, ennobled by visits to an odd—never even—number of churches where they would briefly worship at a side altar, sumptuously decorated in commemoration of Jesus's Deposition from the Cross and Interment. The Maiones visited five churches, completing a route that ran from Piazza Trieste e Trento to Via Pessina, beyond Piazza Dante: a distance of just over a mile that took the entire afternoon and a good portion of the evening to cover, because it also offered an excellent opportunity to admire the plate-glass window displays gussied up for the incoming season, to take note of hats or dresses in the latest styles while the children studied the shops which sold the things they'd most like to receive as gifts for Christmas or their birthdays, the only occasions on which they could expect individual gifts. Even though, most of the time, the gift would consist of a less-fun but far-more-necessary item of clothing.

Time—during the promenade known as the *struscio*, or shuffle, named after the long-forgotten gait of penitent pilgrims who dragged their feet when they walked—tended to stretch out even more because of the many meetings along the way. It was all one long succession of hat-doffings and bowings, exchanges of smiles and hellos, even among those who saw one another every day in their ordinary lives; but the *struscio* was the *struscio*, a special occasion, a feast prior to the feast.

Businesses of all kinds were rolling out the artillery, big, small, and medium-sized. To have a plate-glass window or display space along the route of the *struscio* was an opportunity not to be missed, and it was spectacular to see the glittering array of lights and brass fixtures of cafés and pastry shops such as Caflish, with the waiters standing at the front door, or La Fiorentina, which touted exotic flavors; or bookshops like Sandron, Treves, and Vallardi, from whose windows leapt stacks of brightly illustrated covers of adventure tales depicting tigers and pirates; and shops proffering travel goods, such as Anselmi, where suitcases were featured in an artfully constructed tropical landscape, making window shoppers dream of other worlds. The children stood openmouthed before stuffed parrots and scale models of electric trains that ran through tiny cities, and parents often had to go back and pull them out of their trances with a loving jerk.

The goods on display were not only in permanent establishments; this was a city of movable commerce, and the strolling vendors certainly didn't have to be asked twice to add vivid confusion to the general state of chaos, with wheeled stalls abounding in colors and aromas, or even decorated with just a tablecloth or basket. They rose to the challenge of gleaming plate-glass windows, retorting point by point with their two longtime weapons: the lowest prices and the loudest voices. The air was alive with whistles, shouts, sounds from a wide variety of musical instruments, and colorful expressions, in dialect and in Italian, could be heard touting the goods on offer, seasonal merchandise for the most part. Violets, aromatic herbs, wheat for the *pastiera*, a sweet ricotta-filled pie, and tangerines; but also the *spassatiempo*, a mixture of pistachios, toasted chickpeas, and various seeds and nuts, wrapped in conical sheets of newsprint and carried by children as they walked, and then of course the inevitable pizza, with a handful of anchovies and a spatter of tomato sauce.

Maione set aside a small sum from the anemic family funds for a stop at the Denozza pastry shop, one of the least expensive though every bit as good as the others in terms of quality, located on the upper end of the Via Toledo. The proprietor knew him and reserved a table for him, and there the family sat down for an espresso and a chocolate spumoni for the children—this, for them, was the true purpose of that promenade.

Once they had sat down, the brigadier devoted his attention to his wife, who was reminding the children not to stain their clothing. Ever since lunch he'd had the unpleasant sensation that Lucia was avoiding him, limiting their conversation to nothing but the bare necessities; even his compliments for her extraordinary cooking—which normally got a smile out of her, even when she was angry—this time seemed to leave her indifferent.

Maione knew that asking her what was wrong would only be likely to make her retreat within herself even more; he'd tried, and for a long time, in the aftermath of their oldest son's murder, before she had made up her mind all by herself to go on living, and nothing he'd tried had had any effect. He knew that she wasn't angry with him, and in a certain sense that worried him even more: what worries could his wife have that she was unwilling to share?

He was terrified at the idea that there might be some problem with her health. As he watched her extend a small spoon toward his youngest daughter's open mouth, holding a napkin up to the child's neck and miming the act of swallowing with her own mouth, Maione thought about how much he loved her: it was almost painful, it clutched at his heart, was a desperate burst of anxiety. In his simple mind, that of a husband and a father, the brigadier felt the urge to protect with all his powers the woman who was his main reason for living, mixed with the terror that he might not be up to that task.

For her part, as she fed her youngest daughter, Lucia could feel her husband's eyes upon her. She had no need to turn and look for confirmation: she always knew when he was looking at her, and she had since she was a young girl and he—typical, for a man—hadn't yet even figured out that he was attracted to her. But this time she pretended not to notice, to stave off the questions that he would ask her and above all the answers that she would have to give him.

She didn't know what to do. She had witnessed something awful, she understood that right away; something that certainly concerned a man her husband respected, perhaps even considered a friend: the description matched, and she had seen him once herself when she was visiting Ricciardi in the hospital. But exactly what had she seen? She was unable to understand it.

An arrest? It had many of the hallmarks, but in that case her husband would have told her about or at least she'd have noticed a shift in his mood, and neither had happened.

A kidnapping? In broad daylight, and in the aftermath of a fiery argument? That made no sense to her. And after all, the doctor hadn't called out for help, and he'd certainly had the opportunity, even if it was obvious that he wasn't going with those men of his own free will.

But what was front and center in Lucia's mind was the expression on the face of the vendor who had urged her, for the sake of her own safety and especially for that of those she held dear, to say nothing. To no one. That expression was one of full awareness, and fear. An expression that knew—and said—a great deal more than the few words whispered in the middle of the street.

Lucia wasn't interested in politics, as far as she cared one party was as good as another, but now things were starting to change. Everyday she heard reports of a beating, an injury, an arrest. People said that spies were everywhere, that if you said a harsh word about a public official, or a government institution, there were people who would hurry to inform on you and someone would quickly come calling to ask for an explanation of what you had said. Lucia was convinced that it was best to keep your mouth shut and mind your own business.

Her husband, moreover, was dangerous from that point of view: if he thought something, he'd say it, without apologies. If she were to tell him what she'd seen, he'd feel a responsibility to do something about it, he'd charge off head down, and before you knew it he'd be in the middle of a world of trouble, and she would be wallowing in remorse for having gotten him into the whole mess.

She used a napkin to clean the little girl's mouth, the whole time feeling Maione's eyes on her and pretending she hadn't noticed.

On the other hand, she thought to herself, not to tell him would be tantamount to lying to him; and Lucia had never lied to her husband. And perhaps in the end it wasn't a political matter, and Raffaele could still do something for that poor doctor.

Without turning around, she whispered:

"Rafe', when we go home I have something to tell you. Something important."

Maione's heart skipped a beat.

"Luci', should I be worried? Did something bad happen? Just tell me that, I'm begging you."

She turned to look at her husband, well aware that the only way to reassure him would be to look him in the eye.

"No, don't worry. I just need to tell you about something I saw."

The brigadier peered into her face.

"But are you all right, Luci'? And the children, are they okay?"

She laughed.

"Why, don't you see them, the whole family, right here in front of you? We're all fine, just fine. When we get home, I'll tell you all about it."

Seeing her laugh, cheerful and untroubled, Maione finally felt that knot of anxiety in his chest dissolve. His wife and children were all right; nothing else could get in the way of the Holy Thursday *struscio*.

"Then let's get going. We still have two churches to do before we're done with the *sepolcri*. Benedetta, come here, because it's time for me to tell you the story of the *pastiera*; all your brothers and sisters have heard it before."

## XXXIV

H e came that close to not seeing him at all. He almost overlooked those two brown eyes, gentle and intelligent, staring at the street door and waiting for him.

Ricciardi emerged from police headquarters fairly late, but the street was still full of people who preferred to visit the churches of the *struscio* when the shops were closed, in order to focus on the religious aspect of the experience, which otherwise ran the risk of becoming secondary to more worldly considerations. All that mattered to the commissario, who cared nothing for either religious aspects or window-shopping, was to get home, where he might leave behind his anguish over a murder that he couldn't figure out.

He exchanged greetings with the sentinel, briskly made his way up the short uphill stretch of street that ran to Via Toledo; at the corner he stopped to tie his shoe, and that's when he saw him.

The dog.

The white dog with brown spots, one ear cocked, sitting obediently, motionless as a statue. He was sitting in a nook in the wall of an apartment building, a location that allowed him to avoid the steady stream of people going by, but still keep an eye on the front entrance of police headquarters. That way, he wouldn't risk missing Ricciardi leaving work.

They looked at each other, Ricciardi and the dog. Oddly enough, they were both in roughly the same position, squatting with back straight and knees up, one of them waiting, the other one tying his shoe; they were separated by a forest of legs strolling from one church to the next, between one prayer and the next. Looking at each other, wordlessly speaking about a common friend.

The commissario remembered the first time that he'd seen that dog, on one of the steps of the monumental Capodimonte staircase, next to the corpse of a little boy. He remembered how he had quickly concluded that that death had been accidental, because his hidden sense failed to show him any image of the boy, as it did whenever the death had been violent and sudden. And how the dog, which followed him everywhere and constantly appeared to him in the pouring rain, had instead forced him to carry out a more in-depth investigation, which finally led to an atrocious discovery.

And now here that dog was again, completely out of context.

Ricciardi searched for the shambling figure of Dr. Modo, hoping for the reassurance of his presence; but a tingling on his skin told him that he wasn't going to see him.

He crossed the street and approached the dog. The animal didn't move until Ricciardi stood beside him. Ricciardi noticed that the dog no longer wore the leather collar that his friend had put on him so he wouldn't be netted and euthanized as a stray, as was the custom. Then the dog got up, as if responding to a call, and trotted off up Via Toledo, against the stream of people heading in the opposite direction; every so often he would stop to let Ricciardi catch up.

To tell the truth, the commissario felt a little stupid to be following the dog; after all, Modo had always let the dog run free, off leash, and so the animal could follow his every momentary instinct, chasing down streets at random. But something about this didn't add up: the late hour, for instance, and above all the lack of a collar. Just as the doctor would never have bound him with a leash, neither would he have run the risk of having him seized by the dogcatcher and put down.

The dog headed for the hospital, with Ricciardi at his heels. When he came level with the dark alleys of the Pignasecca, deserted at that hour, he stopped, yelped, and then began to bark insistently; when the man caught up with him, the dog entered without hesitation into the courtyard and headed straight over to a chain from which dangled the collar he'd slipped out of, when he'd set off in the vain pursuit of the car that was carrying away Dr. Modo.

Ricciardi, who had no way of knowing what had happened, unhooked the slender strip of leather from the chain and put it back around the dog's neck, then the dog resumed his sitting position. At that point, Ricciardi decided to enter the building, in order to make sure that Modo was at work and reassure him that his four-legged friend was well.

But Modo wasn't there. At his usual station Ricciardi met a young doctor, who shrugged and said that he'd been summoned by a functionary of the hospital administration to cover a shift.

Ricciardi headed up to the upstairs offices, where he was greeted by an employee who introduced himself as Egidio Montuori, administrative assistant of the Pellegrini hospital. The commissario identified himself, and noticed how the man stiffened as he did. Montuori was about forty and quite ridiculous, with a celluloid collar that rose practically to his ears and a pair of half-frame reading glasses perched at the tip of his long nose.

"I'm looking for Dr. Modo, Bruno Modo. These are important matters of public safety, and I need to get in touch with him."

Montuori looked rapidly around, as if looking for help; then he said:

"Dr. Modo? He isn't here. He . . . he left, a few hours ago."

"He left? And where would he go?"

Ricciardi's tone of voice made clear he would brook no

nonsense, which just made Montuori's situation even more awkward.

"He . . . didn't say, and then, I wasn't here when he left. We, as you may know, we are run by a religious congregation, and at that hour, when they . . . when he left, there was a priest, I don't know which one. I think he went . . . on vacation, yes, that's right. He went on vacation. He said he was leaving town for Easter."

Ricciardi decided that that man was as honest as a one-and-a-half lira coin. He looked him in the eye and said to him, decidedly:

"Signore, you do know that lying to a police officer is a criminal offense, don't you? I'm going to ask you again, for the last time: where is Dr. Bruno Modo?"

Montuori's lower lip began to quiver:

"Commissario, I'm in charge of accounting here. All I know is what they told me, that starting today Dr. Modo is on vacation, and that they'll inform us if and when he comes back to work. That's all I know, and that's all I can tell you."

Ricciardi ran a hand over his forehead. This wasn't making sense.

"Excuse me, but didn't you tell me that he was away for Easter? And now you're telling me that you have no idea when he'll be back."

Montuori spread out his arms.

"That's exactly right, Commissario. We don't know when he'll be back. Please, I can't tell you anything else because I don't know anything else. I have a wife and two small children."

Now Ricciardi really was worried. He left without saying goodbye, and left the courtyard walking hurriedly.

The dog followed him.

Sometimes, against his instincts, Ricciardi allowed himself

to be dragged into evenings out with Modo to chat and drink beer.

The commissario would give in unwillingly to the doctor's cheery and repeated invitations, but afterward he was glad he had: it was a different way of experiencing the city, on hot summer nights, when the enormous red moon hung in the sky as if it were painted cardboard, or when smoky taverns offered welcome haven from the chilly air and biting winds. Invariably, those evenings would conclude with a long stroll during which both men would talk about life, which they viewed so differently; and they'd walk each other home repeatedly, first one, then the other, prolonging their chat when the discussion grew heated, until finally, exhausted, they would say goodnight.

As Ricciardi hurried toward his friend's home, followed by the dog, he realized just how fond of the man he was. His apparently superficial approach to things, his profound involvement in the sufferings of others, his cheerfulness, at once vulgar and cultured, his intelligent irony—all these things had burrowed into his heart, and the thought that the doctor might be in serious trouble brought him a sense of anguish.

Maybe I'm overreacting, he thought to himself. Maybe he really has taken a few days off to get some rest, and right now he's sitting in some horrible tavern down by the waterfront drinking cheap wine and singing filthy songs, and tomorrow he'll laugh at my concerns. Or else he'll come open the door in his nightshirt and make some nastry crack with sexual overtones about the fact that I can't sleep.

Modo lived over near Piazza del Gesù, in an old building that had seen much better days. "It's just like me, no?" he liked to say, with a laugh. Ricciardi had never been through the front door, but according to his friend's descriptions, the apartment had always belonged to the Modo family and by now the place was too big for him.

As he approached the apartment building, the dog yelped

and shot past him. The commissario hoped that the animal had sensed the doctor's presence: but the man pacing back and forth in front of the street door, hair rumpled and evidently very worried, wasn't Bruno Modo.

It was Brigadier Maione.

# XXXV

How is he?"

"Fine, I think. Now he's sleeping."

"Sleeping how?"

"How else is he supposed to sleep? He's just sleeping. He tosses and turns. He mutters, he cries. But he's sleeping. Like always, ever since . . . like always."

"It's nice out here. Look at that moon. For the first time, you can see that spring is here."

"I don't understand you. Do you realize the situation we're in? You're thinking about the moon, about springtime. And meanwhile the world's caving in on us."

"You're the one who doesn't understand. Nothing's happened at all. Everything is normal, perfectly normal. This is the only way he'll be able to recover and go back to doing what he was doing before. And everything will go back to normal."

"I wish I could be like you. I wish I could always think things were going to turn out for the best. But I don't; I think that everything's going to go to hell in a handbasket. The police . . ."

"Oh, don't make me laugh, the police! The police don't understand a thing, they've never solved a single case, and you think that this one time . . ."

"That one guy, I don't like him. The commissario, the one with the weird eyes. You talk and he stares at you, hard, no expression. As if he was digging into your body."

"I'm telling you again, they've never solved a case. If you

don't let yourself get rattled, if you stay cool, they can't charge you with a thing. You have to be like a card player, you know? Like when you have a winning hand and you have to make sure no one knows."

"Ha, ha . . . How funny you are. After all, you're not the one who has to worry."

"Ah, no? And why not? Aren't we both in the same boat? If the boat goes down, we're all going down with it, you know? It's not like some of us will make it and some won't."

"The brigadier worries me too. He's a sly old fox. One of those guys who pretends to be an idiot so they won't draft him, but when the time comes . . ."

"Brigadier, Commissario, even if it was the Duce himself: if they don't have anything, they don't have anything. And they can't charge you with nothing."

"Maybe you're right. The worst thing is the face, her face. I can't get it out of my head."

"So why, why did you insist on looking at her? Couldn't you . . ."

"Sure, I could just as well have left her the way she was. But in the end, I don't know . . . it just seemed like too much, to leave her like that. So I pulled away the pillow."

"Pointless pity. For a whore, for an ordinary stupid whore who would have ruined your life and your future. A future that we earned, a future that we built, day by day."

"But I see her again, and I'll keep seeing her. Not that I'm repenting, obviously. We did what we had to do. But to see her like that, afterward . . . afterward, it was terrible."

"Now it's going to be a test of nerves, and you can't afford to be weak. Neither you nor I can afford to be weak. We have to protect our future. That's why we need to remain calm and unruffled. We can't worry about anything or anybody, least of all the police, who couldn't find a murderer if he bit them in the ass."

"You think not? But, you know, the commissario . . ."

"I told you, nothing at all. Nothing to worry about. If anything, are we sure we haven't made any mistakes? For instance, is there anyone who might have, I don't know, seen something by any chance, or have . . ."

"No, I told you. I was very careful, no one could trace it back to me. Seen from outside, nothing outside of the ordinary happened that day. The clients were there and, you know, there's a constant flow of people, young and old. There was music, everyone was thinking about . . . in short, everyone was minding their own business, that's what the place was designed for."

"Well then, like I've told you lots of times, we should just keep calm and collected and wait for time to pass and heal all wounds. And then, when everything is back where it should be, we can start looking forward again. And it will be as if that whore had never been born."

"She'd said that she was going to give her answer on Easter Sunday. Just think, on Easter Sunday!"

"I'll say it again: it's going to be as if she'd never been born."

"But she'll go on existing, every time I try to go to sleep."

"No. Because it was something we had to do. Now try to breathe. And look at what a beautiful moon there is tonight."

## XXXVI

Maione went over to Ricciardi; he was extremely agitated.

"Commissa', then you know about it too! I was about to come to your house to call you, even if it's past midnight. What are we going to do now? Who can we go to? We can't even be sure that Garzo isn't involved; that idiot's a master when it comes to things like this . . ."

Ricciardi was so surprised to see the brigadier there that it took him a while to stanch that flood of words:

"Hold on, hold on, Raffaele. I don't know anything, tell me: what are you doing here at this hour?"

Maione stopped, perplexed:

"Excuse me, Commissa', but if you don't know anything, then how . . ."

Ricciardi pointed at the dog.

"I found him, sitting obediently on the Via Toledo, when I left police headquarters. As if he was waiting for me. So I went over to see at the hospital, but an employee there told me that Bruno had taken a vacation, for Easter. It struck me that the man was afraid of something, he was hesitant, he kept contradicting himself and he seemed worried, at a certain point he even told me that he had small children, as if that was supposed to help me understand why he wouldn't tell me anything more. That's when I got worried, and I came here."

"He's not here, the doctor; I've been ringing the doorbell for the past half hour."

"What about you? Do you want to tell me why you're here? Maybe we're both worried for no reason, while Bruno is actually someplace like Il Paradiso, drinking and playing cards."

Maione adjusted his collar. For some reason, the fact that he was in civilian clothes in the presence of the commissario put him ill at ease.

"Commissa', I really don't think the doctor is anywhere having a good time; this is serious. Very serious. I think our friend has been taken by the Fascists."

The phrase fell in the lonely night like a bottle from a balcony. Though he'd barely whispered it, Maione still looked around the deserted street to make sure no one had overheard.

"What do you mean, by the Fascists? And how do you know that?"

Continuing to whisper, Maione told him what Lucia had witnessed in the hospital courtyard.

". . . and so, as you can see, it was a full-fledged arrest. With an unmarked car, officers in plainclothes, maybe even packing concealed weapons. Just like in those American movies, you know? The part where the music gets louder."

Ricciardi tried to think clearly.

"And you say that your wife saw them argue, but she didn't hear what they said, is that right?"

"Yes, Commissa'. She was far away, they were at the opposite end of the courtyard and she was outside the gate, and then there was the dog, chained up and barking."

"In fact, I found the collar still attached to the chain. They must have chained him up when they got there, otherwise he would have done what he did at Viper's funeral and defended Bruno. So that makes me think that the argument they had this morning has something to do with it: those four idiots must have been the ones who informed on him."

"You think so, Commissa'? I had assumed that they might know something at police headquarters. Maybe that dope Garzo has a piece of paper sitting on his desk and he chose not to tell us about it. Or it could even be that brown-noser Ponte, his lapdog, maybe he knows something. If that's the case, I swear that I'll smack him so hard he'll forget the way home! I'll . . ."

Ricciardi shook his head no.

"I don't think anyone at police headquarters knows anything about this. Those people move through other channels. We need to figure out exactly what happened, and if things are the way we think they are, then we need to find out where they're holding him and for how long . . ."

Maione agreed grimly.

"I know. They take them to the islands. Ponza, Ventotene, Elba. Who knows where. The luckiest ones . . . We have to find him, Commissa'. Right away. And we have to free him."

Ricciardi grabbed the brigadier's arm.

"Yes, that's right. But we have to move very cautiously, because these people aren't playing around. You have children, you shouldn't put yourself at risk. Let me take care of it."

Maione pulled free, indignantly.

"Commissa', how can you think such a thing of me? What kind of a man do you take me for? My wife told me that, when it happened, a vendor standing nearby told her: Signo', you should mind your own business. And that's why she waited to tell me, because she was worried that I might get myself into trouble. But how many friends do you have, in life? Real friends, I mean. How many? Two, three? The doctor is a friend to me. And if a friend is in this kind of situation, I don't go home and climb into bed and pretend everything's fine. Fascists or no Fascists. And as for the children, Commissa': if you teach your kids to live one way, then how can you set the opposite example? Don't you agree?"

His reasoning was airtight, and Ricciardi knew exactly how hardheaded Maione could be. On the other hand, the risk of stumbling into charges of aiding and abetting or, worse, conspiracy, was very real, and he couldn't allow the brigadier to put his own freedom at risk. So he tried to involve him in a way that would do him the least possible harm.

"All right then. Here's what we'll do: tomorrow morning early, before you come in to the office, run by and see that girl-friend of yours who knows everything inside and out, and try to figure out where they're holding him. I'm going to go check things out in a certain place, and maybe if I'm lucky I'll be able to get some information."

"Yessir, Commissa'. And please, don't do anything reckless: you know I'm not the only one who runs in without looking where I'm putting my feet. As for the dog, I'll take him home with me, for now. It's something I promised the doctor."

## XXXVII

A bit of night, but not for sleeping.

A night for rumpled white hair resting on a wooden plank, in the dark, others breathing in a large room, who knows where and who knows why.

A night for tangled thoughts, firm beliefs, and enormous fears, challenges and defeats and sensations, firm and fixed at the center of the heart.

A night for a clean conscience, for a forehead held high, for a straight back, for convictions confirmed by everything that has happened; and a night for a troubled conscience over the suffering of friends, over the suffering of the patients left in uncouth, inexperienced hands.

A night for fears over the day to come, over the road that will lead far away, over the battles that will be left unfought.

A bit of night, what little remains.

A night for green eyes wide open, staring into the darkness, confronted by an emotion he didn't know he'd been nursing.

A night for strategies and movements, a night for silence as images scream in his memory.

A night for searching after faces and names to trap in the mind, to be asked and even supplicated.

A night for fears over the day to come, over the lanes to be traveled, over the battles that will have to be fought

A bit of night, spent waiting.

A night for one hand resting on your chest, like every night, making sure you'll still be there when she wakes up.

A night around your children's beds, looking down on their perfect sleep, their mouths half-open before the clouds and stars and the future that your hands will know how to build for them.

A night for uncertainty, for weakness in the face of a friend's potential pain and suffering, in the face of the silence that may surround him.

A night for fears over the day to come, over a steep climb to be undertaken first thing in the morning, over a battle that remains to be won.

As soon as this bit of night that remains is over.

# XXXVIII

The sun had been up for less than an hour when Brigadier Maione knocked on the door of the last apartment on the top floor of the last apartment house on Via San Nicola da Tolentino.

It took almost two minutes for the door to open on Bambinella's puffy, bleary eyes, which emerged from the dim light.

"Who on earth . . . Oh, Holy Mary, Mother of God, Brigadie', is that you? What's happened, who's dead?"

Maione had no time to waste.

"Hurry up, Bambine', let me in. And wake up, splash some water on your face and wake up, I need you clear-eyed with good reflexes."

The *femminiello* stood aside to let the brigadier come in, hastily smoothing down her hair.

"Tell the truth, your wife kicked you out of the house, didn't she? And now you don't know where to go, and you thought of me. How romantic! But don't worry, there's always a place for you at my table. As for the bed, trust me, you'll never sleep better as long as you live. I've got a queen-size bed, big enough for the kinds of acrobatics . . ."

Maione put his hands together, as if in prayer.

"Bambine', I'm begging you: you see it, that I'm begging you? I've never begged anyone, but I'm begging you this morning: you need to shut up and listen to me. Because today there's no time for fooling around, a very serious thing has happened and we need your help, which is the only reason I'm not going to kill you right now, which is what I feel like doing. My wife didn't kick me out, and before I'd move in with you I'd try every doorway in every alley in the city of Naples. I'm just here to ask for your help, and I need you to listen to me."

Bambinella was more than a little struck by Maione's tone of voice.

"Brigadie', now you're really starting to worry me. Let me make a cup of ersatz coffee, we'll sit down and talk."

"No, no ersatz coffee. I need to ask you for information, information I need very urgently. Sit down and listen to me carefully."

Bambinella sat down gracefully in the usual bamboo chair, carefully draping her silk nightgown. On her face was a dark five o'clock shadow, and her eyes bore the marks of faded makeup; she felt she owed the brigadier an explanation:

"Don't look at me, please, Brigadie'. My client just left, not even half an hour ago, and I'd planned to redo my makeup after catching at least an hour's sleep. That man is just terrible, a bricklayer from the San Lorenzo quarter, he tells his wife that he's working nights as a security guard to make a little extra, but that's not how it is at all, I can't imagine how she can bring herself to believe him . . . All right, all right, I see your point, this is urgent. Tell me all about it."

Maione stared at her, rabid with anger.

"Now listen carefully: do you remember Dr. Bruno Modo? He was there yesterday, at the funeral, if you want to call it that, of Maria Rosaria Cennamo, in Via Chiaia."

Bambinella giggled.

"Ooooh, sweet Jesus, do you think I'd have to see him at Viper's funeral to know Dr. Modo? Everyone in Naples knows him, he's such a good doctor and so attentive to the needs of the poor. To say nothing of his fond, shall we say, patronage of the finest bordellos in the city. There was a girlfriend of mine who used to see him practically every day at Il Pendino . . . Eh, Brigadie', *mamma mia*, what on earth are you doing with that!"

Maione had pulled out his revolver and placed it delicately at the center of a small side table.

"Well, I'm not going to die of liver disease, so I'm afraid you're going to have to die instead, Bambine'. You see this pistol? It's loaded. And I swear to you that the next time you start telling me the story of your life, or someone else's life, I'm just going to shoot you and be done with it. Because among other things I can just say I came up here to arrest you and you attacked me, which in a sense would even be the truth, because if you don't shut your trap and listen to me, first I'll shoot you and then I'll arrest you. Have I made myself clear?"

The *femminiello* stared in fear at the handgun, and nodded her head yes. Maione seemed pleased.

"Ah, at last. Now then, you saw that there was a set-to with four Fascist blackshirts, on the one hand, and the doctor and yours truly on the other. Now, we have information to the effect that just yesterday, in the late morning, the doctor was picked up at the hospital, against his will, by at least three men in an unmarked black car. I need to find out who these men were and where they took the doctor, and if I can, why."

Maione's questions fell into a profound, unusual silence. Bambinella pointed to the weapon on the table; then she extended two fingers with unnaturally long nails to the middle of her mouth and made the universal sign that indicated a sudden, frightened inability to speak.

Maione sighed, picked up the revolver, and put it back into its holster.

"But look, I'll pull it right back out if you start up again. Now talk."

Bambinella grabbed a fan decorated with an elaborate drawing of a dragon and started fluttering it in front of her face.

"Madonna, how you frightened me! You've taken ten years off my life, Brigadie', you know that I'm very afraid of guns!"

Maione roared:

"You don't have ten extra years of life to lose, Bambine', believe me!"

"I don't have ten . . . Ah, I see. Then let's get to the point: you're going to have to give me a few hours of time, Brigadie'. From what you tell me, this here is serious, you're right when you say it's urgent. Because if the two things are connected and the doctor has been abducted by the Fascists, inside of a day at the very most they'll put him on a train or a ship and send him far away, like they do all their prisoners. And I'd have to say, in this case, it sounds like the doctor really was picked up by the Fascists."

Maione nodded.

"Yeah, that's what it looks like to me too. Well, how do you intend to proceed, Bambine'? This isn't your normal territory, and since I'm planning to murder you myself with my own two hands, I can't afford to let you run risks."

"Oh, at last, a sweet, kind word: you're worried about me, eh, Brigadie'? But you shouldn't worry, there are plenty of Fascists in this town, and you can always find a few with some interesting vices. For instance, I know one of them that just goes wild every time that I . . . well, that's neither here nor there right now. In any case, I already know a few of the first contacts I'm going to try, and don't fret, I'll be careful. You just have to give me a few hours."

Maione stood up.

"We'll see you here at your house around noon, then. And I'm serious about this, Bambine': I've never asked you for a more important favor."

The *femminiello* got to her feet, with grace and elegance.

"Never fear, Brigadie'. I'm happy to do it; the doctor is a good man and he deserves all the help in the world. But first I need to get made up, and get these filthy whiskers off my face: if I want to get us the information we need, I'll have to look my best."

# XXXIX

Ricciardi waited, concealed in a recess between two buildings.

When it became clear to him that there would be no point in trying to chase after sleep, he'd gotten out of bed, put on his clothes, and left the apartment while the night was still far from yielding to the dawn.

The deserted streets had walked with him, his rhythmic steps echoing in the cool damp air that still lacked a clear identity, in that indecision so typical of spring, when it feels as if it's still hovering between winter and summer. Every so often, Ricciardi would cross paths with some night owl returning home, tipsy and giddy, or else early birds riding rattletrap bicycles.

No shortage of dead people out and about, not that there ever was. A little boy at the end of Via Foria, who had fallen off the back of a streetcar where he'd hitched a ride, cadging a free trip to who knows what useless destination, with a huge dent in the back of his head and a broad bleeding wound on his back where he had been dragged along the pavement, who kept muttering prophetically: *Maronna, Maronna, mo' caro 'nterra*— Madonna, Madonna, I'm going to fall down. A motorcyclist near the crossroads of Via Sant'Anna dei Lombardi and Via Toledo, wearing a leather helmet and a pair of oversized goggles from which ran a black tear of blood, laughing obscenely as he said: *Faster, even faster*. Any faster than that'll kill you, Ricciardi retorted bitterly, to himself.

The commissario was very familiar with that hour that really wasn't anything at all, that seemed never to pass, that was no longer night but not yet morning. That hour was a territory with its own weather and its own people, with borders and lights and shadows that would vanish soon enough, leaving no trace. He knew it well, because often his dreams took his breath away and he was forced to wander the streets, in search of a peace that he knew to be little more than a mirage for his tormented soul.

The grief and pain of others became his own. The curse was simply this: it was impossible for him to nestle comfortably in that cocoon of selfishness that everyone is endowed with at birth. Everyone, except him.

Why that fate had been visited on him was something he'd never know. The motorcyclist who had gone too fast, the reckless little boy who'd taken a tumble off the streetcar, and the thousand others just like them were free now: not him. And he never would be free.

He thought of Viper. Ever since he'd learned about Modo he hadn't thought about her, but then what had happened to his friend demanded urgency, and for the rest of the day that investigation could wait.

It was a strange murder, though. Usually, they had to look for a motive, something that might have driven someone to commit such an atrocious act, so contrary to human nature; here there was a veritable jungle of motives.

A murder dictated by passion, but carried out in a rational manner: otherwise the murderer would have left some trace of his or her presence, some bit of evidence, an object; he'd have made some mistake—that's always what happens when you let yourself be swept away by an emotion that clouds the mind to the point of murder. But instead, nothing. There was nothing.

Maybe the murderer really had been good. Or maybe he had just been lucky. Ricciardi just couldn't say.

In the end, he'd found the place and he'd settled in to wait.

As he was waiting for his audience with Achille Pivani, he thought back to the circumstances that had first led him to make the man's acquaintance. The previous summer, during his investigation of the murder of a noblewoman, he'd chanced upon evidence of an intimate friendship that the woman's step-son was carrying on with a strange party functionary, a man from the north whose duties were top secret and who seemed to possess enormous knowledge about anyone and everyone: even about Ricciardi himself.

On that occasion he'd understood that Fascism was a very complex phenomenon, and that the seemingly fanciful tales that circulated about OVRA—the notorious secret police agency that beat back all anti-Fascist activities, real or imag-ined, with stealthy brutality—were, if anything, understating the case. Through a dense network of informants, made up for the most part of ordinary citizens, strolling vendors, doormen and concierges, office clerks and housemaids, OVRA gathered information and reports that revealed a picture of practically everybody's social and political attitudes, first and foremost those of prominent members of society. And once the picture was clear, OVRA struck mercilessly.

Pivani was a slender, impeccably dressed man, about forty years old, with a calm voice, well educated and intelligent; their conversation had seemed to Ricciardi something like a fencing match, a sort of pas de deux, during which neither had grazed the other, though both were poised over a potentially lethal abyss. In other circumstances, in another universe, the commissario might even have liked that unhappy, introspective man; but Pivani had the sinuous, death-dealing charm of a rat-tlesnake.

Ricciardi remembered quite clearly that at the end of the one conversation he'd had with Pivani, right in party head-quarters, the building outside which he was now waiting, the man had urged him to try to persuade Modo to rein in his public statements. He'd never forgotten those words, which had, with the benefit of hindsight, echoed in his mind as a threat as soon as he'd learned from Maione just how his friend had been arrested. Now he was going to ask for an explanation of what had happened, even if it meant putting himself at risk.

A man in a black shirt showed up whistling a tune, unlocked the front door, pulled out a chair, and sat down at the entrance, digging a sheet of paper and a cigar butt out of his pockets. Two other men showed up shortly thereafter, and after a few wisecracks they headed off upstairs; a window swung open on the fifth floor, where Ricciardi remembered the party offices were located.

He had decided in advance that he would only make himself known when he saw Pivani arrive, so that he woldn't have to spend much time in the midst of hostile Fascists. He didn't have to wait long: after a couple more minutes, a subdued voice came out of the shadows behind him and said:

"*Buongiorno*, Commissario. Quite the early riser, I see; but then, that's not unusual for you, from what I've heard."

Without turning around, Ricciardi replied:

"*Buongiorno* to you, Pivani. The wise man never puts off till tomorrow what he can do today, as they say. I need to speak to you, and urgently."

The voice from the shadows murmured:

"So I see. I should tell you that I was expecting your visit, though perhaps a little later in the day; and that it struck me as best, both for you and for me, not to speak in my office. There's a café that opens early, right here on the corner. You head on over, and I'll join you in a few minutes: probably best not to be seen walking together in the street."

## XL

Ricciardi chose a table inside and ordered an espresso. The café was small and not fully visible from the main street, therefore offering a degree of shelter from the eyes of passersby.

Pivani came in almost immediately, sat down across from him, and gestured to the waiter for another espresso.

"I have to tell you, Ricciardi, that if I were to leave this city the thing I'd miss most would be the coffee. It's so much better here than anywhere else that I'd just have to give coffee up entirely."

The commissario stared at him without speaking: he had no intention of carrying on a friendly conversation with the man who, in all likelihood, was keeping his good friend under lock and key.

Pivani must have sensed his thoughts, because he said:

"I see you're angry with me. I understand you. I'd feel the same way if I were in your place. But I assure you that you're mistaken."

Ricciardi's expression remaineded unchanged.

"Are you saying that I should just take it in stride? I should accept the fact that an unmarked car, with three bodybuilders aboard, pulls up and grabs one of the finest human beings I know, a professional who dedicates his life to helping those who suffer, and takes him who knows where under threat of violence?"

Pivani waved his hand dismissively.

"All these inaccuracies. There were four people in the car, not three, including the driver. The car was unmarked because it was rented, and the organization that carried out this operation certainly doesn't place its insignia on automobiles. Last of all, there was no violence. Your friend, who may be impulsive but is also intelligent, quickly understood that any attempts to escape would be unsuccessful, and so he resigned himself to his fate."

Ricciardi leaned forward and hissed:

"Pivani, don't try to sugarcoat the pill: I want Dr. Bruno Modo freed immediately, and allowed to return to the extremely important work that he does for society. This is still a free country and . . ."

The man giggled briefly.

"Oh, is it? I'm honored that you should think so, Commissario. Not everyone would agree with you. Your friend, for instance, certainly wouldn't. And forgive me, but I doubt that you're in a position to demand anything. We're not sitting here, I've never met you, and this conversation never took place, nor will it ever, as you well know. For that matter, you know that without having to be told. All I need do is whistle once."

With those words, he turned and looked at the plate-glass window. Ricciardi saw two well-dressed men out in the street, leaning against a wall and chatting idly.

Pivani went on:

"If we're here, it's because I've allowed it. And the main reason I'm allowing it is that I'm curious. I'm interested in the human aspects of my . . . my profession: they help me to better understand the things that happen, to interpret them. And to act accordingly."

Ricciardi's face was an impassive mask.

"Ah, so then we're an experiment, is that it? Lab rats. Insects in a maze. But I'd be careful if I were you, Pivani. Rats and insects, in big enough numbers, can be quite dangerous."

The man laughed happily.

"Look at that, you're actually threatening me now! Quite interesting. But you didn't come here this morning to argue with me, did you? You came to secure your friend's release. And yet you have no intention of begging or pleading, instead you threaten me. Just what are you hoping to gain in this way?"

Ricciardi stared at him, unblinking.

"I'm not threatening you, Pivani. I'm hoping that someone, even in a brutal and slithering organization, will take responsibility for putting a very special man back in the place where he can do his work. That's all."

Pivani mulled that over, deep in thought.

"Brutal and slithering, you say. I know it can seem that way. All the same, believe me, compared with our counterpart organizations in other countries, we're nothing more than a musical combo. I've seen things happen, elsewhere, that I wouldn't even know how to describe to you, so great is the horror that, as you know, all forms of wanton violence inspire in me."

Ricciardi didn't want to lose sight of the crux of the matter:

"But don't you believe that the most intolerable form of violence is to deprive of his freedom a man who hasn't done anything wrong, who hasn't hurt anyone?"

Pivani spread both arms wide:

"On the question of whether he's done anything wrong, if you'll excuse me, I beg to differ. You're a man of the law, no? Then you'll recognize that all rules, however ridiculous and absurd they may seem, must be obeyed. But now we're wasting time."

Ricciardi stared at him, baffled.

"What do you mean by that, that we're wasting time? How do you mean?"

Pivani finished his coffee, a look of bliss on his face.

"Mmm, how delicious. Now then: our organization has a

rather complex structure. There are different jurisdictions, various branches that are in charge of different sectors. The one I head is not the one that . . . picked up our friend the doctor."

Now Ricciardi was disoriented:

"What are you talking about? Then why would you know everything about it, every tiniest detail!"

"That's quite another matter. It's my job to know everything, every tiniest detail. As for picking up the doctor, no, that wasn't us. We were informed of what happened yesterday morning, during that pathetic parody of a funeral for the murdered whore; one of the young men, the dimmest of the bunch, just to be clear, is the son of a rapidly rising Fascist official who works in Rome. He put in a call to his father, and the mechanism that was thus set in motion resulted in the doctor's arrest. The unmarked car with four men aboard set out from the capital. That's what happened."

Ricciardi tried to gather his thoughts.

"So you're saying that Modo was taken to Rome?"

"I never said that. He may well still be here; but he won't be here long."

The commissario wanted more information.

"Then who can I speak to? What can I do to help Bruno?"

Pivani gave him a sad look.

"You can't imagine how often I receive informants' reports, how many I've received about the doctor. I even decided to investigate in person: I've gone to see him work, I've eaten where he eats, I even followed him to that place where the girl was murdered. And I've seen the two of you together. And I made up my mind that he is a valuable man, a good man, honest and caring." Here he paused and went on in an undertone: "Whether or not you believe me, I wrote an official opinion. In summary I said that persecuting people like him was counterproductive for Fascism's image, that we'd only create martyrs and that martyrs are always dangerous. He slipped through the meshes of a net that for now remain fairly large. But yesterday . . . he was unlucky. He ran into the wrong people. And when the brigadier pulled out his revolver, well, that wasn't very smart: still, though, a knife was pulled as well, and the informant who told us about the incident mentioned that detail too, and one thing balances the other, so your friend Maione got off, because we do make an effort not to kick up too much dust in our dealings with law enforcement. For the doctor, however, there was nothing that I could do."

The commissario waited. Two young women entered the café, laughing at some joke they were sharing. Pivani looked at them, saddened.

"How lucky the young are, especially in springtime, no, Commissario? The season of flowers. The season of love, for some. But not for everyone."

Ricciardi was reminded of the pain that Pivani was forced to suffer thanks to an emotional attachment, as Ricciardi had learned by chance some months ago. The functionary fell silent for a moment, then went on:

"I want to make it clear once again that this conversation never took place, but I also want to tell you that among your exceedingly slender group of non-work-related acquaintances, there is a person. This person, whom you keep at arm's length much more than she would like, has a certain amount of power. I don't believe that she's even aware of it, but she's very much beloved by an extremely important woman, a close friend of hers. They are like sisters to each other."

A beautiful, tormented face appeared before Ricciardi's eyes, as it bit its lower lip to keep from crying.

Pivani continued:

"I don't know what it is that this woman feels for you, Ricciardi. But I would say, to judge from her behavior and above all from the fact that she moved to this city, that whatever it is, it's quite powerful. The lady is subject, by order of the highest authorities, to close and constant surveillance in order to ensure that no harm can come to her. In the context of that surveillance, she has been assigned a . . . a functionary, let us say. This gentleman, who is in a certain sense a colleague of mine, could serve as a privileged conduit as far as the episode that interests you is concerned. Have I made myself clear?"

Ricciardi nodded, somewhat uncertainly.

"So what you're saying is that, through Livia, I should get into touch with this person, is that right? By asking to meet, having a talk with him . . ."

Pivani laughed:

"No, no, you've got it wrong, completely wrong! He doesn't exist, any more than I exist. He would never talk with you, he'd even deny ever having had any contact with your lady friend. You mustn't even try to enter into contact with him, in fact, if you did, that would be highly detrimental to the doctor's well-being, because it would reveal a weakness in the system, which is of course impossible. The only way is to arrange for the lady to speak with him. He is . . . like a guardian angel, he can only interact with her, and no one else."

Ricciardi thought quickly.

"But what if she were unwilling to help me? What if she had . . . certain reasons to feel resentful toward me?"

Pivani shrugged philosophically.

"In that case, the doctor's fate would be sealed. I can't think of any other possible way of saving him."

The commissario stood up, leaving a bill on the table.

"Let me treat you to this coffee, Pivani. You keep showing yourself to be different than you ought by rights to be. And I have to thank you for your advice. One last question: how much time do I have?"

Pivani pulled a watch out of his vest pocket and held it at arm's length.

"My God, I'm going blind with old age; I'd say half a day, maybe a whole day. And let me thank you, Ricciardi, for the coffee: if I actually had drunk it—which is to say if we had ever really met, which obviously is something that didn't happen— I'd have said that it was excellent."

# XLI

M aione found it impossible to believe that only a day had passed since Viper's funeral, in part because of the sleepless night he'd just spent.

The dog had refused to come upstairs; he was sitting in the courtyard, motionless, as if waiting for someone, and that's how the brigadier found him the next morning—his water bowl in front of him, his food untouched—when he went downstairs early in the morning to go see Bambinella. The animal immediately trotted after him, following about fifty feet behind, and followed him to police headquarters, stopping at the corner of Via Imbriani and Via Toledo, exactly where he had waited for Ricciardi the night before.

To the brigadier, the presence of the dog was a constant, urgent reminder of the fact that the doctor was a prisoner. The animal, with his level, intense gaze, seemed to be saying: how dare you do the same things you usually do, the work you do every day, when right now someone could be transporting "him" far away, in chains? How can you let everyone prepare for the holiday, let them bake and buy pastries, when for all we know "he" may be spending Easter in a cell?

The brigadier missed his mock fights with the doctor, the constant exchange of insults. He was not at all willing to give them up, and he was ready to break the world open with his bare hands: but he had to act as if nothing were amiss, because it was impossible to know whether the Fascists had spies even inside police headquarters, and whether they might hasten the process of transferring the doctor if they thought that the commissario and Maione were taking steps to prevent it.

At eleven, when his anxiety and concern for Ricciardi, who still hadn't shown up, and for the time that went ticking inexorably past made it hard for him to breathe normally, he decided to go early to call on Bambinella.

In general, he took care to travel the route to Via San Nicola da Tolentino late at night, to minimize the chances of being seen on his way to pay a call on the *femminiello*. He did it to protect her, well aware that in that city even an empty *vicolo* could have hundreds of watchful eyes, and as many attentive ears, and most important of all, hundreds of mouths eager to report to the wrong people that an oversized police brigadier was on his way to gather information. That day, however, he was willing to run the risk: the situation demanded it.

Luckily, Bambinella was ready for him and had been watching for him from the window. As soon as she saw him coming up the hill she started waving her long fingers, with their painted nails, shrieking like an eagle; Maione decided that that idiot wanted to alert the whole neighborhood and waved angrily at the *femminiello* to shut up, then walked in through the street door and climbed the steep stairs. He took them two at a time, which took less than half the time and left him more than twice as out of breath; by the time he got to the top of the stairs, he couldn't get out so much as a word.

"Ah, here you are, Brigadie', it's a good thing you got here early, any minute now one of my clients, the one who works as a fishmonger, you know the one, he brings me fresh anchovies when he doesn't have the money, which is always, his wife is a harpy who takes every last cent from him, of course, she is his wife, she does have every right, but still he's in love with me and he can't resist, so what's a girl supposed to do, shouldn't I take pity on him? And after all, anchovies are as good as money, it's something to eat, no? But are you all right, Brigadie'? You're white as a sheet. Why don't you sit down, and I'll get you a glass of water. I have big news for you. Believe you me, when Bambinella gets busy she always gets what she's after. That's why I told you this morning that I had to get ready: this wasn't information I was going to find through one of my girlfriends, this information was coming directly from a client. Here, there you go, drink this. Do you feel better now?"

Maione drank down the water in a single gulp, and finally felt his heart climb down from where it had been pounding between his ears and return to its normal spot. In a hoarse voice he said:

"Bambine', I'm going to tell you once, and only once: don't start digressing. Get it? No digressions, or I swear that's the end of you, even if it means I don't get a speck of information. So tell me, now, just who is this client of yours? Is he reliable? And what did he tell you?"

"Brigadie', all right, I promise not to digress: but you have to let me talk the way I talk, otherwise I might skip some important detail that could be useful. Agreed?"

Maione sighed, resignedly.

"Go on. Do it for the sake of Our Lord Jesus Christ, who will soon rise from the grave: go on. But do it before Easter, I beg of you."

Bambinella giggled.

"You're always joking around! All right then, a year or so ago I met this man, not exactly young, from Taranto. Well dressed, a gentleman. I met him in a store run by a girlfriend of mine that . . . oh well, I'll get on with my story. This man comes up to me and gives me a pinch on my bottom, it was hot out and I was wearing that little light dress, the black one with the red pattern, you know the one that I mean? No? Do you want to see it? All right, I'll go on with my story. Anyway, that day I was a little on edge and instead of just laughing it off, I hauled off and slapped him one in the face, all five fingers, *bam!* Silence falls in the store, everyone's looking at us, and he puts his hand up to his face and you know what he does? He gives me a great big smile and says: 'What a temper!'"

Maione ran a hand over his face.

"Bambine', I've made up my mind. I'm going to have to kill you. Please don't take it the wrong way, but I just have to kill you."

Bambinella raised one hand.

"No, Brigadie', you can't kill me, first I have to finish my story. So we start seeing each other and he becomes a customer of mine. I should tell you that nearly all my customers come in part just to talk, because their wives won't listen to them and, as you know yourself, I am a very good listener."

Maione began coughing violently.

"Hey, Brigadie', for pete's sake, don't choke! So anyway this guy starts telling me about how he used to be in the militia and then they transferred him here and gave him a new assignment; he even tells me what it is but then and there I forgot. But then, just yesterday, when he was supposed to come see me, he comes by to tell me that he can't because he has something else to do. And what did he have to do? Go on, ask me, ask me: what did he have to do?"

Maione rolled his eyes skyward and, resigned, repeated in a singsong that was a fair imitation of the *femminiello*'s voice:

"And what did he have to do?"

"He told me: I have to take delivery of a shipment that's going to be brought in by certain colleagues who've come down from Rome. From Rome, you get it?"

The brigadier suddenly became very attentive.

"What does that mean? It could be anything."

"No, Brigadie'. It can't mean just anything. Because when you got here, I finally remembered my friend's assignment. And do you want to know what my friend's assignment was?"

"Bambine'!"

"Oh, I'll tell you, okay, I'll tell you: he's in charge of the temporary detainment of arrestees for political offenses. In practical terms, he's the superintendent of the secret—he says 'special'—division of the militia in charge of the barracks where they keep the prisoners they plan to send into internal exile, like on the islands of Ponza or Ventotene. He's told me the story lots of times, but I just listen out of one ear because I've always got plenty of things of my own to think about . . . but for you, and just for you, that one ear works perfectly well!"

"So how can you be so sure that the doctor is there? If the shipment was coming from Rome, then that can't be him, because they picked him up down here."

Bambinella giggled again, her fingers covering her mouth.

"Good work, Brigadie', I thought the exact same thing. But I also thought that my friend could provide me with a little information. You should know, and this detail is important, that there's this one thing I do to him that he loves, something that, let's say, requires both sides of my nature, the womanly side but also the . . ."

Maione leapt to his feet:

"Halt! Hold everything! I don't want to know what you do with your friends, I'm only interested in knowing what he said."

Bambinella pretended to fan herself:

"Oh, *mamma mia*, Brigadie', you're such a bore! Let's broaden our views a little, after all this is 1932, not the Middle Ages! Anyway, it didn't take much, given my beauty and my special qualities, to find out that those guys came down from Rome just to pick up someone from Naples. And that this certain someone was none other than our dear doctor."

"And how can you be so sure?"

Bambinella put on a solemn expression.

"Brigadie', don't you dare doubt my talents. When I tell

you that I know, it's because I made him get out the documents and check for that name: he carries the documents with him everywhere in a little locked briefcase because he told me that he's worried that if he leaves them at work someone will steal them."

Maione stared at her, horrified.

"Don't you realize the risk you ran? What if he thinks, I don't know, that you're someone who's trying to dig up secrets or something like that?"

"No, Brigadie', don't worry about a thing. I wouldn't have made it to my age out on the streets in a city like this if I wasn't a girl who knows how to take care of her own business. I told him that a girlfriend of mine was supposed to be operated on tomorrow at Pellegrini hospital by this very doctor, and that he was the only one she trusted because his assistant was an ignorant donkey, and that someone had told us that they'd taken Modo away in a black car. And believe me: at times like that, if I want, a guy like that, I can get him to recite the recipe for *casatiello* bread backwards."

"What can I say to you, Bambine'? You are my saving grace. I'm bound to kill you, one of these days, but you're still my saving grace in the meantime. Now, I need you to tell me just two more things: where is he, and how long will they be keeping him there?"

Bambinella put on a sad expression.

"Here comes the bad news, Brigadie'. They're holding him with a dozen or so other prisoners that they rounded up in the past fifteen days, at the barracks of the port militia. He says that there's a large room for that purpose in the cellar. They'll keep them there until the arrival of the ship that will transport them to the island of Ventotene."

Maione rubbed his hands together.

"That's bad news only to a certain extent. He's still here, and I know that barracks, the commissario and I were there at

Christmas on an investigation. All we need is enough time to figure out what to do next."

Bambinella sighed.

"The really bad news, Brigadie', is that the ship is coming in the day after tomorrow. Right on Easter Sunday."

# XLII

When he got back to headquarters, panting and out of breath, Maione found Ricciardi waiting for him by the front entrance.

"Come on, let's go. I'll buy you lunch."

The brigadier immediately understood that his superior didn't want to be in the office when they talked about what had happened to Dr. Modo; on the one hand he appreciated his caution, but on the other, it seemed worrisome: the commissario wasn't usually so circumspect.

When they reached the corner of Via Toledo, the dog, sitting in the shade, got to his feet and followed them. Heading toward Gambrinus, Ricciardi said:

"He hasn't moved from that spot since this morning. It's as if he knew."

Maione grumbled:

"Well, maybe he really does know what happened. And he'd like to tell us, but he can't."

When they reached the café, they found a table inside. It was lunchtime by now, and the place was almost full. There was no piano because it was Good Friday, but music was provided by a strolling violinist who was playing for coins just out front of the café's veranda. The air was mild and sweet-smelling, the sun was warm and bright.

Ricciardi and Maione ordered quickly to get rid of the waiter, and then started to swap the information they'd obtained.

The brigadier told Ricciardi about his two conversations with Bambinella.

". . . so now we know three things, Commissa': that the doctor was picked up by the Fascists, but that they weren't Fascists from here and we need to figure out why that was; that they're keeping him at the barracks of the harbor militia, whom we know very well; and above all that we have today and tomorrow to do something about it, because this coming Sunday the ship is going to dock and they'll take him away to Ventotene."

Ricciardi had listened with rapt attention, leaning forward to make sure he didn't miss a word.

"Good. What I did was take a stroll over to that place where I went to check out the status of Ettore Musso di Camparino, you remember, the murder from last summer."

Maione started.

"Commissa', what are you saying? You went alone, again, to that place? But why didn't you tell me, we could have gone together and . . ."

The commissario had been expecting Maione's reaction, and he'd prepared an excuse:

"The person I intended to question would never have spoken with two people; he wouldn't have run the risk that what he said to me could be confirmed by a third party. Anyway, he was waiting for me. Just think, he wouldn't even speak to me in his office, we went to a nearby café."

"And what did he tell you, Commissa'?"

Ricciardi summarized what he had learned, leaving out only Pivani's mention of Maione's role in the brawl at the funeral.

"Then that's the reason they came all the way down from Rome to arrest him."

"So the guy even gave you a free piece of advice, Commissa'. Certainly, the fact that Signora Vezzi is sweet on you is hard to miss; in fact, if you don't mind my saying so, since we're already on the subject, I've always hoped that your friendship with her might grow into something more, she's a beautiful woman and, it seems to me, a fine person as well. So now what are you planning to do?"

Ricciardi stared into the middle distance. He seemed lost in a painful memory. The violinist struck up the tango that Modo had said he wanted to accompany Maria Rosaria Cennamo, aka Viper, on her last earthly journey.

A man, seated with two young women at a nearby table, began to sing along in a fine tenor voice:

"*Y todo a media luz, que es un brujo el amor, / a media luz los besos, a media luz los dos. / Y todo a media luz, crepúsculo interior. / ¡Qué suave terciopelo la media luz de amor!*"

Ricciardi thought back to his friend's doleful singing, and felt the ferocious fangs of nostalgia sink into his heart. Out on the street, from a vantage point where he could see and be seen, the dog was staring at him, one ear straight up.

But he also remembered the last time he'd seen Livia, right there at Gambrinus, and how he had insulted her, and how the doctor had upbraided him for it. Friendship, love, passion, penumbra. Half-light, like soft velvet, as the song said.

"I know that I need to go and talk to her, and I know that I need to do it right away. But believe me when I tell you, Raffaele, that it's harder to do this thing than it was to go right to the headquarters of the local Fascists to grab their little Duce by the lapels. This morning I wasn't afraid, but now I am."

Maione didn't understand the reason for that fear:

"But why, Commissa'? The Signora is a wonderful person, you'll see: she'll understand the problem and she'll be glad to give us a hand. Do you want me to come with you?"

"No. This is something I have to do on my own. First of all because it's what's right; second because if there's a chance of Livia saying yes, it'll be precisely because I beg her. It's complicated."

"Never in life, Commissa'. When you love someone, it's a simple thing, and it's part of human nature. If I love a person, I want that person to be happy. If there's something that's making that person unhappy, and I can do something about it, there's not a thing in the world strong enough to keep me from doing it. You'll see, as soon as the Signora hears what happened, she'll be the first to want to help us out."

Ricciardi wished he could share the brigadier's optimism.

"No, Raffaele. Unfortunately the thing is complicated because I complicated it myself. The last time I saw Livia was right here, and Bruno was there too: I made a stupid wisecrack, and I insulted her."

Perhaps he had wanted to punish her, he thought. Or discredit her.

"But why did you do it, Commissa'?"

Ricciardi shrugged his shoulders.

"Perhaps because you were just a little jealous of her?"

Ricciardi again said nothing. Then he said:

"I'd better go right away, there's no time to waste. I'll see you later, in the office."

## XLIII

Rosa was delivering the cooking lesson from her chair, pulled up next to the kitchen table.

"The *minestra strinta*, that's something he loves. The ingredients are all sitting right here, I prepared them especially to let you take a look at them, one by one: chicory, swiss chard, and these right here are the cardoons. Now we're going to boil them, then we drain them nicely, and finally we dry them in this towel here, you see? We twist the towel tight, which is why it's called *minestra strinta*, tight soup or squeezed soup. Then we put it all in a pan with the hot oil, the garlic, the chili pepper, and the potatoes, which we've already boiled and mashed very thoroughly. Did you see all that? Is everything clear?"

Enrica looked at the vegetables and the other ingredients, and replied sweetly.

"Yes, Signora. It's all clear. As usual, something simple and delicious, like everything you cook. And if you tell me that he likes it, then I'll learn how to make it. The problem is whether all this serves any purpose, or not."

"And just what is it that you mean by that, Signori'?"

"What I mean by that is that frankly I don't understand this man, Signora. I have no experience with men, that's true: but I do have a married sister, I have plenty of girlfriends, and I do go occasionally to the movies. I listen to songs, I talk to people. And my mother . . . my mother never talks about anything else, how important it is to have a man by your side, that I'm well on my way to becoming an old maid, and so on and so forth.

And if a man really is interested in a woman, then he makes that known. He tries to see her, he speaks to her, he gets as close as he can. He sends flowers, he talks to her parents, he tries to make friends in common. But this man does nothing."

"But that isn't true! Didn't he write you a letter? And isn't it true that every night he goes to his window to gaze at you?"

"Yes, this is true. And it's also true that I can feel it, that he's interested in me and that he likes me. I can see it. I'm not so beautiful, and as I told you, I have no experience: but a woman knows it, when someone likes her."

"There you go. So?"

"So, something's not right. There must be a reason that keeps him from making himself known. He's shy, that's true; and he's also very reserved, I understand that. But too much time has gone by, even a shy man by now would have found a way, however roundabout, to talk to me differently, to arrange for us to go out together. I'm telling you, something's not right."

Rosa sighed. Her eyes roamed, looking at nothing.

"He was a strange child, you know? He always played alone. There were plenty of other children in the baron's castle: the children of the farmers, of the housemaids, more noise than you could possibly imagine, they made more noise than the chickens in the henhouse. Not him. He was beautiful and, as you know, very intelligent. And he talked and talked to me and to his mother; he told us about all the things he imagined and we listened to him, whole hours at a time spent listening to him. But not with the other children, no, he didn't play with them . . ." She stared at Enrica. "There's something, yes. Something in his head, in his soul, I couldn't say. A sign, a mark of some sort, that forces him to be by himself. I may be ignorant and old, but I'm not senile and I know perfectly well that there's something. But my young master is good and kind, sweet and caring. It's not right that just because he thinks he needs to live his life alone, he really should have to."

Enrica listened, toying with a stalk of swiss chard.

"So what should I do? If I wait for him, I really do run the risk of waiting forever, because he might never be able to overcome this barrier. If I don't wait, then I'm giving up on the man of my dreams. Because I know that he's the one, the man of my dreams. I can feel it in my belly, the way it twists every time I think about him. And I can feel it in my legs, the way they tremble whenever I see him."

Rosa slapped her open hand flat on the tabletop, making the lemons jump.

"Then listen to what your legs and your belly are trying to say you need to do! If he has something in his head, and it's keeping him from making a move, then it's up to you to take the initiative."

"If he likes me because I am the way I am, then why should I change? I'm a thoughtful, normal person. I tried a different approach, on Christmas Eve, and you know it. I don't even know what came over me, I would never do that kind of thing. But I felt the need to wish the love of my life a merry Christmas, and that's what I did. And ever since then he seems to be closer to me, he has more of a . . . smile about him, even when he doesn't smile at all. But he never asked me out. I have the impression that at night, when he comes home and sees me leaving this apartment, it makes him happy, but that's not enough."

Without realizing it, she had begun to cry. The tears were streaking her cheeks and her glasses fogged up slightly. Rosa felt a pang in her heart.

"Signori', I beg of you, don't be like that; you shouldn't even think these things. Why, in your opinon, did I come looking for you? Don't you think that I worry day and night about what will happen to my young master, when I'm dead and gone? And what do you think, that I just walked out into the street and grabbed the first girl I saw? He wants you, nobody but you. And if you want him, then you have to go out and get him. Before some other woman steps forward and, taking advantage of some weakness of his, takes him and makes him miserable for the rest of his life."

"But if he wants me, why on earth would he give in to another woman?"

"The danger, Signori', is always there. Certain women have . . . resources, shall we say. And if one of these women, like that widow from up north who goes around town in a car with a driver, you know who we're talking about, finds the way, then he's lost. For example, my young master is good-hearted: so good-hearted. His conscience is a dangerous thing; if she convinces him that she's suffering terribly without him, then his conscience might start bothering him. That's a danger."

Enrica wiped her eyes.

"What can I do to keep that from happening?"

"My lovely girl, you need to take action. Let's cook him this meal: on Sunday, he has to work, he always works on holidays, so you can eat Easter lunch with your own family. But that night you can come to dinner here. You can eat with him, the things that you've cooked for him. That way that knucklehead will start to understand what it means to have a person close to him, and you can toss your hat in the ring, so to speak."

The girl sat openmouthed.

"Me? To dinner, here? Impossible, how on earth could I do that? And after all, no one's even invited me. I could never do it."

Rosa put on an offended expression:

"What about me? Are you saying I'm no one? I live here, I can certainly invite a person to dinner if I like. So I'm inviting you, and if you refuse to come, then you've insulted me and I can no longer speak to you. Are you trying to insult me?"

Enrica stammered:

"Me, insult you? No, never, absolutely not. But . . ."

"Good, then it's all taken care of: for dinner, on Easter Sunday. Now, let's get busy, we have less than two days."

# XLIV

We'd better get busy, Ricciardi thought. We don't have much time.

Two days at the very most, and the doctor would be loaded onto a ship and taken to Ventotene. How many times, joking around with him and Maione, had Modo said: if only they'd send me into internal exile; sunshine and salt water, and I'd never have to look at your ugly mugs again.

As he was walking up Via Monteoliveto, on his way to see Livia, he felt conflicting emotions surging in his heart; sooner or later perhaps he would have gone to see her, to apologize for his offensive wisecrack. But most of all he wondered about the answer to Maione's question: why had he said what he did to Livia? What did he feel for her?

He chased all those thoughts from his mind: he needed to focus on winning his friend's freedom.

He knew nothing about the true nature of Livia's relations with her friends in Rome. He didn't know what result her request for help would have, even if he did manage to talk her into making it. He didn't know how difficult it would be to figure out which path to follow. He didn't know how Modo was doing, and whether or not it was already too late.

He didn't know anything about anything.

Livia couldn't seem to find the will to get out of bed.

She was furious at herself, really furious. For years she'd sworn to herself that she'd never leave so much of herself at

anyone else's mercy, and that never again would she give someone else absolute power over her freedom.

When she swore that oath, she'd been close to death.

She thought back, lying in the darkness of her bedroom.

She remembered the months after her son died, when she
couldn't come up with a single reason to get back on her feet
and start walking through the world again. When she had
turned to her husband, a hard, selfish man, who had only
been able to tell her this: so you didn't even know how to do
this for me. Placing the blame on her, though he was the one
who was never there, he was the one who had never skipped
a performance even to be at the bedside of his ailing child, nor
given up a single opportunity to travel, to spend the night out,
in pursuit of the immense and undeserved talent with which
nature had bestowed him. He had accused her of failing to
take adequate care of the child, of having paid too little attention to the progress of the illness that had taken that sweet
angel.

She lay shut up in darkness for weeks and weeks, wishing
with all her strength for the death that she hadn't been able to
seize with her own hands: a thousand times she'd been on the
verge of gulping down an entire bottle of sleeping pills and
then slipping down, down, down into sleep, never again to
reawaken.

Livia remembered. She remembered perfectly.

When she'd finally stood up and opened the shutters, it was
spring, just as it was now. She'd dragged herself over to a mirror, taken one look at herself, and sworn that she'd never let
herself be reduced to this state again. She banished suffering
from her heart; in exchange, she'd ushered in a harshness that
was utterly unlike her. She became a different woman, now
capable of sailing safely through life, passing unharmed
through a shark-infested world.

She'd done that.

So now what was keeping her closed in the darkness of her room, unable to eat, no idea whether outside it was day or night?

She was furious at herself, for the weakness she thought she'd long since abandoned in the mists of the past.

And she was furious at Ricciardi, at his chilly indifference, and at what she had glimpsed in his green, pain-filled eyes, or perhaps what she had only imagined.

Now she was bound and determined to go back to Rome, but she was afraid of returning to her old life. She wasn't up to it: it felt like setting out to scale a mountain.

Still, she'd do it. She owed it to the memory of her little Carletto, because if losing him hadn't killed her, nothing could kill her now. Even if the image of that trick people called love was dead to her now.

She heard a knocking at the door. She said: leave me alone.

The housekeeper uttered a name.

In a fetchingly furnished drawing room, Ricciardi stood waiting to learn whether Livia would see him.

He remembered that apartment.

He'd felt a pang in his heart, as he stood outside the door. He remembered a night of incessant rain, the immense weight of his grief, the usual grief that had swollen, that night, to intolerable proportions. He remembered the way he'd shivered feverishly, his distorted sense of reality, the mortal loneliness that was killing him. He remembered a door opening, and then a bed, a cool hand on his scalding hot forehead.

And he remembered the scent, a scene of spices, at once savage and sophisticated. And the feel of soft, welcoming, moist flesh. Smells and tastes, a slow fall, like a feather's as it flutters to the bottom of an abyss. A pair of large, happy eyes, a soft mouth opening in a smile, as he realized with a new burst of pain that he'd be unable to keep that promise, that he was twice a traitor: he'd betrayed the trust of a person who wasn't there, and the hopes of one who was.

He asked himself what had brought him back there again. And he was reminded of the doctor's frank and boisterous laughter, his hat pushed back on his head, the shock of white hair uncovered, the doctor's hand on his shoulder. Right, that's what he was doing there.

The housekeeper had come back to say that the Signora wasn't well, and he'd felt as if someone had clutched his heart in their fist. He'd insisted. The woman had told him to wait there.

And he'd been waiting for a good ten minutes, when the door swung open and Livia walked into the room.

## XLV

With a stab of emotion, Ricciardi found himself face to face with a woman quite different from the one who had fled Gambrinus just two days ago.

Livia wasn't made up and her hair had been swept back hastily. She wore a dark red dressing gown, tied at the waist with a sash, and a pair of low-heeled shoes. But her clothing, the absence of the usual care she put into her appearance— these weren't what struck the commissario to his very soul.

It was her eyes.

The woman's gaze was blank.

He was used to seeing cheerfulness, passion, confidence, and even sudden bursts of anger in those eyes. He knew her look of defiance, her look of unease. But to see those eyes drained, weary, devoid of hope hit him like a punch in the nose.

They stood face to face, and gazed at each other for a few seconds. Then Livia waved him to an armchair, perching gracefully on the corner of a sofa, at a safe distance from him.

"What a surprise. I have to say I hardly expected to see you today. To what do I owe this visit?"

Ricciardi lacked the courage to speak. To see her in this state was more than he could handle: he was accustomed to defending himself from her, to erecting barriers against her impulsive passions, and now there she was, chilly and remote.

In the face of his silence, Livia said:

"Forgive me for receiving you looking like this. I have a terrible migraine that's been tormenting me for . . . for two days, and this is the first time I've been out into daylight since it first hit. I'm not exactly the ideal hostess today."

Ricciardi shook himself.

"No, you should forgive me, actually. I show up here without any advance notice—not even on the job do I burst in on people like this. But I needed to . . . I need to speak to you, Livia. About a very important matter."

There wasn't so much as a flicker of interest on the woman's face.

"I'm all ears. I have to imagine that, for you to come here, it must have been pretty urgent."

The commissario ignored the irony that dripped from her words. He clutched once again at the picture of his friend and worked up his nerve to go on.

"You're right. And you have every reason to be angry with me: my behavior the other day was inexcusable. I can't even explain it to myself and, believe me, I've done my best to try to understand what came over me."

Livia gazed at him without expression.

"Don't worry about it. I didn't think it was particularly strange; perhaps the only novelty was that there was a third party present, but the behavior was the same you've always shown me. As far as that goes, I have no cause for complaint: you're a perfectly consistent man."

"That's not true. I'm only sorry that you should think such a thing, which couldn't be further from the truth. I understand that it might seem that way, but you must believe me: it isn't true. It's just that I . . . I'm a strange person, that's all. I don't open up. I can't open up, not to anyone. Much less to a woman, and a woman like you, who would have every right to happiness. If I hold you at arm's length, I do it for your own good."

She laughed with bitter irony.

"Just who do you think you are, to claim the right to decide what's best for me? God almighty, perhaps? Forget about it, Ricciardi. I'm old enough to understand when a man doesn't like me, without further humiliating myself in his presence. But listen, why don't you tell me why you're really here? I have no doubt it's a serious matter, otherwise you'd never have come."

Ricciardi heaved a deep sigh.

"Yes, that's right. I have a reason, and it's a very serious one. And in fact it has to do with the person who was with us the other day; the man in whose presence I stupidly insulted you."

Livia furrowed her brow.

"The doctor? Why, what's happened to him?"

The commissario told her what had happened, leaving out nothing. He told her what Maione had been told by his wife and by Bambinella, and he told her about the call he paid on Pivani.

". . . it was him, confidentially, who told me that the only person I could turn to is you. And so here I am, precisely to ask for your help."

Livia had listened with growing interest, and now she was positively fuming.

"Why, who do you take me for? Do you think I'm, I don't know, a spy for the Duce or a Fascist functionary? I'm very sorry for the doctor; I like him and he struck me as a nice person, but what the devil do you think I can do to help?"

Ricciardi bore that dressing down the way you would a summer cloudburst.

"I know perfectly well you have no political connections. That's why what I said the other day was just an idiotic joke, and one uttered by a fool. But this Pivani told me that you, most likely without being aware of it, are very dear to someone important in Rome; and that for this reason you have been assigned, for your safety, an agent who works for the same branch that is about to ship Modo off to internal exile."

Suddenly, before Livia's eyes there appeared the image of a distinguished-looking man, middle-aged, carrying a leather portfolio. She muttered under her breath:

"Falco."

That was the name he had given her, along with an address where, if she ever needed help, she could arrange for an envelope containing a sheet of white paper to be delivered. She was afraid of the man; behind that nondescript exterior lurked a cold, dark mind, as well as a perfect catalogue of information about her that not even she knew. It was from him that she'd learned all about Ricciardi, unable to resist the temptation to learn whatever she could, even though she instinctively wanted to keep that strange man as far away from her as possible.

Ricciardi nodded.

"I'm begging you, Livia: I'm begging you. If it were for me, I swear to you, I would never have come here; but Bruno is a wonderful human being, who does more for his fellow man than all the Fascist officers in Rome put together. We can't— you can't let him be thrown who knows where just because of the ideas he has. I'm begging you."

None of the ice in which Livia had shrouded herself melted. But the woman said:

"I doubt I have the power you attribute to me; the Roman friend to whom your Signor Pivani was probably referring is a person with whom, for the most part, I talk about clothing and jewelry, with a little gossip thrown in about which of our friends in common have new boyfriends. And yes, it's true that on several occasions I've seen a man—I don't even know whether the name he told me is actually his Christian name, his last name, or a nickname—and he mysteriously seems always to be perfectly informed about everything."

"And would you know how to get in touch with him? There is no time to waste; based on the information we've received, the ship is sailing on Sunday. Easter Sunday."

Livia retorted bitterly:

"That ship won't be the only one leaving Naples on Easter Sunday. I've decided to leave town too. You'll be rid of my irritating presence once and for all."

The news washed over Ricciardi like a gust of icy wind. He understood instantly that he didn't want Livia to leave.

"You . . . if you've made that decision for your own reasons, then there's nothing I can say. But if you're leaving on my account, don't do it. Don't do it. I . . . I really don't know what to say, but I'm begging you, don't do it."

Livia looked at him for a long time, baffled. Trying to understand whether what her heart was telling her was the product of what she was hearing or the product of what she wanted to hear.

Then she said:

"I'll try to get in touch with him. I'm doing it for the doctor, because of the impression I had of him and because of what you've told me about him. I very much doubt I'll be able to do it, but if I am, you'll have two reasons to rejoice: first because your friend will be set free, and second because it will mean that the other day at Gambrinus you were right."

Ricciardi ran a hand over his face.

"I thank you. This matter now takes precedence for me over everything else. But if this is resolved, as I hope it will be, I'll come and talk to you, I promise. And I'll try to persuade you that I never believed those words I said, that I'm nothing but a stupid idiot. And that I know how to appreciate a fine sensibility and a good heart, the few times I find them."

Livia said nothing, struggling to tamp down the excitement she could feel clutching at her throat. God only knew how many times she'd dreamed of hearing those words, of having at least the shadow of a chance with that man. But the wound was still too fresh.

She stood up.

"Don't think twice, it has nothing to do with the two of us. You asked me for help, and I'm willing to do what I can. I hope to have news for you soon, in which case I'll give you a call. You just be ready."

Ricciardi stood up too.

"Whatever the result, I thank you, Livia. You could have kicked me out without a second thought, and I would have deserved it: for me to come here, after insulting you, to ask you to help me by reaching out to the very same friends my stupid insult was aimed at. And instead you decided to listen to me all the same. I won't forget it."

He started to leave, but then halted on the threshold and said, without turning around:

"And I haven't forgotten a single moment of what happened in this house the last time I came to see you. Nothing. This is the second time that I've found, inside these walls, a hope that I lacked when I arrived."

And he left, leaving Livia caught uncomfortably between the past and the future.

# XLVI

You look the night in the face, Doctor.

You can tell that a few people around you are actually sleeping. You're always amazed when you see what human beings can get used to; what they can put up with.

You look the night in the face, and it looks back, impassive. The night is accustomed to more than this, after all. It's moved over more serious misery, it has covered up far worse yearnings.

There's a high school teacher, over there, a Calabrian. He's a homosexual, that's why he's here. He says that he has no political beliefs, but for all you know he's actually a Fascist and they took him anyway. He won't say how they caught him, but from a few of the hints he's dropped you think that it must have been with a student, in the toilets. He sleeps and he snores, mouth open. As the saying goes: the sleep of the righteous.

And there's a university student—you did your best to treat a nasty gash on his forehead—who speaks in monosyllables.

And there's a shepherd from Avellino who cursed at the dedication of a statue of Old Bull Head, as they call the Duce.

And others, who have thoughts that now constitute crimes punished by exile in a concentration camp.

Because, you tell the night, that's what we're talking about: a concentration camp. And you're about to be shipped to one of those camps.

Who knows when you said something out loud, who knows what you did and when, within hearing of vigilant ears which hurried off to report. Perhaps it was just the other morning, at

Viper's funeral, when you spoke to those four drunken thugs. The good you've done doesn't matter, it doesn't matter who you've been or who you are.

Do you remember the night, Doctor? Do you remember it on the Carso, when the chilly morning sunlight found new corpses strewn on the ground, when the mortar marked time with greater precision than your wristwatch? Perhaps the night was less frightening then.

At least then you knew who the enemy was, and you fought him. Now someone out in the street might perfectly well tip his hat as you go by and then turn around and report you.

Someone's crying softly. Wives, children: at least you don't have that regret. At least you're not leaving anyone behind.

For some reason you find yourself thinking about the dog, Doctor. And you hope that Maione will take care of him, as you had the good sense to ask him to do.

Maione, Ricciardi. Sunshine and people.

God, how you miss your life, Doctor.

Now that they're taking it away.

You think you're close to the water, you can smell it in the air. The air also smells of diesel fuel from ocean liners, and every so often you hear voices calling. The port, probably. So it's going to be a ship that takes you away, along with the high school teacher, the shepherd from Avellino, and the other poor bastards.

For no good reason, you think back on Viper, on her laughter and her beauty, lost now. Seven days ago you were at Il Paradiso, drinking and laughing and playing cards, and she walked past and you blew her a kiss. Too bad about her, and too bad about you.

How you miss it.

How you miss a world you never thought you loved so much.

The night, Doctor.

The night that won't end.

## XLVII

Livia sprang into action immediately.

She didn't want to think about the personal implications of what Ricciardi had said, nor did she wish to cultivate hopes that might have to be crushed underfoot as soon as they germinated; but she did sense a new euphoria washing over her.

And after all, she'd told the truth: she liked the doctor. She'd liked him instinctively the first time she'd met him, with Ricciardi, in the aftermath of her husband's murder, and that opinion had been reaffirmed in the few minutes she'd spent with him during that unfortunate episode at Gambrinus.

Livia didn't think of herself as a Fascist, or for that matter as an anti-Fascist. Politics, as she had said on that occasion too, was of no interest to her; anytime she was at a party or at the theater and her companions started arguing about politics, she lost interest and thought about other things. Still, she was convinced that there had to be something wrong if a man like Modo, open-minded, intelligent, and, as Ricciardi said, kind to his fellow man, were to be incarcerated, sent into internal exile, or whatever it was they had in store for him.

She'd taken an envelope, written her own name on it, and inside, in accordance with the instructions that she had been given, she placed a blank sheet of paper. She handed the envelope to her housekeeper and told her where to take it—a nearby apartment house, where she was to give it to the doorman.

Then she went to the mirror: she was greeted by a sight that filled her with horror. She immediately set about fixing her appearance, hardly suspecting that Ricciardi had never before found her so beautiful.

Not even half an hour had gone by when she heard her housekeeper knock at the door again. There was a visitor, and the gentleman had declined to give his name.

She found Falco standing by the window, looking down into the street. When she walked into the room, he said without turning around:

"How beautiful springtime can be. Even in the city, the air is fresh and you can sense it. It's the smell of hope, don't you agree?"

Livia sat down in an armchair.

"*Buonasera*, Falco. Thank you for coming immediately; not that I had any doubt you'd be prompt, of course."

The man bowed his head. He was of average height, well and soberly dressed in a dark double-breasted pin-striped suit; he gave off a faint whiff of lavender. His thinning salt-and-pepper hair was combed back, and he seemed to be freshly shaven.

"Signora, of all the tasks that my job requires of me, your summons is certainly the most welcome. And let me take the opportunity to compliment you on your new hairstyle, which highlights the loveliness of your features."

Livia, in spite of herself and in spite of the tension she felt, burst out laughing.

"Careful, Falco! I see a bit of gallantry peeking through the chinks in your armor! I'll wind up thinking you're human."

Falco sat down across from her.

"At last, I'm tempted to say. It doesn't happen often, sadly, that anyone takes us for human. In any case, to what do I owe the invitation?"

Livia waved her forefinger:

"I should scold you, though: you don't seem to be worried in the slightest, in spite of the fact that this is the first time we're meeting at my request. I might have needed you for some very ugly reason, no?"

The man shook his head.

"The last report was from the day before yesterday, and you came home by car without any problems. At the very worst, you might have been feeling uneasy, but nothing serious. Am I wrong?"

Livia changed demeanor, her face darkening.

"I don't like to be reminded of the fact that I'm constantly being watched. Nor is it particularly nice of you to remind me."

"You're quite right. But it's also true that I take special care of you, and I only wanted to reassure you: nothing bad can happen to you, as long as we discreetly watch over your well-being."

Unfortunately that's not true, Livia thought. But she said:

"Then you must know that I received a visitor today."

Falco stood up again, went to the window, and looked out.

"Yes, you received a visitor. I was informed by the same person who told me about your invitation. I hope that the person who came to call on you here didn't bother you in any way."

She replied in a cutting voice:

"I continue to feel that these matters are none of your business, Falco. And they're none of the business of the person who asked you to watch over me. The person who came to see me, and let me add that I was very happy to see him, brought a matter to my attention that I feel I need to discuss with you, and urgently. That's why I summoned you here."

Falco continued to look out the window, saying nothing. Then he said:

"As you think best, Signora. I'm here to listen and, if I can, to obey your every wish."

Livia took a deep breath.

"I have the idea, Falco, that you already know everything I'm about to tell you. If you want to hear it explicitly, then I'm asking you to help free Dr. Bruno Modo, whom you're holding for no good reason in some location you know well."

Falco turned to look at her.

"All right then, Signora, let us speak in terms of pure conjecture. Let us say that I know the person you mention, and let us suppose that I know that he is under arrest and being held in a place familiar to me: how can you be so certain that there is no justification for it? Don't you think there might be reasons, and important ones, why this has happened?"

The woman puffed out her cheeks:

"Please, Falco. We both know perfectly well what the reasons are. My friend, my visitor, told me everything, and I trust him. Blindly."

"You trust him. Blindly. So much so that you moved here from Rome for his sake, in order to pursue him with no thought for your pride. So much so that you allow him to be utterly unfeeling about the pain he's causing you."

Livia leapt to her feet, furious. The feline impression that she always gave, in the elastic gracefulness of her movements, was accentuated by her anger.

"I ought to throw you out of here," she hissed, "and put in a phone call to Rome immediately, telling them loud and clear what you've just dared to say to me. Don't you ever dare say such a thing again, understood? Never again!"

The man blinked.

"Forgive me. I beg you to forgive me. It's hardly professional to say so, but I believe that a person like you doesn't deserve to suffer, with the life you've had. And for the woman that you are."

Livia calmed herself, and sat back down.

"In that case, you'll understand that the fact that I've called you, instead of calling Rome directly, shows how much I trust in your sensibility as a man."

"Yes, and I thank you for that. Moreover, I must admit that I admire the work that the doctor does, the way he puts his heart into helping people. This is still my city, after all. That's the reason we've turned a blind eye to certain of his behaviors and to a great many statements he never abstained from making in public. But this time matters have gone, as you know, well over our heads."

Livia leaned forward.

"I know that, Falco. But perhaps it's not too late to do something about it. Is it true that the transfer is scheduled for Sunday morning?"

The man stared at her without answering. Then he said:

"I have no idea how your friend came by this information, which even I don't have. But yes, it's possible. The ship. . . the conveyance that is scheduled to transfer the prisoners could arrive at any time between tomorrow and Sunday, in fact."

"In that case, we only have a few hours. I have to know whether I can count on you, Falco: otherwise I'll have to call Rome directly; and that is something I'd rather not do. It would mean having to explain too many things, and I would have to draw on credit that may not even be available to me. Dolls like me, as you know, are never forgiven for talking about serious matters."

"You are no doll, Signora. You are a wonderful person, endowed with an incredible talent: I heard you sing, once upon a time, and I know just how incredible."

This time it was Livia's turn to be surprised:

"Really? And when was that? I haven't sung since . . ."

". . . since the tragic death of your son, yes. But in another life, I allowed myself to indulge in the pleasures of the opera house. And it was my good fortune to see you."

There followed a silence heavy with memories. Then she said:

"In that case, in the name of the pleasure that you had that day and in the name of . . . this strange, secret friendship of ours, if you can help me, please help me. I'm begging you."

Falco fell into a thoughtful silence.

"All right. I don't know what effect this may have: I assure you that we must deal with people who can have very unpredictable reactions. And I don't even know whether there is any likelihood of success: but we'll try. With the greatest goodwill, we'll try."

"I thank you, Falco. I thank you in advance. I understand that it isn't easy, and I understand how complex the work you do must be. How do you intend to go about it?"

"I don't know yet. I'll have to try to identify the proper contacts, and I have to come up with a reason why it woud be more costly to detain the doctor than to free him. Possibly the pigheadedness of your friend and his brigadier, their continued insistence, will be considered valid justifications. I couldn't say. You wait to hear from me—and I assure you that you will—but not for at least twenty-four hours. And in the meanwhile, take it from me: don't do anything. Do you promise?"

Livia looked at him; now she would have to decide whether or not to trust that man. She decided to do it.

"All right then. I'll wait for you here, at home. And I'll wait for you to tell me where I can go to collect the doctor. After that, you only need tell me what I can do to repay you for this immense favor that you're doing."

Falco picked up the leather portfolio and hat that he'd set down on a counter.

"If I do manage to pull this off, and believe me, it will be quite a challenge, then I will ask you to sing for me. Just once."

# XLVIII

Ricciardi didn't like telephones.

He'd never managed to become comfortable with that instrument of communication, out of which came a metallic and inexpressive voice that made it impossible to capture the half-tones, the hesitations, and most important, the look in the eye that allowed him to understand what was being hidden behind the words. And then, there was the awareness that all conversations could be heard by the switchboard operators, who theoretically only connected the lines by inserting a plug into a socket but who could actually break in at will, which seemed to him to rob all conversations of confidentiality.

But at times the telephone was necessary: he was relieved when he got Livia's call. She had told him in a whisper that "the letter has been delivered" and that "we can only wait for an answer." She had assured him that he "would be the first to hear" and that she would contact him via "a visit from her chauffeur" to police headquarters, but no sooner than Saturday night. In the meanwhile, "there was no need for them to talk to or see each other."

The woman's voice seemed not only metallic, but also flat and expressionless. He'd been surprised and chagrined at how distant she'd seemed: it was clear that the wound he'd inflicted was still open, though she had given him the help he had asked for.

Ricciardi wondered whether her decision to leave the city, which Livia had mentioned in the same conversation in which they'd discussed Modo, was definitive. And he wondered why it gave him such a pang of sadness.

Hadn't he hoped most of all that she would finally come to terms with the fact that his heart wasn't his to give? Hadn't he hoped she'd finally forget him, that she might find someone more compatible?

Those thoughts took his mind back to Enrica, to their slow but unequivocal courtship, the afternoons that the young woman was spending with Rosa, and to their encounters at the front door at night. How to square that desire, that sweet and uneasy yearning, with his sadness at Livia's departure? What was happening to him?

He'd always told himself that love was completely alien to him, as distant as the face of the moon, but now he was face to face with not one but two emotions he couldn't explain.

Suddenly he felt suffocated, and he decided to leave the office. Just then, all the bells in all the churches started ringing, and their peals were joined by the tooting of the horns of the ships anchored offshore and moored in the port. Eleven o'clock, Holy Saturday.

Easter had officially come to town.

Ricciardi headed off to Via Chiaia. Getting closer to the scene of Viper's murder might perhaps give him some new ideas, or at least help to take his mind off other thoughts.

The street as always betrayed the spirit of the city, which had changed as if someone had thrown a switch: in place of contrition and mortification there was a swelling, generalized euphoria charged with anticipation. The sound of church bells, silent for days out of respect for Christ dead on the cross, now announced to the world that what was done was done, and great things could now be expected: the Savior would be reborn, He would redeem mankind from its infernal fate, and all would be well.

The festive sound of pealing bells was meant to tell the city that all the bad things plaguing it would come to an end sooner or later: the economic crisis that had brought hundreds of shopkeepers to their knees, the poverty that gripped nearly all the families, and the diseases caused by poor sanitary conditions; and that unpleasant thoughts could be put off for two days, while they awaited the miraculous discovery of Christ's empty tomb.

The radio stations continued broadcasting only classical music, as they had for nearly a week and would continue to do until the following day, but the serious, doleful sacred melodies had been replaced by surging symphonies.

The strolling vendors had resumed calling their wares to the city's women with renewed urgency, and now, in the streets, the roving butcher, apron spattered with blood, pushing a cart loaded high with knives and cleavers, ready to slaughter lambs, kid goats, and chickens destined for the paschal table, could be seen. From the railings of the balconies and half-open shutters, children who had become fond of the animals they had raised and fattened for months stared down in horror at those bringers of death, whose shrill whistles and jovial cries announced that the time had come.

The very air itself was laden with new scents: they came from kitchens bustling with feverish activity. The aromas of orange blossom water, cinnamon, vanilla, boiled wheat, and lemons elbowed their way through the rich smells of coffee, grilled fish, and the thousand other fried foods that generally reigned supreme, along with the tang of draft horse manure and exhaust fumes from trucks and cars. But the smell that dominated came from the ovens, where women brought their *pastiere* and *casatielli* to be baked, the queens and kings of the impending feast.

There was still none of the noise that would come from children shouting and playing; even the street urchins, the *scug-*

*nizzi*, were sworn to silence in honor of the coming holiday: the metallic echo of the isolated *troccola* excepted, their noisy games were still forbidden. But it would be only a few hours now before they burst out into the streets in swarms, with balls made of crumpled newspaper or rags bound together with twine, the best possible representatives of the young new season that had just arrived.

The commissario absentmindedly noticed the change, and saw that the suicide outside Gambrinus, incongruously dressed in his heavy winter jacket, went on, undaunted, calling for his lost love, even though he was already beginning to fade like an old photograph. Some things don't get swept away by the spring winds, unfortunately, mused the commissario.

On the other hand, at the corner by Il Paradiso, not far from the *vicolo* where the tradesmen made their deliveries, the accordionist had resumed playing at full force. The instrument, broken by the drunk Fascists the morning of Viper's funeral, had been patched back together and now played just as well as it had before, under the nimble fingers of its proprietor. Ricciardi was pleased to see it, and he tossed a coin into the man's plate: a misdemeanor he was willing to encourage. Amused, the commissario noted just how skillful the man was at pretending he'd noticed the coin only from the sound, and not because the eyes behind those smoked-glass lenses actually saw perfectly well.

Just as he was about to walk on, he noticed someone stepping out of the small side door and he drew back into the shadows to wait and see who it might be. The ample silhouette and the matronly gait immediately told him that this was Madame Yvonne, heading off briskly in the direction opposite the one from which Ricciardi had come.

The commissario waited a few seconds, then set off after her. He certainly had none of Maione's skill at tailing people, but the woman seemed quite unaware of her surroundings and she didn't notice him. She was walking hastily, sticking close to the wall, wearing a black hat with a short veil that just covered her face, taking short quick steps, her heels striking the broad paving stones with a burst of sharp reports. She crossed paths with two women who glanced at each other with raised eyebrows and a man who shot her a faint smile, taking care that the woman on his arm not sees. In neither case did Yvonne show any sign of having noticed. Ricciardi reflected that perhaps he and this woman had more in common than one might guess: they both lived on the thin line that separates light from dark. She, who dealt with whores without being one; and he, who did much the same with criminals.

She wasn't strolling, she was clearly headed somewhere: her pace was too determined. Ricciardi identified the destination when he saw her slow down and move closer to the wall, peering into the windows of Vincenzo Ventrone's shop.

## XLIX

They stayed that way for a while, sharing the same posture a few yards apart: Ricciardi observing Yvonne, who was in turn observing the interior of Ventrone's store, working to improve her vantage point by small, incremental adjustments.

Then the woman was forced to give up; her shoulders sagged under the weight of disappointment, and she slowly turned to retrace her steps.

At that point the commissario pulled up next to her. The *maîtresse* gave him a sidelong glance without slowing down.

"Oh, great, now you. What do you want with me this time? Can't a poor woman even go out for a walk without having the police in her hair?"

Ricciardi adjusted his gait to match the woman's.

"Hardly, Signora. I just spotted you from a distance, and I wanted to say hello."

Yvonne grimaced.

"And what a lovely hello. Forgive me, Commissa', but this is just not the day for it, with all the problems we have. By the way, when are we going to be able to use Viper's room again? You can't imagine how many customers want to see it, but I have to keep it closed until you say otherwise."

Ricciardi replied confidently:

"Signora, for now I can't give you that permission. Until we understand what happened, it's important that everything remain just as it was at the time of the murder."

The woman snorted.

"Commissa', I'm sorry about what happened to Viper. I'm really sorry, truly. But life has to go on, and I can't afford to do without any available resources right now."

"You need all your resources, eh? Ventrone was a very nice resource, and apparently that's one you're having to do without."

Yvonne stopped and lifted her veil.

"And just what is that supposed to mean, Commissa'? What do you know about it? Maybe the Cavalier is coming to see us all the same, even after Viper's death, for all you know."

"It's simple, Signora. Why would you need to go to his shop in hopes of running into him if he was still coming to Il Paradiso every day the way he used to? And since they tell me that Cavalier Ventrone isn't feeling well, or so he claims, and isn't even coming down to the store . . ."

The woman ran a gloved hand over her face.

"You already know everything, don't you? Then what are you asking me?"

Ricciardi shrugged.

"Nothing at all, Signora. I was just wondering why you had to speak with Ventrone. Perhaps it would help me to understand whether there's some reason that man is no longer in circulation."

They'd arrived at the building where Il Paradiso was located. Madame began to cry. She wasn't sobbing, nor was her voice broken; tears simply began to streak her cheeks, and she did nothing to wipe them away.

Ricciardi looked around uncomfortably, and he was reminded of Livia at Gambrinus; he seemed to have a special talent for making women cry.

Madame opened the door with a key that she carried on a small chain under her shawl, and she headed up the staircase; the commissario followed her. Given the hour and the day, the bordello was immersed in an unusual silence veined with Lysoform and stale cigarette smoke. When she was close to her customary post with the oversized cash register, Yvonne finally felt comfortable:

"Commissa', you don't know. You couldn't possibly know. I was in the profession, like so many others; I did it until one day I couldn't do it any longer, and the funny thing is that it didn't happen to me on the job. He, Tullio's father, was . . . well, he never really had a job. And he didn't have the money to pay me; but he was nice, and he was funny. Oh, how he used to make me laugh . . . A whore's life is no laughing matter, as you know, Commissa'. But he told jokes, he acted out scenes, he did perfect imitations, and I had so much fun, and if he made a move, well, I didn't say no. And when I happened to get pregnant, he didn't leave. He certainly could have left, no? It would have been easy. I was a whore, it could have been anybody. But he stuck by me."

Ricciardi pulled out a handkerchief and handed it to Madame, who distractedly dabbed at her tears.

"And he wanted a place of our own, for our son; only he didn't know how to make money, and since he was good at cards he gave that a try and he started to win. But then he started to lose, until one day they killed him. In broad daylight, one afternoon, they killed him. When does that ever happen, Commissa', that loan sharks come and kill someone in the afternoon?"

A lamb, on a nearby terrace, emitted a high-pitched bleat that sounded like the cry of a baby.

"And now my son has started gambling too, right where his father left off. Instead of thanking Almighty God for how things turned out, the way that the two of us have managed to make do on our own. And I can't stand the idea that he might wind up like him."

Ricciardi listened attentively.

"And how do you think you can stop him, Signora? By continuing to pay off his creditors, with money you extort from whoever you can blackmail?"

"Commissa', I don't blackmail anyone. It's true, I do take advantage of the friendship of some of our most loyal customers, I ask them to give me a little something in advance; but I give the girls their share out of my own pocket, and I assure you that they're not going without, no, not at all."

"And the most important of these customers, the one who was most willing to provide these, as you call them, advances, was Ventrone, wasn't it? Look at that, coincidentally the one whose business was most vulnerable to gossip and backbiting."

"Do you really think that I would blackmail Ventrone? No, Commissa', I'll say it again: I don't blackmail anybody. The Cavalier is an old client, perhaps one of our dearest ones, and a friend. It's just that his son . . . you've met him, haven't you? He's a young man, but he has the mind-set of an old one. All that contact with priests, ever since he was little—maybe he's become a little bit of a priest himself. I'm sure that it's him, that he's locked his father up at home so he can't come see us."

Ricciardi tried to grasp the meaning of those words.

"Why, do you think that even without Viper the Cavalier would come all the same?"

Yvonne laughed mockingly.

"Commissa', you need to listen to me: if someone is disposed to come to a place like this, they'll just come, no question. It's not a matter of this whore or that whore, it's just the place. Ventrone, like so many others, used to come here even while his wife was alive, in fact, when his wife died they came to tell him right here in this drawing room. And there's nothing wrong with that, if you think about it: when you're grieving, you look for a place where you can concentrate on other things. It's not the sex, it's the state of mind. If Ventrone could come here, he would, the way he did before Viper, and the way he will again, long after the pleasures of the flesh are a distant memory. You're not the kind of man who would come here, I know that. But if you did, you'd see how many people come even though their thingy is only good for peeing, and they pay plenty of money to hide behind a curtain or under a bed, just to hear and watch and especially to remember. And what's so bad about that? It's not as if the only thing we're allowed to do in this life is suffer."

If only certain forms of suffering could be avoided, Ricciardi thought. If only all you had to do was give someone money, in order to stop seeing. Even if only for an instant.

"Then why did you go looking for Ventrone? If you're sure that he'll come back, that it's just a matter of time, why did you go to the shop this morning?"

"I was hoping not to see him at all in his shop. Because if he wasn't there, it would mean that he was still afraid to to be seen here. And if he was there, then it meant that he was going somewhere else. Men like him, Commissa', they just don't give up coming to a brothel. Not for long."

Ricciardi understood that he wouldn't be able to pry any more information out of the woman.

"Signora, just as there are men who can't stop coming to the brothel, there are others who are slaves to the card tables. Your son, as you know, is heading down that path, and he owes considerable sums to some nasty people who, luckily, given his youth, will no longer extend credit to him; but if that's the way he was heading, let me tell you from experience, sooner or later he'll start back down that path. Keep him on a short leash for now. He'd be well advised not to be seen in certain parts of town."

The woman sighed.

"What do you think, Commissa', that I haven't tried? He's turning into a full-grown man, he's been coming into places like ours for years now. He's an adult. A mother can't do much in this situation. I can't keep him locked up in his room."

And Ventrone, with his advances, had been helping to pay off the debts that young Tullio was running up at the gaming tables, Ricciardi thought to himself.

"Another thing, Madame: Coppola, the fruit vendor, has he come back? Have you seen him again, since the murder?"

"No, Commissa'. The only reason he came was to see Viper, he's not the kind of man who would patronize Il Paradiso or any other cathouse. He's a different kind of person; nothing exists for him but his work and his family. In fact, he never really came for Viper: he came for Maria Rosaria, the *guaglion-cella*—the little girl—from Vomero whom he'd known when she was young and whom he wanted to marry. He paid for his time just so that he could see her. He didn't even come here to deliver fruit, until the one time he came and ran into her by chance. And it would have been better for everyone if he'd never run into her at all."

"And why do you say that?"

"Because the only new thing that happened was that Peppe asked Viper to marry him, in fact. And she died as a result. And no one knows what she had decided to tell him. In any case, no, he hasn't come back. He's not one of those men who can't live without seeing pretty girls, even if it's only for fun. Just to spend time in a place that's playful, amusing. To keep from dwelling on one's troubles. You should come here yourself, sometime, Commissa', lots of your colleagues from police headquarters do it. And after all, you could come with your friend: the doctor."

Ricciardi pulled out his watch and wondered anxiously, for the thousandth time, whether what Livia was doing would have the hoped-for effect and what he would come up with if it didn't.

And suddenly, the tiny window that had been laboriously creaking open in his mind over Viper's murder slammed shut.

L

As always, Maione had arranged not to be on duty during Easter Saturday and Sunday: the children loved that holiday so much, and the family had its own little traditions. The brigadier, though, couldn't have foreseen that he'd be riddled with anxiety and eager for news about the fate of Dr. Modo, so he was distracted and unusually taciturn.

Lucia, who knew the reason for her husband's bad mood, watched him anxiously, careful not to alter what she usually did on Holy Saturday in the slightest, also because this was the first Easter that the young Benedetta would spend with them. She'd even whispered to Raffaele, as he pulled his watch out of his pocket for the hundredth time, that he should pay more attention to the little girl, who doted on him specially ever since he had brought her home with him the previous Christmas; he'd nodded his head, lost in thought, then he'd called all the children over, taking the smallest into his arms.

"Now then, while *mammà* makes it, I'll tell you the story of the *pastiera*. Do you want to hear it?"

As if at an agreed-upon signal, Lucia started laying out on the table all the ingredients necessary for the preparation of the pie: shortcrust pastry dough, mixed and kneaded in the early hours of the day when everyone else was still asleep; the sheep's milk ricotta, in a basket of woven straw; the wheat, boiled in fresh milk; refined white sugar; lard, eggs, cinnamon, and lemon; candied citron and *cucuzzata*, the squash marmalade for which Lucia was so renowned; and the tremendously delicate orange blossom water, made by steeping the blossoms of the bitter orange tree in hot water and then filtering it: the true scent of springtime in Naples.

Every noise from below, every passing automobile engine brought Livia to the window where she scanned the street to see if someone was coming to her front door with news from Falco. For hours, the woman had been prowling her apartment like a lioness in a cage; anxiety was swelling in her chest minute by minute.

She had urged Ricciardi to wait and not to contact her. But right now she wished he was at her side, not out of fondness but for support.

She wondered once a minute whether Falco would be successful, and even though she had every reason to believe him, whether he'd actually make the effort. She had decided to trust him, but in all likelihood, she told herself, it was out of necessity rather than any real conviction.

She stubbed out her umpteenth cigarette in the crystal ashtray. The lack of sleep and food combined with the tension, making her head spin. The future was full of uncertainty.

Enrica was looking to the future with a renewed faith. For the first time since she realized that she was in love with Ricciardi, she had some hope of persuading him to open himself to a genuine relationship, giving body and words to the tender gazes they exchanged every time they saw each other.

Rosa's invitation to dinner on Sunday, after an initial burst of anguish, now seemed exciting. She would go, of course she would. She'd sit across the table from him, they'd eat and talk, and at the end of the evening they'd say goodnight with an *arrivederci*.

She had made a decision: she wanted to make something with her own hands. She wanted this Easter to be different from the others, for her and for him. She would prove her love in silence, not with words but with flavor: the finest flavor that she knew how to create.

She'd make her *pastiera*.

As the children of the Maione family stood gaping at the array of delicious food that Lucia had laid out on the table, the brigadier said:

"Long, long ago, when this city was young, there was nothing here but a small fishing village by the sea. And from the sea came almost everything there was to eat, fish, shellfish, mussels, everything. But then one day came a terrible storm, and the fishing boats couldn't go out anymore; the storm went on and on, the weeks passed, and by then the people had used up their stores of food, there was nothing left."

Maione punctuated his account with all the requisite sound effects, thunder and lightning, towering waves. Even the older children, who'd heard the story a dozen times, were still captivated and listened openmouthed.

Smiling, Lucia expertly mixed the ingredients.

Smiling, Enrica mixed the boiled wheat, lard, milk, and lemon zest together in the stockpot.

She was thinking that the true meaning of love is in sharing. Not that she was an expert, she reflected, but who ever said that you have to experience something to understand it completely?

She, for instance, had read widely and dreamed extensively about love. She'd listened when her girlfriends and her sister confided in her, and she'd watched romantic movies accompanied by heartbreaking scores at the movie house near Piazza Dante, and on hot summer nights she had heard the sweet serenades of lovers. She knew everything about love.

And she knew—as she methodically mixed the batter to

eliminate all clumps, one eye on the wall clock to mark the ten minutes prescribed by the old recipe—that disappointments only drive a person away from love; that love has no need of experience to come into being and to grow stronger, in fact, if anything, experience hardens and embitters you.

Perhaps it's better not to be so experienced.

That's right, she thought, taking the stockpot off the heat.

"That's right," Brigadier Maione told his children. "The sea wouldn't hear of it, he wouldn't calm his stormy waves. And since springtime had come and the children were hungry, the fishermen decided to venture out anyway, even if the tempest was still howling. The wives and children were despondent at the thought of their fathers and husbands daring those waves that towered higher than their houses. Every night they gathered on the beach, in the driving rain, and prayed and wept and despaired, imploring the mean old sea to send back their papas with their boats. What should I do, should I stop or do you want me to go on?"

With his skills, he held the children's attention while, with just as much of her own, Lucia's nimble hands composed their own symphony, blending ricotta and eggs, vanilla, cinnamon, sugar, and orange blossom water. She noticed with a hint of pride that though Maria and Benedetta were listening to every word of Raffaele's story, they weren't missing a single thing she did.

Go on, she thought.

Go on, said the children, in chorus.

"Come in!" said Livia, startled by the light knocking on the living room door.

She had just nodded off in her armchair, overcome by exhaustion. Her heart leapt into her mouth, her eyes darted to the pendulum clock hanging on the wall. Early, she thought. Still too early.

The housekeeper appeared at the door, uncertain.

"Signo', excuse me. May I?"

"Yes, what is it?" Livia asked brusquely.

"I beg your pardon, Signo'. You haven't eaten in two days and . . . I mind my own business, you know that, but it breaks my heart to see you like this, especially now that Easter is on its way. So I just thought, since I make it at home the day before Easter because then I come to work and I don't have enough time, well, I just thought . . ."

The woman's dithering was starting to annoy Livia.

"Clara, just say what you have to say: you just thought what?"

"I just thought: this year, I'm going to make a small one, just for my signora. And I've brought it to you."

"What is it, what did you bring?"

The housekeeper pulled out a small bundle and, blushing, extended it to Livia.

"The *pastiera*, that's what I've brought you, Signo'. A special pie that we make in our city."

"Our city," said Maione, "was small then, like I told you. But the children and the women were the same as they are now: when they cried they sobbed so loud that it was impossible not to hear them. And in the end a siren, or mermaid, which is to say, a woman with a long fish tail who lives under the sea, Parthenope was her name, came out of the water and said: Why on earth are you crying and sobbing day and night, so I can't get a wink of sleep?"

The little girl who was sitting comfortably in his arms, hugging him tight, said:

"Because they wanted their fathers!"

"Good girl, that's exactly what the children said to the siren Parthenope. And since she was a good siren, she took pity and said: lemme see what I can do. And she plunged back under the waves and went to speak to her father, the Sea. She told him that all those wives and children were waiting for their men to come home so they could get to eat and hug them again."

Lucia kneaded together the dough with the kernels of wheat boiled in the milk, adding the *cucuzzata* and the candied citron cubed fine. Her son reached out a hand to snatch a piece, but she was faster than he was and gave him a light slap, saying:

"Not yet!"

Not yet, Enrica said to herself under her breath. It's not yet time.

She thought that she'd understood how Luigi Alfredo worked: it was counterproductive to try to drag him out of himself, forcing him to do or say things that didn't come naturally.

She didn't want to employ strategies, she wouldn't even be capable of doing so. As she rolled out the pastry dough in the pan, careful not to leave it any thicker than a quarter inch, creating the hollow that, like a woman's womb, would accommodate the mixture of boiled wheat, ricotta, and a myriad of scents and spices, she thought about herself and about the man she loved, and she thought about the pie she was making: something complex, intricate, and difficult that would lead to something else, something that would be much more than the sum of its parts.

Enrica smiled.

Livia smiled, a little tightly, and thanked her housekeeper. Her short nap had left in its wake many new thoughts, dense as clouds heavy with rain.

She wasn't only anxious at the thought of the doctor; there was also her uncertainty about the future, what she should do tomorrow, whether to leave town, as she had decided after a sleepless night, or stay, and take another chance at winning herself a tomorrow.

She looked at the slice of that strange pie that her house-keeper had made for her, and for an instant she was tempted to just toss it into the trash can: the last thing she wanted to do right now was eat. Then the sweet smell of orange blossoms wafted to her nostrils, and her empty stomach rumbled.

"The Sea rumbled," said Maione, "because he didn't want to let the fishing boats get home, he was having too much fun with his tempest. Also, he was hungry, and that made him grumpy. Parthenope, who knew him well, hurried back to the mammas and children assembled on the beach, and they had a meeting to decide what to do next. That was when the littlest girl of all had an idea: since it was springtime, and the Sea didn't know that, she thought it might help to show him all the wonderful things that come with that season. And so they prepared lots of bowls full of all the earth's bounty: ricotta and flour, symbols of the fertile countryside; eggs, symbols of how life renews itself; wheat kernels boiled in milk and orange blossom water, symbols of the meeting of plants and animals; sugar, the symbol of sweetness; and spices, a symbol of distant peoples and the brotherhood that grows thanks to the sea. And they put everything out, right next to the beach."

Lucia began to cut the remaining dough into long strips; she'd set it aside just for this purpose. As she worked, she listened to her husband's full, orotund voice and thought how much she loved him.

"During the night, the waves swept all those gifts down to the bottom of the sea; Parthenope, who'd been waiting for them, mixed them all together and made a pie and gave it to her father. He ate the whole thing, one slice at a time, and once his hunger was placated, he got over his anger and calmed down, till his surface was flat as a tabletop. And so the boats were able to return home, piled high with fish, and the children threw their arms around their fathers. Since then, every time that springtime comes back around, the mammas think back to that day and make the pie that Parthenope prepared. And we eat it!"

Lucia watched Raffaele as he wrapped his arms around the children; Benedetta came over to her and gave her a kiss, and so she let her place the last strip of dough on the *pastiera* which was now ready to be taken to the oven for baking.

She smiled at the girl, and decided that Benedetta was wonderful.

Wonderful, thought Enrica as she looked at the *pastiera* that she would take to Ricciardi's home tomorrow, for their first dinner together.

Wonderful.

Wonderful, Livia thought to her surprise, savoring the last bite of the slice of pie that her housekeeper had given her. This pie is the best thing I've ever tasted. And for a moment she felt the vise grip of anxiety loosening. Perhaps it was even possible to look to the future with a hint of optimism.

Wonderful.

Wonderful, thought Maione as he watched his wife hugging their new daughter. She's a wonderful mother.

And as he mused over the idea of how intolerable it would be to lose her, his thoughts wandered to the doctor and the crushing loneliness that he might be experiencing at that very moment; he pulled his watch out of his fob pocket, and wondered how long it would take, and what they would do if Livia's friend were unsuccessful.

There was nothing to do but wait.

In the dim light of the falling night, Ricciardi sat in the chair in his office, his green eyes wide as he stared into the empty air before him.

How long would it take? And, most important of all: how would it turn out?

There was nothing to do but wait.

Nothing to do but wait.

Outside, Easter burst silently into the spring.

## LI

L ivia had made sure that the apartment house's front entrance would be manned by her driver after the building's doorman locked up, to be sure that Falco's long-awaited arrvial would be noted immediately; in the end, her precautions proved pointless: around three in the morning, the phone rang right by her head; she'd curled up in the armchair and dropped off into a light and troubled sleep.

She jerked awake, emerging suddenly from the confused dream she was having. She answered the phone on the second ring, her throat twisted in anguish.

On the other end of the line, a man's voice spoke, cold and metallic:

"The package you're waiting for will be delivered in one hour at the San Gennaro wharf, down at the port. Be there to take delivery."

She couldn't tell whether it was Falco's voice, but she suspected it was not. He hung up before she had a chance to reply. She stood up fast, and her spine protested painfully; massaging her back, she went to summon her chauffeur.

The sharp rapping at Ricciardi's office door found him wide awake, all his senses alert, tormented by a growing tension. A rumpled Maione looked in through the half-opened door.

"Raffaele? What are you doing here, if you're not even on duty?"

"Commissa', I just couldn't bring myself to stay at home. At a certain point, the hundredth time I'd tossed and turned in bed, Lucia told me: listen, go to headquarters, at least that way I can get a little sleep. And then there was the dog, out in the courtyard, who would howl every so often, like a wolf. So I got dressed and we came over here, me and the dog."

Ricciardi already had his overcoat on.

"Is there news?"

"Yes, the Signora's driver just got here. He says that we have to be at the San Gennaro wharf, down at the port, inside an hour; it's the wharf next to the militia barracks, remember? The man doesn't know anything else. He left, saying that he had to hurry back to his boss."

"All right, let's go. And let's hope that Livia stays home, there's no reason for her to risk it."

Maione smirked:

"If I know anything about her at all, I'll bet that the Signora isn't the kind to mind her own business."

The journey from police headquarters to the harbor was a brief one: it took them less than fifteen minutes. They decided not to take any officers with them: either things would go smoothly or they wouldn't go at all. Behind them, at the customary distance, the dog was following silently, one ear up, trotting along close to the walls.

Maione said:

"Happy Easter, Commissa'. Happy Easter."

Although it lay shrouded in darkness, the port was still bustling with activity. Two ships were loading cargo, with groups of longshoremen making their way up gangways carrying enormous wooden crates on one shoulder, while steam from the ship engines curled upward from the smokestacks. Another vessel was just docking, amid the shouts of the men mooring it. A number of fishing trawlers were returning from their day's work, gathering the nets that were left dragging overboard until the last moment.

The barracks of the port militia, named in honor of Benito Mussolini, stood darkened except for the front entrance and two windows, lit up on the ground floor. From a distance it was possible to make out the silhouettes of two sentinels standing stiffly at attention, on either side of the front door.

Maione and Ricciardi set themselves up in a niche halfway between the barracks and wharf number 2, where a medium-sized vessel was tied up, the engines idling quietly, rumbling softly in the night, like a phlegmy old man lying fast asleep. There were no signs of activity onboard, but there was a light on deck.

Ricciardi looked around. Not far off, in the flat water just off the wharfs where ships were loaded and unloaded, he glimpsed the ghostly image of a young man under the surface, his arm tangled in a hawser that had kept him there long enough to drown. The image of the man had almost entirely dissolved, so he must have died some time ago. From his black mouth, wide open and gasping for a breath of air that had never come, the young man kept uttering the word: *Beer!* In an imperative tone of voice, as if he were sitting in a tavern and calling it out to a passing waitress. The commissario wondered why on earth, as the filthy harbor water was filling his lungs, the man's mind had turned to the name of that beverage. But he sought no answer: he'd given up years ago trying to understand the procedure of last thoughts; he only wished to never listen to another one. Never again.

After a few minutes, a hundred yards or so away, they saw a car pull up, let someone out, and then pull away again. The brigadier nodded his head at the commissario, as if to say: See? I told you so. Shortly thereafter, Livia walked over to them.

Even after nearly two days without a wink of sleep, she was enchanting. She wore a pair of slacks, flat shoes, and a lightweight dark wool sweater; her hair was short and she wore a beret, which would have made her appearance more masculine, but her generous figure and lithe gait left no doubts about it: she was more womanly dressed as a man than were practically any of the women in evening gowns who filled the Teatro San Carlo for gala events.

"Nothing yet, right? We're early, he should be here in half an hour."

Ricciardi scolded her harshly:

"What are you doing here, Livia? You shouldn't have come. This could be dangerous, don't you know that? To be down at the port, late at night, is already dangerous under normal conditions: but tonight, with everything that's going on . . ."

The woman shot back in a no-nonsense tone:

"I hardly think you have any right to tell me what I should or shouldn't do. And after all, my contact arranged this, and the doctor—if everything goes smoothly, and I certainly hope it will though I can't be sure of it—will be released if and only if they see me. Therefore, actually, you should be thanking me for having come; as for your being glad to see me, well, that's something I've given up hoping for."

Maione coughed with embarrassment. Ricciardi replied, in a more considered tone of voice:

"I'm grateful to you, very, very grateful indeed. I'm grateful that you took care of all this, and for putting yourself on the line. Don't think I don't know, and I'm very sorry for the anger you feel toward me. Even if I can hardly blame you for it."

The brigadier called out to get their attention.

"Look out, there's movement in the barracks."

Livia looked around and pointed to a stack of empty crates:

"Hurry, let's hide behind that stack."

The front door had swung open, and now a line of men was shuffling out. There wasn't enough light to make out their faces. From the way they held their arms crossed in front of them, it was clear that the ones in the middle were in chains or handcuffs, and the men around them, craning their necks cautiously, must be their guards. As soon as the longshoremen loading one of the ships tied up along the wharf saw the line of men emerge from the barracks, they set down their crates and hightailed it aboard the ship; Maione decided that it must be a healthy habit for them, avoiding being witness to those processions.

Now Ricciardi was upset: if it turned out that Modo was in that line of men, then their efforts to free him had failed. Livia realized what he was thinking, laid a gloved hand on his arm, and squeezed gently.

It was the dog who alerted them, hidden a few yards away by a tangled pile of ropes. He let out a short yelp, drawing their attention to a pair of figures that had just stepped out of a side entrance to the barracks, and were now heading toward them.

Ricciardi started to stand up and leave his hiding place, but Livia stopped him with a hand, whispering:

"Don't move. I'm the one who has to go, otherwise they'll get scared and refuse to release him."

She got to her feet and walked toward the two men, while the others proceeded in single file toward the waiting ship.

# LII

The men stopped a dozen paces or so away. One of the two—it was now clear both to Livia, who was standing in front of the crates, and to Maione and Ricciardi who were still crouching behind them—was Dr. Modo.

Hatless, his white hair was illuminated by a streetlamp, and his face appeared to be marked by deep suffering. His arms were crossed in front of his body, and his white lab coat covered his hands like a folded overcoat. The open, tieless collar of his shirt revealed a pulsating throat, as if he were swallowing constantly.

The man standing beside him was tall and large, and he was dressed in a fine double-breasted pinstripe suit, topped by a broad-brimmed hat that covered his face. He had locked arms with the doctor, like one old friend supporting another who is slightly drunk.

The ship had finished loading, and three men returned to the wharf down a gangway which was immediately retracted behind them.

The man spoke to Livia, in a voice marked by an out-of-town accent that struck Ricciardi as Tuscan.

"*Buonasera.* You would be . . ."

Livia stood motionless, tense, her legs spread slightly. To Ricciardi it looked as if she were about to lunge for the man's throat at any moment.

"You know who I am, I believe. I'm here to accompany the doctor, once you've left. Soon, I hope."

The man in the suit snickered derisively.

"Sure, I know who you are. They told me who you are. Congratulations, Signora: you may not be aware of it, but you have achieved a minor triumph this evening. But let me tell you something, and I want to tell your friend here the same thing: some things you can only get away with once. Just once. So don't tempt fate."

The menacing tone made the man's whisper as chilling as a shout. Modo swiveled his head toward him, a flash of anger in his eyes, and from the darkness Ricciardi silently prayed that for once he'd restrain his fiery temperament and keep from doing anything rash that might upend everything they'd done to win his freedom.

As if he'd heard him, the doctor once again dropped his head and stared at the ground. Livia took a step forward.

"Are you planning on spending much more time giving us life lessons, or will you let us go?"

The man laughed softly again and with a quick dart pulled a key from his pocket, removed the handcuffs from the doctor's wrists, and shoved him in Livia's direction. Modo staggered, doing his best not to lose his balance.

The dog emerged snarling from the shadows and lunged at the man with the broad-brimmed hat, tearing away a substantial piece of pin-striped trouser cuff with one sharp bite. The man swore and one hand shot toward his pocket.

Just then the imposing uniformed figure of a brigadier of the Naples police appeared in Ricciardi's field of view; he strode briskly out of the darkness and toward the three figures:

"Ah, and what do we have here? A police officer is out patrolling the wharf, early in the morning, resigned to a solitary stroll, and he suddenly finds himself in the midst of a nice gathering of friends. How are you this fine morning, Signo'? Oh, what a lovely surprise, Dr. Modo! Are you taking your dog out for a walk, is that what we have here? Do you know this gentleman, Dotto'?"

The tension was palpable. The dog continued to point the man, growling, the scrap of trouser fabric dangling from his mouth like a fake tongue. Livia smiled nervously. The doctor kept a hand on the animal's back, softly petting him.

The ship blew a short burst of its horn, announcing its imminent departure, and pulled away from the wharf.

After a long pause, the man in the hat pulled his hand out of his pocket very calmly. Then he said:

"No, Brigadier. I just happen to work around here, and I was out getting a breath of fresh air. And the doctor, no, I've never met him before; so naturally he doesn't know me either. I'm heading back into the barracks, after all, I've said all that I needed to say. Just one more piece of advice: keep this dog on a leash. *Buonasera.*"

The drowned man, from behind Ricciardi, called out faintly: *Beer!* Livia burst into tears of relief.

As if he too had heard the dead man's call as clearly as Ricciardi had, Modo invited everyone to come with him to a tavern that never closed, not far away.

Once the man in the hat had left, Modo stood watching the ship that should have been taking him away as it steamed out of the port. He said nothing. Maione was supporting Livia as she calmed down, and Ricciardi walked over slowly. When the ship was finally swallowed by the darkness, he said to his friend:

"How are you, Bruno? Are you hurt?"

Modo looked at him as if he had only just then noticed his presence, and said:

"In a certain sense, Ricciardi, I am. And badly."

Now, warmed by a familiar setting and his third glass of wine, Modo was starting to relax.

"I'd given up hoping, you know. I assumed that those sons of bitches would just take me away, destroying my life the way they did to those poor wretches who were locked up with me. Bastards, those damned bastards."

Maione put a hand on his arm:

"Dotto', first of all, you need to calm down, because it's all over now. Then you need to understand the lesson, though: these people have you in their crosshairs, you heard that nasty piece of work with the pistol, no? If it hadn't been for Signora Livia, here, who managed to get you out, we'd have never heard from you again."

Modo smiled at Livia, the only one who was drinking with him. Her hand was still trembling slightly, but her eyes had regained their usual confidence.

"I only did what I had to, Dottore. But the brigadier is right: these are dangerous people. They know everything about everyone, they're capable of tracking down any scrap of information that they need to ruin people's lives. You have to be careful."

The doctor patted her hand.

"Lovely lady, I'll be eternally grateful to you. I was afraid, yes. I hated like hell being torn away from my life, and from my friends, even if they're of a pretty crappy quality and smell of police stations. But this experience did teach me one thing, and that is that ideas should be nurtured, if they're borne out by the facts: and my ideas have been fully confirmed."

Ricciardi sighed:

"Very good, now we can rest assured that if you vanish suddenly some night, we'll know you're safely ensconced at the bottom of the sea with your ankles tied to a large rock. Did you even hear what that guy said? Don't you care about your patients, about the people who rely on you, about us, who for some mysterious reason like having you around?"

Modo gazed at him fondly.

"So there's a heart beating inside the casket you live in after all. I'd be tempted to tell you that the whole thing was a charade designed to force you to display some human emotion, but you'd never believe me because you're suspicious at heart, like all provincials. And in fact, do you know that in the group of miserable wretches who were being held in the barracks cellar with me, there was a man from your neck of the woods, not far from Benevento?"

Ricciardi objected:

"Hey, I'm from the Cilento, at the far end of the province of Salerno. We have nothing to do with Benevento."

Modo waved his hand vaguely.

"Sure, sure, all right, from around there, a country bumpkin just like you, in other words. And do you know why they were sending him into internal exile?"

The commissario sighed:

"I'm not from the country, I'm from the mountains, but go ahead and tell us."

"Because he had told, in public, in his small town, the following joke: a factory worker went to buy some apples, and when he realized that the newspaper in which the grocer had wrapped his fruit featured a photograph of Mussolini, he asked him, in a worried voice, to use some other section of the paper, because otherwise he was worried that Il Duce would eat even his apples."

Ricciardi started to object, then heaved a sigh as Livia and Maione burst into laughter.

"Come on, Bruno, I can't believe that's why he was arrested."

Modo was perfectly serious. He leaned forward and said:

"Ricciardi, you don't get it: things are terrible. They call it "undermining the image of the head of state," and they behave as if it's a serious crime because they claim that it harms the image of Italy as a whole. They've gone crazy. And that's not the funniest thing I heard in there!"

Maione was wiping the tears from his cheeks.

"Really, Dotto'? Do you have another joke as good as that last one?"

Ricciardi scolded the brigadier:

"Raffae', please, don't encourage him, otherwise we won't be able to stop him, and he'll wind up behind bars once and for all."

Livia was happy to let the tension loosen, in part because she sensed another source of anxiety at the pit of her stomach, ready to replace the first.

"Yes, Doctor, tell us: what other ridiculous reasons did they have for locking people up?"

Modo took a long drink of wine.

"Well, there was a teamster, a man who drove a cart. A poor wretch whose only concern in life was how to feed his ten children. Well, this guy used to spend time at the workers' club for railwaymen and trolley drivers, you know, the one up at Monteoliveto, because with his little cart and donkey he used to deliver coal to the train station. So one day last month, at the club, they inaugurated with full honors a new plaster bust of our leader, Old Bull Head, and this poor fellow finds himself attending the event, with everyone in dress uniform clapping when they unveil the bald-headed bust. And he thinks to himself, well, maybe they just didn't have the money to include the hair. You get it? He had no idea who the bust was supposed to be."

Maione and Livia had started to chuckle. Modo went on:

"Well, he just wanted to help out the head of the club, and he'd seen how proud he was of that bust; and so, late one night, he decided to make up for the club's monetary deficencies, so he cut off his donkey's tail and he made a magnificent toupee for the egghead himself, and he slaps it right on, in the middle of the head. The next morning the custodian unlocks the club at opening time, and he finds old Thunder Jaws himself wearing a wonderful donkey-tail hairpiece, perfectly combed and brushed. Of course, the teamster was immediately arrested and shipped off to internal exile."

Maione burst out laughing.

Livia burst out laughing.

Ricciardi suddenly understood who had killed Viper.

## LIII

S uddenly, everything was crystal clear. The connections were clear, what had happened was clear, and how it happened was clear as well.

It took tremendous effort for Ricciardi to keep from leaping to his feet and running straight to police headquarters; but there was no rush. And he didn't want to undercut the first moment of peace and safety in three days for Modo, Maione, and Livia, and for himself as well.

When they got out of the tavern it was broad daylight, and it was Easter Sunday. The church bells, finally free, filled the air with their chimes and the streets began to fill up with little old ladies in black shawls, heading for the churches where they would preside over all the celebrations.

Modo ran his hand over his face, and felt the stubble that demanded the attentions of a razor.

"*Mamma mia*, Signora, I can't believe I let you see me in such bad shape. I hope you'll forgive me. I usually take better care of myself."

"Don't think twice about it, my dear doctor. First of all, you have the best excuse possible; and then, after all, I'm certainly not at my finest either. I've had a few bad days, though nothing to compare with the experience you've just had."

Maione added:

"You know, I'm suddenly starving. It's a good thing that today is Easter Sunday, if it was still Lent I'd commit a sin and go straight to a restaurant. In fact, Dotto', I wanted to tell you that I swore an oath last night, privately: if the doctor is freed, then he's coming to our house for Easter dinner. My wife Lucia has made a *pastiera* that's so good it can talk."

Livia lit up:

"Ah, the *pastiera*! That's the pie my housekeeper brought me yesterday, because she was worried I had eaten so little over the past few days: it's a wonderful thing, that pie. Even as overwrought as I was, I ate two slices, and I can't wait to eat some more."

They were outside the doctor's building now, in Piazza del Gesú. The large church, its façade covered with diamond, was dressed up for the holiday, and the faithful were gathering for the first service.

Modo said:

"I never thought I'd see my home again so soon. And I'm grateful to you, truly grateful, my friends. If I weren't such a tough old battle-hardened army doctor, I swear I'd start crying. But since I know that if I were to do such a thing you'd march me straight back to the barracks, I'll spare you. Brigadie', thanks for having taken care of my four-legged friend, it seems to me that under that coat he might have even gotten a bit fatter. And thanks for the invitation, which I gladly accept: I'll catch a couple of hours of sleep, get a shave, and wash up, and I'll see you later in the home of the lovely Signora Lucia."

After which he went over to Ricciardi and, after gazing into his eyes for what seemed like a long time, gave him a hug.

"I'm sorry, Ricciardi. I'm afraid you're just going to have to tolerate this hug." Then he bowed to Livia: "Allow me to pay my most sincere respects, Madame: and my heartfelt gratitude. It's a double blessing, to be so devoted to a woman of such beauty: I am surely the beneficiary. I hope to see you again soon."

The woman returned the bow with a graceful curtsey.

"It's been a pleasure, Dottore. And who knows, perhaps we will see each other again sooner or later."

Once Modo had vanished through the front door, followed by his dog, Ricciardi turned to Livia:

"I hope you'll forgive us, Livia: Maione and I have to run, we have a very important matter to attend to. But I thank you too, truly. I'll be forever in your debt, for this deed you performed, and which I certainly didn't deserve."

"I'm very happy with how things turned out, mostly for the doctor, who truly is an extraordinary man. As for you, I just hope that what happened will help you to understand a little something about me, and about yourself as well. Happy Easter."

She turned to go, but Ricciardi impulsively called after her:

"Livia, listen. You mentioned a celebration, a special Easter performance tonight at the Teatro San Carlo. If you still plan to attend, I'd be delighted to accompany you."

She stood motionless, her back to him. She wasn't sure she'd heard right; and after all, she'd made up her mind to leave town, hadn't she? She'd decided to abandon that ridiculous illusion, to stop humiliating herself for a man who didn't want her. And even that invitation, she realized a second later, wasn't it merely the product of his gratitude for her help in freeing the doctor? Wasn't it too little, too late, for a new beginning?

No, she answered her own question. It wasn't too little, too late.

"You know, Ricciardi, I'd decided to leave, and I was planning to spend the evening packing my bags. But all things considered, that's something I can just as easily do tomorrow morning; perhaps after another slice of that wonderful pie. All right then, invitation accepted. I'll expect you at my place, at nine."

And she left, taking care that neither man could see the joy lighting up her face.

Once they were alone, Maione immediately spoke to Ricciardi:

"Commissa', just what is this important matter we have to attend to? I'm not even on duty, and if I'm late for Easter dinner this will be the time that Lucia finally slaughters me and serves me up roasted, with a side dish of potatoes, instead of the kid goat."

Ricciardi was walking briskly toward the office.

"I've figured it out, Raffaele. I've figured it all out. I've figured out what happened, and why. I've figured out who killed the poor girl, and how, and even the mistakes they made. I need to confirm a few things, but I've figured it out."

Maione was having a hard time keeping up with him.

"Commissa', then help me figure it out too. Tell me what we need to do."

And Ricciardi told him, continuing to stride briskly, dodging all the people pouring out into the street to celebrate Easter and springtime, the *madonnari* who were using colored chalk to draw scenes of Jesus blessing Mussolini on the sidewalks, beggars playing mandolins and ocarinas, black blindfolds over their eyes, and the thousands of strolling vendors setting up shop outside the churches.

He told him everything, speaking of passions, emotions, and cash.

He told him everything, of murder caught as always midway between hunger and love.

He told him everything, and when they reached the entrance to police headquarters they were once again full of strength and energy, as if they hadn't spent two sleepless nights, as if they hadn't just dealt with so daunting an experience. They were hunting dogs, and after bounding aimlessly through fields, they'd caught scent of their prey and were prowling, bellies to the earth, ready to lunge at its throat.

Maione rubbed his hands eagerly.

"Fine, Commissa'. That explains everything. All right, what's our next move?"

Ricciardi followed the thread of his thoughts.

"Here's our next move: you go with two officers to pick up the murderer, without making too much of a fuss. Be careful, this is likely to be something that won't come entirely as a surprise, though with every passing day the sense of safety is probably growing."

"What about you, Commissa'? What are you going to do?"

Ricciardi smirked.

"I'm going to go spend a little time at the bordello. Everyone has been telling me that's what I should do, so this time I really will. Maybe I'll be able to pick up some confirming evidence. I'll see you afterward, at headquarters; move fast, and you'll get home in time for lunch and your wife won't have to cook you."

## LIV

O nce again, Ricciardi walked up Via Toledo and then Via Chiaia, heading for Il Paradiso.

Springtime had decided to welcome in Easter dressed in her very best. The air was sparkling like a *vino novello*, and was every bit as intoxicating and treacherous, full of scents and promises that spring had no intention of keeping. He could hear singing from the apartments overlooking the street, women busy with final holiday preparations or finishing up some spring cleaning, and men shaving by the light of day for a change, the mirror hanging from a hook out on the balcony in the first whiff of the new season: voices both off-key and gloriously melodious, deep and high, all talking of love.

The commissario tried to put himself into the mind of Viper's murderer. Now that he was certain of the killer's identity, he could rule out what he had first theorized as a motive, a burst of rage or some accumulation of contingencies: the murder had been premeditated, prepared and planned out. Therefore the murderer must have walked this very same route, calm, the same as all the other pedestrians walking beside him on that magnificent Sunday morning.

Ricciardi mused on how often he wound up close to someone who was planning to put an end to a human life. He went past the ghostly image of the suicide outside Gambrinus who stood murmuring: *Our café, my love, our café, my love.* He was starting to fade, and before long he'd vanish just as the memory of him would, to be replaced by some new and despairing emotion. I prefer the dead, thought Ricciardi: their thoughts are blunted and by now useless, but at least they're obvious.

He reached Il Paradiso, but he didn't go in; instead he walked a little farther and stopped at the corner of the side alley, the *vicolo* that ran past the small door that served as the tradesmen's entrance. He found himself standing in front of the accordion player, with his dark glasses and his little metal plate of coins.

The man accompanied the music that his nimble fingers drew from the instrument with a few of the words of the song, modulated by his half-open lips. The position of his head, pointed toward some indeterminate point between the roof of the building across the way and the sky, was the very picture of blindness. No doubt about it, thought Ricciardi: he was a master at maintaining his fiction.

Noticing the commissario standing motionless before him, the accordionist raised his voice and begin singing with conviction, in a fine baritone: "*T'aggio vuluto bbene, a tte, / tu m'e vuluto bbene, a mme. / Mo' nun ci amamm' cchiú, ma 'e vvote tu / distrattamente pienz' a mme!*"

The song ended with an elaborate arpeggio and a passing matron dropped a coin in his plate; without shifting the direction of his eyes, the man thanked her. Ricciardi remained motionless.

The man went on playing, but his discomfort was making itself clear. Finally he stopped, his dark lenses pointed at some distant point straight ahead of him. Ricciardi said, in a low voice:

"We need to talk."

The man nodded his head yes but didn't get up. So Ricciardi sat down on a step near him.

"Let's not waste each other's time. I know you're not blind, and I'd ask you to drop the pretense, which I care nothing about and about which, I assure you, I'll do nothing in the future. I'm here for something else."

The beggar nodded.

"And I know exactly who you are, Commissa'. I was hoping to have a chance to thank you and the brigadier for defending us, the other day, against those Fascists who came dangerously close to ruining my accordion, and what would I have done then? Luckily the damage was light and I was able to fix it."

"What is your name?"

The conversation was conducted in whispers and the man hadn't altered his posture at all.

"Francesco Lo Giudice, but they call me Ciccillo. Ciccillo 'o Cecato, to be exact."

"'O Cecato, eh? Ciccillo the Blind Man. And how long have you been pretending to be blind?"

"When I was a boy I fell ill and for a while I couldn't see very well. That was exactly when I learned to play the accordion, from an uncle of mine who was a strolling musician. He'd take me with him, so folks would take pity on the little boy with the bandaged eyes and would be more likely to give us charity. Then I got better, but when people see that you're normal, they say: go get a job. As if playing the accordion and making people happy wasn't a job."

Ricciardi considered the matter and deep down, he had to agree.

"So this is your regular spot, right? This is where you always work?"

"Yes, Commissa'. And it's a good spot. The police, given the fact that there's a bordello right here, generally leave me alone; lots of people pass by, and they stop to look in the shop windows; and there's a restaurant right there, with a good-natured waitress who always gives me leftovers."

"And you were here last Monday, weren't you, when . . ."

"When Viper was killed, yes. Such a shame. You have no idea how beautiful she was, when she'd come out of that door and walk past me, you have to believe me, the temptation to turn my head and watch her even just from behind was almost irresistible."

In spite of himself, Ricciardi began to understand the difficulties of being professionally blind.

"Then perhaps you recall who went in and who came out the little side door leading into the cathouse."

Ciccillo snickered.

"Commissa', I may even pass for blind: but I have a memory like a steel trap, if I do say so myself, and I don't forget what I see."

And he told Ricciardi exactly what he wanted to know.

Il Paradiso was closed for Easter, and that struck Ricciardi as nicely ironic.

Madame Yvonne had greeted him in a nightgown, her hair a mess, her face free of the usual heavy makeup. Wearily she had walked him upstairs to the door of Viper's room, opening it with a key chosen from among the many that clanked on an iron ring.

"Commissa', forgive me if I ask you again: when will we able to use this room again? I'd like to give it to Lily, because word has gotten out that it was her who found . . . that she was the first to see Viper, and there are people willing to pay very good money to make . . . to hear the story."

"I imagine there are. Don't worry, Signora: it won't be long now, not long at all. Now, if you'll be so kind, I'd like to go in alone."

"At your orders, Commissa'. I'll wait for you here."

In the room, everything was just as Ricciardi remembered it; his orders had been respected and no one had moved anything. The stale odor of a closed room, with the heavy traces of

French perfume and disinfectant all but drowned out by the scent of rotting flowers, almost made him gag; he opened the window and let in the fresh spring air.

He shivered slightly when he heard the words of the girl's corpse, as she stood before the mirror and kept repeating: *Little whip, little whip. My little whip.* The little whip he'd looked for and been unable to find. Perhaps now this too had an explanation.

Ricciardi looked at the objects on the dresser, the ones scattered over the bed and on the floor. The pillow that had killed the young woman. The jewel box. The frame with the photograph, which he now knew was a picture of the girl's mother and her own son. Suddenly what Ricciardi knew about the dead girl's life weighed down on his heart, her sadness and her joys. This was no longer a stranger's room, the place where some unknown corpse had been found; now it was a place where a person had experienced pains and passions and emotions.

He took what he needed, and he left in a hurry.

## LV

Ricciardi didn't have to wait long, once he was back in his office. He was sitting at his desk, his thoughts lost in a reconstruction of what had happened, when Maione knocked at the door.

"Commissario, he's right outside. When he saw us coming, he tried to run, but I'd brought Special Agent Palomba, you know him, that kid is fast and he caught him right away. The crowd messed him up a little, those guys, you know what they're like, savages. We had to fire a couple of shots in the air, and that quieted them down."

Ricciardi said:

"I was expecting him. Bring him in."

The door swung open and two officers brought in Pietro Coppola in shackles, the younger brother of Peppe 'a Frusta, Joey the Whip.

As soon as he saw the commissario, the man started right in:

"Commissa', what does all this mean? To come and take a respectable citizen out of his home, on Easter Sunday, what is this, the moving pictures? And after all, I've been perfectly forthcoming the whole time, would you explain to me . . ."

Ricciardi raised one hand to halt the river of words.

"Coppola, let's not waste any time, let's just skip the part where you get indignant. The more straightforward our conversation, the less painful this will be for all of us. You should understand that to bring you in, and in shackles, we must have good evidence."

"Commissario, you've got it all wrong! I don't have anything to do with it, I was just covering up for my brother, who . . ."

Ricciardi opened one of his drawers and set down an object on his otherwise empty desktop. The man fell silent; his lips kept moving as if he were murmuring something, but no voice emerged.

A long silence ensued, at the end of which Coppola slumped forward, as if his soul had left his body. The officer at his side held him up and, at a signal from Ricciardi, sat him in the nearest chair.

The man's gaze was fixed on the object on top of the desk: the inlaid wooden brush, in which what looked like long blond human hairs were tangled.

# LVI

Commissa', in truth, my brother—you never actually met him. The person he used to be, the man, the worker he once was. You never met him.

He's the best young man in the world, or actually, he was. Always cheerful, always thinking about the business, all the work we do he dreamed it up himself. We were poor, we were starving; we had a vegetable garden that didn't even produce enough for us. And as long as he was with Maria Rosaria, when they were kids, they were satisfied with what they had.

That woman, Commissa', she robbed my brother of his will. When he had her, he didn't want anything else.

Then, when that man took her for himself and fathered her child, my brother resigned himself to it and started working, and he changed all our lives.

I don't know if he was doing it was so that he wouldn't have to think about her, or because without her he found other motives, like love for his own family: but he became another man. Little by little, with hard work and sweat, we became what we are now. We all work for the company—you saw my one sister, and the other one that you never met, and I take care of the carts and the animals: but the one who decides, who makes the choices, who points the way for everyone else—that's my brother; without him we're nothing. Without him we'll just go back to being the miserable yokels we were before.

I met Ines three years ago, when we weren't much more than kids. She's not from where I grew up, she came with her sister who, like I told you, is a schoolteacher. We fell in love immediately, but we have nothing, she lives on that miserable salary and I depend on my family. But then I talked my brother into hiring Ines to help us out, and we started to hope. We set a date; at first we'd live together with the family and later we'd build a house of our own.

Everything was going fine, Commissa'. Everything.

And then, the one time I didn't make the round of deliveries to our customers, and let my brother go in my place, they happened to see each other again.

Bad luck, Commissa'. The worst luck. Bad luck for my brother, whose peaceful life ended; bad luck for Ines and for me, because we were forced to forget about getting married; and bad luck even for her, for Maria Rosaria, seeing how things went in the end.

He went out of his mind, went right back to where he'd broke off when he lost her. He stopped working, he spent all our money on her, to spend time with her, to buy gifts for her. We saw all our hard work go into the house where Maria Rosaria's mother lived, which grew, one room after another; while he told me—his own brother—that there was no money for me and Ines to get married, that we'd just have to wait. For a whore, Commissa'. Because that's all she was: nothing but a whore.

But it wasn't her fault, it was my brother's fault. He had become convinced that he couldn't live without her, that he couldn't lose her again; he decided to marry her, if you can believe it.

You don't know what it means to hear those words, one Sunday at lunch: he wanted to marry her. We couldn't get married anymore, Ines and I; and the company would slide into ruin, and we'd lose everything, because my brother couldn't see beyond her and wouldn't have cared about anything else anymore.

That very Sunday, after lunch, Ines and I made our decision. There was only one way to save our future. Only one way.

I could pass undisturbed through the little side door, everyone knew me both because I delivered the fruit and vegetables, and because I often went to call my brother, when he lost all sense of time and forgot about the rest of mankind. It was opening time, when all the girls are busy and no one notices anything. I waited for my brother to leave and I immediately slipped into the room.

I wanted to know what Viper had decided. If she was going to tell my brother no, she'd still be alive now.

But when she saw me, she said: I want to surprise your brother. I'm going to give him my answer on Easter Sunday, in less than a week. I'm going to tell him yes on Easter Sunday. I'll only make him wait until the holiday, and then we'll take back the future that was taken from us.

You understand, Commissa'? They were taking back their future, and taking away mine and Ines's. Love at last, she told me: do you know what love is? She asked me, *me* of all people. A whore who wants to teach me about the meaning of love.

That's when I picked up the pillow.

I didn't realize right away that I'd dropped my horse-grooming brush; when I couldn't find it anymore I just thought I must have lost it while I was driving the cart, it's happened to me before.

I loved Maria Rosaria, you know. I'm not a monster. When I was a child, since I went everywhere with Peppe, she treated me like a younger brother, I still remember.

She used to make fun of us, she'd say: ah, here they come now, *Peppe 'a Frusta avanti e 'o Frustino appresso*. Joey the Whip leading, and the Little Whip trailing behind. That's what she always used to call me, Commissa': my little whip.

I loved Maria Rosaria.

But what I did, I'd do again. A hundred times over, I'd do it again.

## LVII

When the officers had taken him away, Maione and Ricciardi sat in silence. Outside, the sun was setting on the first Sunday of spring.

The brigadier said, as he sat scratching his head:

"Crazy, eh, Commissa'? When you hear the motives people have for murder, they always seem ridiculous. Maybe all he would really have had to do is talk to his brother, tell him what he wanted, they could have found a solution, and now they'd all be nice and cozy, sitting around a lovely Easter table, enjoying themselves."

Ricciardi started in surprise:

"Oh, Raffaele, I'm so sorry, I completely forgot that today is Easter! I made you miss your lunch!"

"Don't mention it, Commissa'; when I left to go pick up Coppola, I did a quick calculation and it became clear that I wouldn't make it in time; so I sent someone to alert both Lucia and Dr. Modo to push everything back to supper tonight, so I've got plenty of time, work is work, and that poor girl deserves respect too. But satisfy my curiosity: how did you know? What made you realize that Pietro Coppola was the murderer?"

Ricciardi sighed, vaguely waving one hand in the air.

"Luck. Pure dumb luck. Do you remember yesterday, when the doctor told that story about the donkey-hair wig for Il Duce?"

"How could I forget, this morning I was still laughing all by myself."

"Exactly. But what occurred to me is that what I thought were long blond hairs on that brush, hairs that I thought belonged to Lily, the prostitute who often shared toiletries with Viper, might not even have been human hairs. And we had already seen hair like that, when Coppola was grooming the sorrel mare, that time we went to Antignano to question Viper's mother."

"That's true, exactly. And then he started whittling a piece of wood, while we were talking to his brother, I remember clearly."

"Right. Then I remembered the blind man with perfect eyesight who plays the accordion out front of Il Paradiso, right on the side where the tradesmen's entrance is, do you remember?"

"Of course I do, the man whose accordion the Fascists broke the other morning. And what did he tell you?"

"He told me that Monday afternoon he saw Peppe 'a Frusta leave the building, happy as he always was when he'd seen his girl; then a minute later, Pietro went in, and he wondered why on earth Pietro would have made a special effort to avoid his brother. But since he's blind, of course, he kept it to himself, because he didn't want to give himself away and lose his source of income; after all he'd seen Pietro go in plenty of times, he was one of the chief suppliers for the brothel's restaurant, so he didn't think it was all that remarkable."

Maione shook his head.

"Incredible. If he hadn't dropped the brush, he might even have gotten away with it. And he might even have sent his brother to prison; after all, he was still the last person to have seen the girl alive. Which is why he defended him so furiously."

Ricciardi checked the time.

"It's almost seven. Go on home, Raffaele, and give Lucia and the children my best Easter wishes."

"*Grazie*, Commissa'. But what are you going to do? Aren't you going to go home and celebrate?"

The commissario heaved a sigh:

"No, I'll write a report on Coppola's arrest and then I'll just be able to make it in time to take Livia to the theater, as I promised I would. We owe it to her, don't we? If it hadn't been for her, the good doctor, instead of eating Lucia's *casatiello*, lucky man, would be sailing toward some godforsaken island and a diet of bread and water."

Maione laughed out loud.

"You're absolutely right, Commissa', I'll have to tell him that, tonight. Oh, that'll steam him! And as for Lucia's *casatiello*, there's a big slice just for you. But what are you going to do about Signora Rosa? I'm sure she's made supper for you, your shift was supposed to be over this afternoon, wasn't it?"

"Rosa's used to it. This isn't the first time I've skipped dinner. She knows that if I'm not back by a certain time, she just needs to wrap up whatever she made. I'll eat it tomorrow."

Maione raised his hand to the brim of his cap in a salute.

"Well then, happy Easter, Commissa'."

"Happy Easter to you, Raffaele."

# LVIII

Springtime has no pity.

She sees herself reflected in the tail end of sunset, draping the night around her shoulders like the finest of capes; she gazes at herself, she admires herself, richly bedecked in new buds and fresh green leaves, and she has no pity.

She has no pity for the elderly woman who sits at a table of covered dishes, thinking to herself that this may be the last Easter in her life, and she's spending it waiting for a footstep on the stairs that never comes, her heart gripped by fear—fear for her own loneliness and the loneliness of others. A heart that gradually weakens, in silence, closed in her chest. Beat after beat.

She breathes in the gusts of air off the sea, springtime does. And she has no pity.

She has no pity for the long-legged young woman with tortoiseshell glasses who spent the whole morning standing in line at the oven in Via Santa Teresa to pick up the *pastiera* that she made just for him, and the whole afternoon choosing which of her three good dresses to wear; and she worked up her courage to ask her mother if she could borrow her grandmother's earrings, and got a hail of questions in exchange, all of which she ignored; and she will spend her whole evening watching the clock, sitting in a chilly chair in an apartment that is not hers, losing every certainty, and she will spend her whole night weeping into her pillow. Believing that her heart is broken forever, feeling a sharp and desperate pang of pain. Beat after beat.

She strolls in the light breezes from the forest, springtime does. And she has no pity.

She has no pity for the woman who once again feels her heart beating in her throat, as she puts on a magnificent silk dress and gazes into the mirror at a topaz glittering between her breasts, hoping that in a nearby heart something more than mere gratitude might live. Hoping that that heart might learn to love, even if it's only a little at a time. Beat after beat.

She stirs the blood in everyone's veins, old women and young, springtime does. And she has no pity.

She has no pity for whole families, gathered around a table overflowing with food, love, and friendship; no pity for all those who embrace and kiss, under the spell of a holiday instituted by men that will go by and come around again, and some will be there when it does, and others will be gone by then. Hearts alone and hearts together. Hearts that gaze at each other and smile. Beat after beat.

She stirs up life and the memory of death, springtime does. And she has no pity.

She has no pity for the man who walks through a city made up of both the living and the dead, trying to ignore his emotions, hoping not to err both in what he does and in what he doesn't do. Shrugging off both his own pain and sorrow and that of others. Thinking all the while that love brings death, and hoping that's not love's only gift. Hoping also that one day he'll be able to listen to every lurch of his heart, without fear. Beat after beat.

But springtime has no pity.

No pity at all.

## ACKNOWLEDGMENTS

This story exists because Severino Cesari and Paolo Repetti asked for it. It was shepherded by Mariapaola Romeo and Valentina Pattavina. Its architecture was shaped by Antonio Formicola and in discussions with Michele Antonielli. Set design and staging by the fantastic Annamaria Torroncelli and Stefania Negro. Scented and nurtured by the expert hands of Sabrina Prisco, of the *Osteria Canali* of Salerno. Overseen from the very beginning and cultivated by the marvelous Corpi Freddi. Like all the Ricciardi stories, it springs from my mother's stories and smiles. All I did was tell it.

## About the Author

Maurizio de Giovanni lives and works in Naples. His Commissario Ricciardi series, including *I Will Have Vengeance* (Europa 2013), *Blood Curse* (Europa 2013), *Everyone in Their Place* (Europa 2013), and *The Day of the Dead* (Europa 2014) are bestsellers in Italy and have been published to great acclaim in French, Spanish, and German, in addition to English. He is also the author of *The Crocodile* (Europa 2013), a noir thriller set in contemporary Naples.